"You owe me something, Alicia Farr," Ian promised threateningly. "And you're going to stay put until I decide how to make you pay."

"I owe you nothing, Ian. That child was conceived under unusual circumstances. Won't you even admit to that?" she replied. Alicia closed her eyes wearily and turned away from him. "What is it you want from me, Ian?" Her tone was close to despair.

"Another child." He said the words with flat conviction, as though there was no possible argument offered. He lifted her into the hollow of his body, straining her to him as though he wanted to fuse her flesh with his. And Alicia had to admit to herself that at that moment there was nothing else she wanted as much. . . .

Dear Reader,

It is our pleasure to bring you a new experience
in reading that goes beyond category writing.
The settings of **Harlequin American Romance**
give a sense of place and culture that is uniquely
American, and the characters are warm and
believable. The stories are of "today" and have
been chosen to give variety within the vast scope
of romance fiction.

An author-editor relationship is explored in this
timely narrative that deals with a medical dilemma.
Jacqui Ashley very competently handles the modern
knowledge of the effects of childhood diseases on
adults and the strength of a mature love.

From the early days of Harlequin, our primary
concern has been to bring you novels of the highest
quality. **Harlequin American Romance** is no
exception. Enjoy!

Vivian Stephens

Vivian Stephens
Editorial Director
Harlequin American Romance
919 Third Avenue,
New York, N.Y. 10022

Love's Revenge

JACQUELINE ASHLEY

Harlequin Books

TORONTO • NEW YORK • LONDON
AMSTERDAM • PARIS • SYDNEY • HAMBURG
STOCKHOLM • ATHENS • TOKYO • MILAN

Published August 1983

First printing June 1983

ISBN 0-373-16020-8

Printed in Canada

Chapter One

Alicia Farr raised the glass of sparkling wine to her lips and inspected the stunning man seated across the table from her with a jaundiced eye, contemplating the next gentle barb she intended to launch in his direction. She wasn't sure exactly what had got into her this evening... why she felt such a strong inclination to prick his facade so unrelentingly... but she had been allowing the compulsion to hold sway over her all night, and with each succeeding glass of wine she drank it grew stronger.

Perhaps it was because this was the first anniversary of her husband's death, and Ian Halsey was the exact antithesis of Ben. She was filled with a sense of injustice that fate had seen fit to deprive the world—and herself—of the gentle sweetness of such a saintly man, while *this* one—a jaded sensualist—was permitted to live and was now sitting across from her, positively vibrating with an almost repugnant vitality.

It wasn't fair! she thought with unaccustomed bitterness. What did Ian Halsey have to offer anyone aside from his ribald tales of sexy adventurism, which, if all accounts were true, were based at least in part on his own life-style? Yet his books sold by the thousands while Ben's poetry had seldom even been published and when it had been, it had made so little money that if it hadn't been for her job, they wouldn't have survived financially.

It was always the way, she thought with cynical frustration. The good died young, while the bad... She eyed the devilish smile quirking Ian Halsey's sensuous mouth as he bent his handsome head down to listen to the twittering of his publisher's enthralled wife. Well, the bad just went on being bad. Alicia finished her thought with a mental shrug.

She chose a moment when the conversation around the table had temporarily died down, then cleared her throat to get her adversary's attention. Ian Halsey looked up, his attractively formed mouth tightening a fraction, his light golden eyes focusing on Alicia with an impervious stare of polite attention that was just short of connoting rude disinterest.

"Tell me, Mr. Halsey," Alicia said, her clear blue eyes widening with innocent inquiry, a gentle smile pulling at her full lips. "Did you mean for your hero in *Savage Pirate* to be quite so immature in his relationships with women as he came across?" She shrugged her shoulders in a disarming gesture. "I mean, if it *was* intentional, I *suppose* I can understand your motivation...." Alicia shot him a quick discerning look from under her thick lashes. "After all, he really was an amoral bastard in every other way as well, wasn't he?"

She didn't miss the slight tensing of his jaw, which was the only sign Ian gave of his annoyance, and which gave Alicia a contented sense of accomplishment. It didn't matter to her in the least that as far as anyone else at the table could tell, Ian Halsey had taken her question in good humor.

A charming white-toothed grin announced his unperturbed sense of humor to the others. "But, of course, Miss...uh..." He gave the impression that he couldn't remember Alicia's name, though she was certain he did. He looked like the sort of man who always identified a perceived enemy right down to the last detail, the better to protect his own back. Alicia suppressed a smile at his tactic, thinking that if this was the best he could do in retaliation for her baiting, he had a long way to go to achieve the status of a worthy adversary.

He covered the lapse smoothly, managing to give the impression that Alicia was insufficiently important enough for him to remember her name, but that he would always remain the perfect gentleman and reply to her stupid questions politely. "That's the charm of my heroes, you see," he drawled, giving the other members of the party the benefit of a devilishly rakish look. "No female reader—and they make up the bulk of my public, of course—would be satisfied with a hero who was a staid sort of fellow...one who indulged in reading poetry to his ladylove and who committed himself to her for all time. That would be very dull, don't you agree?"

He wasn't really asking for her opinion, but Alicia's temper was aroused by his words. Ben had been exactly the sort of "staid" fellow Ian Halsey had described, right down to reading poetry to her—his *own* poetry— and Alicia considered that her husband had been an imminently satisfactory hero. At least he had known the value of making a commitment to another human being—something the man seated across from her would never be able to bring himself to do.

Alicia waited until the rather strained laughter of the others died down. Many of them had known Ben and had seen the sort of relationship that Alicia and Ben had had, so it was only natural that they felt a certain amount of embarrassment for Alicia...embarrassment and sympathy, though not enough to risk incurring the displeasure of the money-making author in their midst. Then she smiled sweetly and shook her head slightly. "Perhaps you're right." She gave the appearance of agreeing with him. "Women do like completely different things in their fantasy lives than they would be willing to put up with in reality. For that reason I'm sure your heroes will continue to be...uh...*financially* successful." The slight emphasis was almost indiscernible, but Alicia was certain Ian Halsey had caught it. Then she administered the coup de grace. "But I would imagine someone like your Brick Devereaux in *Savage Pirate* would be doomed to remain a bachelor in real life. When a woman wants a *real* man, she looks for very different qualities than an ability to swash and buckle, whether *in* bed or out of it."

There was a shocked silence at the table for a moment, following her words, as everyone there was aware of Ian Halsey's much publicized reputation as being his own model for the male characters in his books. But having made her point, and remaining completely unmoved by the flash of savage danger in Ian's golden eyes, Alicia was quick to attempt to relax the atmosphere. After all, she was here as the guest of her boss, Howard Talton, the owner of Talton Publications, and she knew the invitation had been rendered out of a sense of real concern for her tendency to withdraw into herself since Ben's death. It certainly was not a business invitation. She was not yet high enough on the editorial ladder to pretend to any real importance on the staff. Howard Talton was a personal friend, however, which accounted for her inclusion in this evening's entertainment to celebrate the release of Ian Halsey's new book, and Alicia's only regret at having spoken as she had was that it put Howard in an awkward position.

Therefore, she raised her glass of wine and smiled brightly, if not sincerely, at Ian and proposed a toast. "Everyone else has toasted you tonight, Mr. Halsey, and I'd like to, too. Here's to Talton Publications's best-selling author," she said sweetly. "May your present book sell a million copies, and may your well-deserved success continue into the future."

Ian smiled charmingly and nodded his dark auburn head graciously amidst the general relaxation following Alicia's words and the *Hear! Hear's!* of heartfelt agreement. Alicia had to admire Ian's control, as she had the definite sense that he would like to reach across the table and strangle her bare-handed. But his restrained hostility didn't make her regret her baiting of him. She considered him a spoiled, egotistical, hedonistic, intellectual lightweight, and she thought he deserved at least one thorn among the rosy accolades that consistently came his way.

She relaxed back into her chair, suddenly tired of the chatter that resumed around her, the superficiality of her surroundings, and her own bitchiness. She had had far too much wine during the course of the evening and, as a result, her head was beginning to ache and her limbs felt slightly numb. She wanted nothing more than to go home and climb between the sheets of her lonely bed, but since she had ridden to the restaurant with Howard and his wife, Samantha, she was stuck there until they were ready to go.

As she shifted her gaze around the table, noting with disgust the fatuous expressions on the women's faces as they gazed spellbound at Ian Halsey, she inadvertently caught Brian Crossley's eye. Brian bore the distinction of being Ian's editor, and though he and Alicia were normally good friends, it was clear that he was less than pleased with her at the moment. She couldn't really blame him for that displeasure and she gave him an impish smile and a lazy wink, then almost laughed out loud at his resulting scowl. She would have to make her peace with him the next morning, but for the time being she couldn't be bothered. However, when Howard Talton appeared at her elbow and asked her to dance, Alicia emitted an inner sigh, knowing she wasn't going to be given the chance to take her time in making her peace with *him*.

Resigned to accept the scolding she knew was coming, Alicia stood up to accept his invitation, then felt slightly alarmed at the realization that she was skirting the edges of becoming drunk. The fact was vaguely annoying, since she very rarely drank at all and presumably had learned her limit long ago. She couldn't imagine why she had failed to pay attention to her normal quota of drinks this particular evening, but perhaps it had been the result of sheer boredom at hearing Ian Halsey lionized ad nauseam.

Alicia barely listened as Howard administered the expected chastisement for her behavior. She was starting to feel slightly dizzy and disoriented, and it was all she could do to follow his uncomplicated dance steps, much less his conversation. Finally Howard became aware of her lack of attention and frowned down at her with what would have been an intimidating scowl if she hadn't known him so well.

"What's the matter with you, Allie?" he growled impatiently. "First you insult our most important author, and now you aren't listening to a word I say. Are you sick?"

Alicia seized upon Howard's words with gratitude. Indeed, she felt they weren't that far from the truth at the moment. "I'm sorry, Howard," she apologized with meek sincerity. "I'm *not* feeling well, as a matter of fact, and I hope you'll forgive me for my inexcusable behavior."

"What's the matter?" Howard's irritation quickly changed to gruff concern. "Do you think you're getting the flu? It's been going around the office lately."

"Perhaps," Alicia murmured, wincing inwardly at the lie but unwilling to confess the real reason she was feeling under the weather. Howard was already disappointed with her, and she didn't want to undermine his faith in her completely.

"Do you want to go home?" he inquired with solicitous concern. "I can slip away long enough to take you if you feel you should be in bed."

Alicia bit her lip, longing to accept his offer but sure that Howard's wife, Samantha, would be upset if she did. It wasn't a question of jealousy, as Samantha was a friend of Alicia's, too, but rather the fact that Samantha was inclined to get irritated if Howard didn't stay close enough to dance attendance on her. Howard spoiled her abominably in Alicia's opinion, but that was their affair. Her expression brightened as she considered the fact that Howard's offer *did* give her the excuse to get away without being rude. She could take a taxi.

There ensued a short argument when Howard objected, but Alicia managed to convince him that she didn't need his escort. Her task was made easier, she suspected, since Howard appeared to be a little anxious about leaving Samantha in close proximity with the rakish Ian Halsey, as well he might be, considering Samantha's obvious fascination with the author.

"Very well, Allie," Howard relented as he guided her back to the table. "Just let me tell the others where we're going, then I'll take you to the street and have the doorman flag you a cab."

Inwardly Alicia thought the sooner the better. Her legs were developing a distinct tendency to wobble, and her vision was far from clear. At the table she had to concentrate all her attention on retrieving her evening bag and the wispy shawl draped over the back of her chair while Howard explained to the others why she was leaving. She could barely acknowledge their expressions of sympathy.

Suddenly her wandering attention was caught by the deep tones of Ian Halsey's attractively seductive voice wrapping itself around her name. With a frown she blinked owlishly at him as he got up from his chair. "I'll take ... uh ... *Allie* home, Howard," he was saying with suavity. "I have to be on a television set for an interview early in the morning and had planned to leave early anyway to get a good night's sleep." He glanced at Brian for confirmation. "Remember, Brian?" he prompted his editor.

Brian looked for a moment as though he didn't remember any such thing, but at Ian's flashing look he hastily murmured that he did. Ian then graciously disentangled himself from the mingled protestations coming from the others at the table as he moved to Alicia's side and plucked the shawl from her benumbed fingers and draped it over her shoulders. She stood bracing herself to stand upright, frowning in vague dismay at the prospect of sharing a taxi with the man she had mildly abused all night, but her befuddled brain wouldn't supply the necessary words to protest the arrangement. It was too occupied with maintaining her balance, preventing her from making a complete fool of herself by falling on her face in front of the whole crowd.

She never knew exactly how Ian managed to extricate the two of them from the restaurant and into a cab. She couldn't even remember if she had spoken a polite good night to everyone. She had simply drifted along beside Ian's solid, reassuring body, leaning heavily on the arm he provided for support. Somehow she found herself in the back of a taxi, slumped in a corner and drawing in huge gulps of air from the window Ian had opened for her.

When she felt able to speak, she murmured, "Thank you," gasping. "You're very kind." She was unaware of the rather nasty, sardonic smile that greeted her words, because her eyes were closed. But she became aware of Ian's attitude shortly thereafter when he spoke in a tone that echoed the smile.

"I'm always happy to assist a lady in her cups," he drawled sarcastically. "Even an amoral bastard like me picks up a few gentlemanly tendencies along life's way, if only to facilitate the seduction of tender young maidens."

Alicia's eyes flew open and she cautiously turned her head to find the golden eyes raking her with scorn. "I don't know what you mean," she managed with stilted dignity. "I'm ill...."

Ian's harsh laugh was all the more insulting for its quietness. "Oh, yes, I'm sure you are," he responded with more sarcasm. "Too much wine has a tendency to cause that condition, and at the rate you were downing it tonight, I'm surprised you were even able to walk to the taxi. You really know how to put it away, lady, I'll say that for you!"

He ignored the icy look Alicia gave him and his tone took on a mocking sympathy. "Oh, but I forgot," he purred silkily. "You have to drown your sorrows, don't you *Mrs.* Farr?"

"I thought you didn't know my name!" Alicia snapped, then put a shaking hand up to her forehead as her sharp words caused a stab of pain.

"Samantha Talton is a fount of information," he answered with incisiveness. "She told me all about the tragic young widow of the genius poet." His eyes raked her as he shifted in the seat to stretch his long legs more comfortably. "You lost your soul mate, didn't you, poor little Allie?" His smile was grim and his eyes glittered with anger. "I wonder why you haven't fled to a nunnery instead of going the alcoholic route. I believe that's the accepted method of coping with grief for a woman with your lofty ideals, and it would have the added advantage of providing a living monument to your dead husband."

Alicia stiffened at his cutting sarcasm, filled with loathing for the sneering, insensitive man who sat lounging in languid comfort, regarding her with all the cynicism she might have expected from a man of his morals. She was positive he didn't possess one fine characteristic in his whole person, and yet he dared to speak disparagingly of Ben, who had been—

She shut off the sudden pain of her memories with determined effort, forcing herself not to respond in kind to Ian Halsey's mockery. She made herself relax her body, feeling weary to the bone and utterly uncaring of the opinions of the man beside her. She realized he was merely getting back at her, and she couldn't really blame him for that, though she wished she'd never wasted her time provoking his anger in the first place. He simply wasn't worth the effort.

Closing her eyes again, Alicia faced away from him, remaining silent and seemingly impervious to his presence. It didn't take much effort to make her facade of indifference a reality, as she was having to concentrate exclusively on controlling the nausea that was boiling in her stomach from the motion of the automobile. Therefore she was startled when Ian ordered the taxi driver to stop over two blocks away from her apartment. "This isn't right..." she started to protest, but Ian ignored her and dragged her out of the taxi.

She stood shivering and miserable as he paid the driver, and her eyes were eloquent with her anger when Ian turned back to her. "Just what do you think you're doing?" she asked with cold control of that anger. "I am not in the mood for a midnight stroll!"

Ian took her arm in a bruising grip and turned her toward the direction of her apartment, ignoring her attempt to pull away. "I don't really care *what* you're in the mood for," he answered with equal coldness. "I want you to sober up, and this is as good a way as any."

Alicia closed her mouth on a biting retort and allowed him to drag her along the street. Indeed, she had very little choice in the matter, since it would have taken someone much stronger than she to break his grip. She ignored the fact that without his support she would have found it hard to make the journey on her own. Her head was clearing somewhat in the night air, but the rest of her body was still in the grip of the alcohol she'd drunk, and her legs were a very unsteady support for the moment.

The trip was accomplished in deadly silence, and Alicia couldn't wait to get into her apartment and out of Ian's company when they reached her building. She pulled on her arm again, attempting to dislodge his hold on her. "This is my building, and I can make it on my own now," she explained icily when he refused to release her. "Will you *please* let me go?"

"No." His refusal was given almost absently, though with curt determination, and Alicia fought back the urge to scream at him to leave her alone. He accompanied her up the stairs of the building and turned to hold out his hand for her key.

Resigned now to having him accompany her to the door of her apartment, Alicia simply handed him her purse. It was beyond her to search among its contents for the key he was requesting.

Moments later, after an elevator ride that did nothing to settle the queasiness in her stomach, Alicia breathed a silent sigh of relief that at last she was going to be rid of Ian Halsey. He was opening her apartment door, and, in seconds, she would be able to climb into her bed and sleep away the disaster of this night. She couldn't wait!

As the door swung open Alicia held out her hand for her key, expecting Ian to hand it over. "I won't say thank you," she bit out icily. "I think your only purpose in escorting me home was to give you an opportunity to get revenge for my comments this evening. Well, you've said what you wanted to, and now if you don't mind…"

She got no further as Ian grasped her arm and shoved her inside her apartment, then followed her in. She swung around to face him, wavering unsteadily at her precipitate movement, to see him toss her key onto the small table in the foyer. Then, before she could utter a word, Ian grabbed her shoulders and forced her backward until she was pressed against the wall, his body holding her where she stood. Eyes wide, body tense against the unwelcome intrusion of Ian's, Alicia sputtered with the indignation she felt.

Ian reached up a hand to place it over her mouth, his eyes boring into hers, his expression grimly intent. "Oh, no, Alicia Farr," he grated out threateningly. "I didn't bring you home just to *tell* you what I think of prudish, bitchy women who take pleasure in verbally downgrading what I do for a living while they curl up under the covers with one of my books to experience a little vicarious excitement. I brought you home to *show* you what I think of women like that! I'm going to show you what a little hypocrite you are, grieving for your poor, dead, saintly husband on the outside while you long for an entirely different kind of man on the inside!''

Alicia gasped as Ian bent his head to capture her mouth with savagery, grinding his lips against hers with bruising force and punishing her body with the dominance of his own. She wasn't frightened by his actions, simply because she couldn't believe a man of his renown would risk a rape charge just for the sake of relieving his anger. Rather, she was furious at his implication that she would prefer a man of his type over Ben, and she was disgusted at his primitive method of trying to extract revenge for a few insults. It was typical of his character, she thought with scathing dislike as she struggled feebly against him.

The struggling was automatic. The feebleness was caused by the still lingering effects of the wine she had drunk and the weary acceptance that in a physical battle between them, there was simply no contest. She could wear herself out trying to fight him off, but given the size of him and his excellent physical condition, she would get nowhere. Besides, she was certain he would desist from his pointless attack once he had got some of the spleen out of his system. She decided she could help that along by ceasing to resist at all and, suiting action to thought, she let her hands fall to her sides and her body relax against the wall.

A low triumphant laugh greeted her actions, and Ian Halsey raised his head to stare into Alicia's eyes, his own glittering with satisfaction. "It's taking less time than I thought to prove my point," he grated out mockingly, apparently mistaking Alicia's drooping eyelids as a sign of sensuality rather than sheer fatigue. "Aren't you even going to make a show of fighting for your honor?" he mocked. "Or are you too starved for a man in your bed to waste time?"

Alicia gave a deep sigh, opening her eyes wider to give Ian the full benefit of the tired disgust they reflected. "On the contrary, Mr. Halsey," she said with exaggerated boredom and contempt in her voice. "You haven't proven a thing, except that you're bigger and stronger than I am." She saw his jaw tighten and a look come into his golden eyes that should have warned her she was taking the wrong tack with him, but she simply didn't have the energy or the wits to plot strategy right then.

"I assure you I am not starved for a man," she went on unheedingly. "I've had the best there is, and it spoiled me for anything else. I certainly wouldn't attempt to find the same sort of satisfaction with *you*, even if I did feel the need for physical gratification." Finishing her little speech on a dismissing, uncaring note, Alicia let her drooping eyelids close again, naively waiting for Ian Halsey to release her. Consequently she missed the hard purposefulness that appeared in his eyes and the male aggressiveness that tautened his features. She wasn't the least aware that her words had been construed as a direct challenge to his maleness rather than the off-putting dismissal she had intended.

"Is that so?" he murmured with deceptive softness, his gaze roaming her pale features and settling on the soft vulnerability of her mouth. "I think you just settled your fate, Allie," he drawled in that same soft, dangerous tone. "You aren't nearly as smart as you think, are you, my dear?"

His tone finally got through to Alicia, and she opened her eyes, a puzzled frown creasing her smooth forehead. It seemed Ian had only been waiting for her attention, and when he had it, he brought both his hands up to her breasts while he pinned her body to the wall with his thighs.

Alicia's eyes widened in shock and she drew in her breath on a gasp as Ian's thumbs stroked her nipples with a sensuous expertise that was just short of hurting. The unexpected physical reaction she felt brought Alicia's hands up in an instinctive reaction to try to dislodge Ian's. "Stop!" she got out on a strangled note.

A hard smile pulled at Ian's firm mouth, and his gaze was unrelentingly steady as he continued what he was doing and ignored Alicia's feeble attempts to move his hands. The look of reckless determination on his face sparked off the first twinge of real fear in Alicia, though she was still unable to believe that Ian meant to do any more than frighten her. But since, if that was his purpose, he was beginning to accomplish it, Alicia tried to marshal her wits to combat him more effectively than she had managed so far.

"Ian, please..." she unconsciously pleaded, then bit her bottom lip in chagrin at allowing him that small victory. He was the type of man who would only take any show of weakness as encouragement, she felt certain.

"Please what?" he mocked her. "You want more?" His eyes raked her. "I'm more than happy to oblige, I assure you." With that he released her breasts, but even as Alicia was beginning to relax with the relief she felt, he raised his hands to her shoulders to push the material of her dress aside, using enough force so that she heard and felt the rip of the flimsy fabric as the draped bodice parted.

Her shock and fear gave birth to instant fury! "Damn you, Ian Halsey!" she spat at him. "This is an expensive dress, and I can't afford to pay for your childish games!'' Her blue eyes sparkled with animosity as she glared up at him, but anger proved as ineffective at stopping him as had indifference.

His dark eyebrows rose in sardonic amusement. "Then I must remember to buy you another dress to replace this one, mustn't I?'' he drawled infuriatingly, but Alicia's anger was choked off by his next words, to be replaced with a return of her fear. "But this is no game, Alicia,'' he promised in that soft, menacing voice that sent a chill down her spine. "I think it's about time you faced that fact and took me seriously, don't you?''

His mouth came closer with each word, while Alicia watched its approach with all the horrified attention of a small bird confronted with the approach of a snake. She shuddered as his mouth closed on hers and forced her lips apart, but it was too late to take countermeasures by the time she was alert enough to protest the invasion of his tongue.

A moan came up from her throat but was smothered by Ian's insistent mouth as he ravaged her lips. Alicia brought her hands to his shoulders to try to push him away, but he used the opportunity to stroke his palms down her sides to her thighs, then around to her buttocks. He curved his fingers around the soft rounded mounds of flesh and lifted her into the grinding motion of his hips.

Ian's assault brought a dismaying sensual response from Alicia that was entirely physical and which became all mixed up with the churning nausea in her stomach and the pounding ache in her head. She felt overwhelmed by the chaotic sensory assaults she was undergoing, and for long moments, as Ian continued to kiss her and mold her against him, she could only drift with the tide while she struggled to subdue all of her various physical symptoms.

When Ian at last drew back, she noted with one vague, alarmed part of her mind that his breathing was harshening and his body had hardened during his attempts to arouse *her.* Apparently he was getting caught up in his own game, which only increased the chances for disaster inherent in the situation.

"Ian..." Alicia gasped his name as he bent his head to rasp his lips against the sensitive skin of her neck. "Ian, why are you doing this? If you want—" She started to say that if he wanted an apology from her as the price for stopping what he was doing, she was more than ready to give it, but he cut her off.

"Yes, I *want,* Alicia," he growled from deep within his throat. "I want once and for all to make a woman like you face up to what's inside her, instead of condemning me for being honest." He raised his head with a jerk and his eyes flared with a combination of anger and arousal. "I want you to admit you're just as capable of allowing your body to rule you as any man is, instead of hiding behind a sneering, superior morality that's only skin deep!" He took her roughly by the shoulders and gave her a slight shake. "You picked the wrong time and the wrong man to dig your claws into, Alicia Farr! I've had all of that kind of hypocrisy I can take!"

Alicia was appalled at the reaction she had unwittingly set off in this man. Apparently he had been building up for something like this for a long time, and she was going to be the recipient of whatever hostilities he had accumulated. She had, indeed, been at the wrong place at the wrong time, saying the wrong things, and she had lit a fire under simmering emotions she would never have suspected Ian Halsey capable of harboring. Now it was up to her to short-circuit those emotions before she had to pay a far higher price for setting them off than she deserved!

She licked her lips and swallowed down the nausea welling into her throat. "Ian, listen," she panted, pushing against his shoulders with little effect. "I'm sick, Ian. I'm sick and a little drunk...." She tried not to plead again, but in any case her words were having little effect. Ian's hard features were as uncompromising as ever. But she had to *try* to make him realize that she really was ill! "Ian, *please!* I'm really not well...."

A harsh breath of laughter washed over her. "I'll make you feel better," he purred nastily. Then he suddenly stepped back, and Alicia sagged against the wall, but an instant later she was being lifted into his arms and carried into the living room of the apartment, where Ian paused, searching for the bedroom door with his eyes. He headed in the right direction unerringly, and Alicia could only cling to him helplessly, fighting the nausea that was becoming increasingly difficult to control.

When Ian tossed her down onto the middle of her bed, Alicia had to raise a hand and place it over her mouth to choke down the sickness threatening to spill over. She was in no condition to fight him as he began to strip off her clothing with an economy of motion and a frightening speed that were appallingly indicative of how often he must have done so with other women.

Then he stood up and shrugged out of his jacket, tossing it onto the floor. His hands began to unfasten the buttons of his shirt with that same efficiency he'd used on her, and Alicia watched in horrified fascination, using all her will to bring her thoughts to order. Her body was beyond her control and would be absolutely no use to her in preventing what was about to happen, and that left only her mind to help her.

"Ian, I'm going to throw up!" Alicia warned on a note of total sincerity. The pallor of her face and the trembling in her limbs gave force to her threat, and Ian paused momentarily as his eyes searched her face. The fact that the pause was only momentary before he slowly began to draw off his shirt, and the calculating expression on his face were anything but encouraging to Alicia. She was about to throw dignity to the wind and do exactly as she'd threatened when Ian turned away and started across the room toward the small adjoining bathroom.

"We can't have that," he said on a dry note as he disappeared from view.

Alicia lay where she was, knowing she should use the opportunity his temporary absence provided to get up and away, but she felt totally unable to move. She consoled herself with the knowledge that even had she been able to make her body function properly, by the time she found something to put on her nude body and got to the door, Ian would catch her.

She heard water running in the bathroom, and then Ian was back with a glass of foaming liquid in one hand and a dripping washcloth in the other. "Drink this!" he ordered as he tossed the wet washcloth onto the bedside table with little regard for its effect on the wooden surface, then lifted her with his arm into a position to drink.

Choking and gasping, Alicia was forced to drink the liquid Ian held to her mouth before he would let her lie down again. An instant later she felt the cold wetness of the washcloth on her face. She reached up with both hands to press its blessed relief to her flushed skin, reveling in the dissipation of her nausea the drink and the cold wetness were bringing.

She completely forgot Ian for the moment in her

self-preoccupation, until she felt the mattress beside her give under his weight and then felt the long length of his warm body beside her. Startled into an awareness that the danger he represented was far from over, Alicia cautiously lowered the wet cloth from her face and stared up at him as he loomed over her with all the overpowering maleness of his superb now-naked body pressed against her side.

"Feeling better?" he murmured with a cynical smile as he plucked the cloth from her hands and tossed it aside.

Alicia didn't acknowledge his question. She was too busy searching for something... *anything*... to say to deflect him from his purpose. It was obvious that the state of her health was going to prove no deterrent. He had simply gone about making her feel better in order to aid the accomplishment of his objective. The man had absolutely no moral decency to appeal to, apparently, but perhaps he did have a modicum of common sense.

"Ian, I promise you, if you go through with this, I'll have you prosecuted for rape," she assured him levelly. "I have nothing to lose, but you do. The publicity could ruin your career."

She felt a spasm of defeat when she saw the unconcerned smile her words elicited. "Ah, but it won't *be* rape, Alicia," he promised softly as he drew a finger from the base of her throat down to her navel. Alicia shivered at his touch, her inner confusion mounting again as she felt an unwanted physical pleasure combined with fearful loathing for Ian's dominance over her. "Why don't you just relax and accept the inevitable," he coaxed persuasively, bringing his finger back up her body to circle a nipple. "There's a lot of passion underneath your prim exterior, Alicia," he murmured as he dipped his head to brush her mouth with his. "Let it out," he whispered. "You know you want to."

Alicia stiffened as he lowered his head farther and captured the peak of her breast in his mouth. The tantalizing sensations his suckling evoked infuriated her even as they sparked a debilitating warmth in her belly and thighs that chased away her remaining nausea as though it had never existed.

She fought the alcohol-induced weakness in her limbs as hard as she fought Ian's seduction, beginning to struggle in earnest for the first time since Ian had begun his assault. "Damn you, Ian Halsey," she panted as she writhed and thrashed to get away from him. "I don't want you! I can't stand you! Can't you understand that, you egotistical bastard?"

Ian's eyes flashed with hot arousal as he subdued her, and his lips were clenched over a savage smile. "You may not like me, Alicia, I'll give you that," he ground out with a nasty laugh, "but I can prove that you want me."

Ian thrust one of Alicia's arms under his body to immobilize it and caught the other in an iron grip. Then he forced one of his legs between her thighs so that she couldn't move anything but one leg, which proved useless as a defense. He let her thrash around with it until her exhaustion reached its limits and she collapsed, and then he slowly began to explore her with his free hand. He touched her breasts and stomach, his palm and fingers amazingly light and erotic in contrast to the brute strength he was using to keep her where he wanted her.

Alicia recognized the pattern of that roving hand as it traveled slowly, seductively, down her body, coming ever nearer to an objective she knew she couldn't afford to let him reach. The danger that Ian might succeed in seducing rather than raping her was too great, and by now she was resigned to the fact that he was going to use her body one way or another. It only remained to be sure that she maintained a weapon with which to punish him for that use instead of letting him win over her on all counts.

"Ian," she said, projecting calmness into her voice with every ounce of her will. "How do you manage to live with yourself after doing something like this? Are you incapable of feeling guilt?"

Ian's amused look vied with the softening his sexual arousal had imparted to his strong features. "I won't know until later, Alicia." He chuckled with a silky growl. "You're the first woman I've ever had to fight to get to bed."

Alicia closed her eyes wearily, wondering if he spoke the truth and, if he did, how she had had the bad luck to become the first woman he had ever decided to subdue by force.

"However," Ian continued, his voice growing huskier, "I don't think I'm going to need to feel guilty." His voice dropped into a still lower register as he finally reached what he sought and discovered Alicia's unwilling, hated physical arousal. "You can't pretend any longer that this is going to be rape, can you, Alicia?" He whispered her name, nuzzling her ear with his warm lips.

Alicia's first shuddering reaction to Ian's intrusive intimacy turned to a trembling struggle to fight what her body was beginning to demand under his expert manipulation. Her thoughts churned with wild disbelief at what was happening to her. Surely her body and her mind couldn't be so out of tune. To have this reaction to a man she loathed was an insult to everything she'd ever believed about herself and the nature of love...an insult to what had been between herself and Ben. It was intolerable!

Ian didn't give her time to agonize over her tortured thoughts for long. "Don't worry, Allie," he breathed with an exultant satisfaction that scraped her nerves even as it shivered her flesh with a response to his male domination. "This won't hurt a bit...."

Then he was on top of her in one smooth motion that gave her no opportunity to use his release of her arms and legs as a chance to escape, and with that same economy of motion she had noted earlier he used his thighs to push her legs apart and plunged into her, all in one graceful, devastating movement that managed to take her by surprise despite her expectation that it was going to happen.

"No!" She cried the word out instinctively, tensing every muscle in her body in rejection of his possession.

"It's too late for no, Allie," Ian groaned, and as Alicia stared up in horror at the glazed, golden fire in his eyes, she felt him begin the smooth, irresistible motion that imitated the act of love he profaned so casually.

Despite every screaming denial in her mind and heart against it, despite her wild inner assurances to herself that she wasn't like this, that she needed warm, nurturing commitment and love before she could respond sexually to a man's touch, Alicia felt long-dormant instincts slowly begin to function. Ben had been dead a year, and she had thought all her desire for physical gratification had died with him, but her body knew better. Perhaps if she had been her normal self, unweakened by alcohol and fatigue, she could have won over her healthy sensuality with her mind. But she had no strength left with which to fight.

Ian did his part in undermining her defenses as well.

He was enormously skilled as a lover, and Alicia found herself being drawn into his demands and responding to his forceful sexual manipulations. Her mind began losing control with increasing frequency as her body's needs took over.

She heard Ian murmur, "That's it..." in a soothing croon. "That's it, my darling Alicia. Let go...let go...." And with a strangled cry of despairing denial and savage release, Alicia followed his lead and did as he ordered. She let go and flowed into his rhythm with a mindless, passionate striving for the ecstasy he promised with every powerful surge of his smooth muscular body.

When the final release did come, a part of Alicia was sick with the knowledge that she and Ian had reached it simultaneously. They had proven perfectly matched in a physical sense, coming together with an exquisitely coordinated fusion that was technically, if not emotionally, the most satisfactory sexual experience she had ever achieved. Ben's lovemaking had been sweet and gentle and entirely satisfactory to her in her limited experience, but it couldn't compare with the sheer power of Ian's.

But Ian's performance couldn't be termed loving, Alicia realized as a wave of nausea flowed through her as she lay spent in his arms, her skin slick with perspiration, her heart pounding from the strength of her exertion. Ian had used her as though she were merely an object for his gratification, deriving most of his satisfaction from humiliating her rather than from satisfying her.

He levered himself up on his elbows and smiled down at her with lazy self-satisfaction, but at the look of frozen hatred in Alicia's eyes, his smile crooked into a wry coolness.

"Get up!" Alicia bit out the words, wanting for the first time in her life to commit violence against another human being. "Get up and get out before I—" She choked on the words, not wanting to waste another syllable on him.

Ian took his time about it. For long moments he stared down at her, something moving behind his heavy lidded eyes that almost resembled regret, but Alicia knew it couldn't be. He reached a hand to brush the damp tendrils of her wheat-colored hair from her temples, but when she shrank from his touch, his expression closed up and his eyes went coolly blank.

As he finally got up, Alicia closed her eyes and held on to her fast-diminishing control, determined she wouldn't give him the satisfaction of seeing her cry.

"You're taking the loss of your pride rather hard, aren't you?" Ian said in a cool voice as he shrugged into his shirt. "You're only human, you know. You shouldn't—"

Alicia's eyes were filled with icy contempt as she opened them in response to his words and seared him with the blue flames they contained. "I haven't lost a thing, Mr. Halsey." She cut across what he was about to say with deadly coldness. "My pride is intact and always will be. Nothing you did could ever dent it." But even as she said the words, her mind was wailing the silent litany that she *had* lost her pride! She had!

"Oh, I'm aware that I'm not the cause of it," he replied in a dry drawl. "It's what *you've* done that you're finding so hard to live with."

Alicia abruptly turned her back on him, curling into a huddled ball. She bit back the response that threatened to spill out, knowing she would dissolve into hysteria if she started to express her hatred of him. But his words revolved sickeningly in her mind, for she knew he was right. She felt as soiled and sullied as any prostitute who sold her body for money. More so, in fact, for she had sold hers for a few moments of mindless pleasure, and to a man who had made it clear what he thought of her before she had given him what he wanted.

At last she heard the sounds that meant Ian had finished dressing and was about to leave. Her mind screamed at him to hurry...to get out and leave her alone to try to cope with this new self-contempt waiting to overwhelm her.

Ian didn't leave immediately, however. Instead he came to sit beside her on the bed. He touched her shoulder, ignoring the shrinking stiffness of her immediate response.

"Alicia, I'm sorry," he apologized in a deep, weary voice. She was shaking now, and Ian reached down to the foot of the bed for a coverlet to pull over her, though his expression made it clear that he knew her shivers were not due to the chill in the air. "Don't take it so hard," he persisted in a gentle voice. "It's been a long time since you've made love, hasn't it? Since your husband died?" He paused, and when Alicia didn't answer, he went on. "Your body was hungry, Alicia. And your resistance was down because you had drunk too much and were sick." He gave a slight, self-condemnatory shrug of his wide shoulders. "And I didn't give you a chance to control that hunger. I was angry, and I meant to humiliate you...." Again he paused, and again Alicia was silent, gritting her teeth and forcing down the sobs that were tearing at her throat.

She didn't see Ian silently shaking his head in anger at himself, or the very real regret in his eyes. "I won't apologize again, Alicia," he murmured on a deep note, his voice expressing that anger, not realizing that Alicia took it to be directed at her. "You're in no mood to accept it, and I can't blame you." His grip tightened on her shoulder for a moment and then he got to his feet. "But give yourself a break, Alicia. You didn't damage anything but your pride, and that will heal if you give it a chance to. You're not the first person to discover that you can't always live up to your own image of yourself." Alicia was beyond detecting the self-mockery in his tone and she couldn't see the tight self-disgust in his expression.

"Good night, Alicia," he murmured softly. He hesitated for a moment, surveying with sad eyes the huddled picture she made, then he turned on his heels and left the room, closing the door quietly behind him.

His exit was the signal Alicia needed to let go of her stoic control and to give in to the tears that washed over her in racking paroxysms of grief and anger and self-disgust. She was unaware that Ian still stood just outside her door with his head bent and his fists clenched, listening to her cry out her misery. His face wore a haggard expression of self-condemnation that would have afforded Alicia a great deal of savage satisfaction had she seen it.

But she couldn't see it, and after a while, when Ian had satisfied himself that Alicia's sobs were easing, he moved quietly away from the door and let himself out of the apartment to walk for long hours through the silent, empty streets of New York.

And back in her lonely hell she had created for herself, Alicia pulled the covers higher over her shaking shoulders and fell into an exhausted sleep that gave her the only peace she was to know for the days and weeks of torment that stretched endlessly ahead of her like a dark tunnel into eternity.

Chapter Two

Alicia called in sick the next morning, and it wasn't a lie. Apart from a classic hangover, she was suffering from mental and emotional depression that rivaled what she'd felt after Ben's death. At least then she'd blamed blind fate for what had happened. Now she had no one to blame but herself, and since it was the first major disappointment she'd ever suffered with regard to her own actions, she was unequipped to deal with it.

As she faced the drawn paleness of her face in the bathroom mirror, she reflected with wry bitterness that the age of thirty was no time to have to come to terms with the fact that she was as fallible as the next person. She had been a classic good girl all her life: a model daughter, a model student, a model wife, and, until last night, a model employee. What, in God's name, had happened to her all of a sudden?

Her features hardened as she reflected that Ian Halsey had happened to her. The man had provoked her into a veritable string of unpredictable behavior, all the way from turning her into a catty bitch, which was definitely not her style, to undermining her lifelong belief in herself as a person embodying all the finer instincts that went hand in hand with a strong moral fiber and an upright character. What a myth! She smiled bitterly, her bruised, swollen mouth turning down at the corners. Ian Halsey had entered her life and, in the space of a few hours, had shown her she had no more claim to moral superiority than a common streetwalker!

And she hated him for it. That was something else she hadn't experienced before—the burning, lacerating acid of hatred stirring in her guts and branding her mind with a whole new bitterness she couldn't have contemplated twenty-four hours earlier. Some deeply buried emotions she hadn't even realized she possessed had been brought to the surface under Ian Halsey's tutelage, and they writhed in her consciousness like the proverbial snake in the Garden of Eden.

Alicia turned away from the mirror, feeling more sick in mind than in body, and walked slowly to the kitchen to fix an unwanted cup of coffee, her movements lethargic and listless, completely contrary to her usual briskness of motion. As she waited for the water to heat she wandered aimlessly from counter to table, her eyes vague and unfocused, her fingers restlessly fiddling with whatever came to hand. When the kettle screamed, it made her jump in reaction, as she'd forgotten she'd even put it on to boil.

Later, sitting at the table, sipping the coffee she didn't taste, tears slipped down her cheeks unheeded as she wondered how she was going to put her life back together when she was so completely changed inside. How could she go on doing the same things in the same way when she was a different person now?

Her glance focused on the wall clock, and a memory of something she needed to do struggled for recognition. And then she remembered. Ian Halsey would be on television in a few moments, giving an interview so that all the "little" people in the world could have the benefit of seeing him and hearing him and envying his success. Alicia's eyes narrowed and her forehead crinkled under her puzzled frown. Seeing Ian Halsey again, even on television, was the last thing she wanted in the world. So why was she thinking of it at all?

The hair of the dog? she thought cynically. Did she need to look at him once more to try to dissipate some of the damage he'd done as carelessly as he would throw the remains of a meal in the garbage once he'd finished with it? Her fists clenched as she debated the wisdom of giving in to her inclination to turn on the set and stare at the face of the man she hated. The prospect held some of the same fascination for her that she imagined gripped people at the scene of a tragic accident. There was both a pull and a sense of repulsion warring for dominance. In the end the pull won, and Alicia got up and moved toward the living room and the TV, almost like a sleepwalker in the grasp of a nightmare.

The program was just beginning as the set came on, and Alicia walked to the sofa to huddle on one end, her knees drawn up, her arms wrapped around them and holding on with a tenseness that invaded her whole body. She felt an actual physical jolt when the camera focused on Ian's strong, masculinely distinctive features, which looked drawn and pale under his normal tan this morning.

Alicia stared at him, unable to turn her eyes away from that face, images of what had happened between them the night before flashing in and out of her mind with anguishing force. She studied him with all the attention she might have given to some dangerous species of alien that threatened her very life.

At first she didn't hear the give-and-take of the interview. She was too intent on *seeing* Ian to hear him. But gradually, as her heart steadied to an approximation of its normal beat and her breath began to fill her lungs again, she forced herself to listen, instinctively wanting ammunition to fuel the hatred his image instilled.

The interviewer was good, projecting neither animosity nor favoritism, asking discerning questions and allowing Ian to actually answer them before he went on to the next. Alicia tensed slightly as the interviewer began to discuss the nature of Ian's work. Since she considered that Ian's work was substantially an extension of his character, Alicia wanted to hear how he justified both.

"Mr. Halsey," the interviewer began, "there are a lot of people who consider your books to be intellectually lightweight, catering to the baser instincts we all have rather than trying to uplift the reader to a higher plane of consciousness. How do you reply to such criticism of your work?"

"Well, Ben," Ian began, giving Alicia a decided jolt at hearing that name on his lips. She remembered for the first time the name of the interviewer, and with a lightning flash of irony she conceived the idea that this interview could be construed as a debate between the ethics of her late husband and Ian's own—if he had any. She relaxed slightly, a twisted smile on her lips, fully expecting to view with contempt Ian's forthcoming justification that she was certain would lack any real veracity.

"You say a *lot* of people consider my books in a negative way," Ian went on. He shrugged his magnificent shoulders, and a faint smile tugged at his sensuous mouth. "I can only say that judging from the sales figures, there are a lot of other people who view them differently." There was a spattering of laughter from the studio audience, and even the interviewer's craggy features lightened in a smile. But when the camera returned to Ian, his expression had changed to thoughtful introspection. It gave his face an attraction Alicia rebelled against.

"There's a market for my type of book, Ben," Ian said quietly. "And because there's a market, there must be a need. I don't see anything wrong with fulfilling that need. People come in all shapes and sizes, with diverse capacities and interests. I've never been able to figure out why one segment of society feels they have the right to dictate to another what they should or shouldn't eat, drink, think... or read."

A wry smile curved the firm contours of Ian's mouth and his eyes flashed with dry amusement. "Do you think it has to do with a need to feel superior?" he asked rhetorically. "If so, I can think of better ways to feed one's ego than to have to put someone else down in order to raise yourself up."

Ian faced the camera directly then, his eyes seeming to bore into Alicia's. She drew back slightly under the onslaught of that look, already feeling slightly uncomfortable from the impact of his words. They struck her in an area where she was most vulnerable—her own sense of fairness, and her tendency to adopt an attitude of superiority because her interests had always been of an intellectual vein. She was one of those people who considered Ian's books lightweight material, and she didn't like having her conclusions held up to objective scrutiny. It was an uncomfortable challenge to look at herself as a snob, and she didn't need any more shakeups to deal with than Ian had already given her.

"Wouldn't it be better if people didn't always feel the need to label things and people?" Ian continued in that same thoughtful vein. "I confess, I've always had a tendency to live and let live, and it disturbs me when I come across someone who feels they have the right to judge me or anyone else. And it isn't only a tendency to judge others, but themselves as well." He shrugged charmingly. "Human beings are not and never will be perfect. And yet they insist on setting that impossible goal for themselves and others."

He shook his head then, his dark auburn hair falling across his forehead from the movement, giving him a curiously vulnerable look. "Sorry to get off the subject," he apologized to Ben, the interviewer. "What I'm trying to say, I suppose, is that I have no intention of apologizing for my work. It doesn't need justification. It is what it is, and people either like it and buy it or they don't. I view it as entertainment that fills a need, and as long as it sells, I can only assume a lot of other people do, too."

Alicia blinked at that. It was such a simple statement of fact, and the basic truth behind it shook her. When she had turned on the set, the last thing she had expected was that Ian Halsey would make her feel better about herself. She didn't quite know what it was she *had* expected, but certainly not exposure to a philosophy of life she'd never taken seriously before. But then, she had never needed the healing gift of mercy for her own shortcomings before. She had always lived up to her—and others'—expectations.

She felt a little disoriented by the changes in her beliefs that she was undergoing, and for the next few moments she lost out on the discussion between Ian and Ben. Then her attention was brought sharply back to the set as she heard the interviewer mention Ian's private life.

"There's a lot of speculation that your stories are based on your own private exploits, Mr. Halsey," Ben said, grinning. "How true is that? You're a bachelor, I believe, and all the women on the staff have been swooning since they heard you were coming on the show, so I assume you have no problems in conducting...uh...research for the more erotic portions of your books."

There was laughter and whooping from the male members of the audience and titters from the females. Alicia unconsciously tensed again, her face grim and anguished as she wondered if she would someday end up in one of Ian Halsey's books, perhaps as the classic example of the protesting female who succumbed to the hero's seduction.

Ian's expression closed up momentarily at the question, and then, as if realizing that he had a part to play, he flashed the devilish smile that was so effective with most women, Alicia supposed, though not with her, she thought grimly. Never with her.

"I'm a bachelor, yes," Ian drawled, amusement glowing in his eyes as the women in the audience gave a collective sigh. "And that's all I'm going to say about that particular subject."

The audience groaned, and the interviewer chuckled, but when the noise died down, Ben persisted. "Come now, Mr. Halsey, you're among friends here. We won't tell anybody your secrets." He laughed as he spread his arms innocently. "Just tell us what you like in a woman," he coaxed. "I'm sure the females in our audience are dying to hear."

Alicia grimaced in disgust at the loud yelling that backed up the interviewer's statement, bitterly deciding that she knew exactly what Ian Halsey liked in a woman: subservience, cowlike devotion and respect, and the ability to keep her mouth shut—not to mention a willingness to please him in bed! She smiled bitterly. On second thought, the woman didn't even have to be willing...just in the wrong place at the wrong time.

Ian looked directly into the camera again, and Alicia shrank back unconsciously, having the same feeling as earlier that he was speaking for her benefit, which was patently ridiculous! He had probably forgotten she existed!

"Honesty," he said on a clipped note that took everyone by surprise with its seriousness. "I'm not a fan of women who lie to themselves and everyone else about what they're really like." He shrugged, looking tired and momentarily disgusted. Then he raised his golden eyes to the camera again, and Alicia felt a pull at her senses that she rejected with all her might. "And kindness," he added calmly. "We can all use a little of that."

His answer left the audience subdued, not being what they had expected, and the interviewer hastily broke for a commercial. Alicia sat frozen where she was, pondering Ian's words. He had insisted last night that she was like many women he had apparently come in contact with who denied their own natures and indulged in hypocrisy in public, then slipped under the covers with one of his books for some "safe" excitement. But the description hadn't applied to her, though Ian hadn't known it. She had never felt the things he ascribed to her until— She bit her lip and clenched her hands at the memory of how she had responded to him the night before— Until Ian Halsey had taken her to bed and had proved she had a capacity for passion that she had never suspected.

Alicia jumped up from the couch and began to pace the room, hugging her stomach with her arms, determined to think things out no matter how painful the process. A little wildly she wished she *were* like the women he had described. There was nothing inherently wrong with behaving circumspectly for the benefit of others while harboring secret desires that could be fed harmlessly alone under the covers with a spicy book. In fact, it seemed a healthy way to deal with the reality of human nature. Certainly no one would recommend that instead of fantasizing people act out their secret desires. The whole fabric of society would unravel under those circumstances!

But Alicia had never felt the need to fantasize. Not that it was anything to feel superior about, it was just a fact. During her teen years she had been too busy with her studies to date much, and when she *had* dated, she had been much more interested in lively conversation than in groping in the backseat of a car. She had met Ben in college, and it was his nature that had drawn her rather than any physical need. The need had grown, of course, as her love for him had developed. She had always thought the sexual part of their marriage was wonderful. Ben's sweet tenderness had nurtured and comforted her, and she had enjoyed the subdued passion he could invoke in her, without ever really thinking too much about it, other than experiencing a certain feeling of relief that she wasn't frigid. She had been accused of it by disappointed suitors and had half begun to believe it herself until Ben had shown her otherwise.

Now she knew that there were other kinds of sex than that which sprung naturally from spiritual love, and the knowledge that she was capable of enjoying— no, *reveling,* she corrected herself bitterly—in purely carnal satisfaction was galling. It destroyed an image it had taken her thirty years to accumulate...an image of sweet chastity, pure femininity, and the redeeming sense of being *above* such things.

Well, Alicia thought with a sad sigh, Ian had shown her she wasn't above much at all, and if she was going to get on with her life, she had better learn to accept

her own feet of clay...or at least come to terms with
them if acceptance was impossible.

Her attention was drawn to the TV again as the commercial faded and Ian's powerful body and features appeared on the screen. The cameraman had drawn back
to include both Ian and the interviewer in the shot, and
Ben was speaking, winding up the interview. "I wonder
if you have any last words for us, Mr. Halsey." He
grinned invitingly. "I always like to give my guests a
chance to leave a few words of wisdom with the audience before we close the show."

The camera panned in on Ian's face, and Alicia
stared impassively as a slow smile curved his mouth.
His eyes were warm and humorous, showing clearly
that he found it pretentious to impart wisdom to anyone. Nevertheless, he spoke in a comfortable drawl,
giving a little wave of his hand to the camera in fare-
well. "Go easy on yourselves, friends," he advised
casually, "and on your neighbors as well."

The camera panned back, and the studio was filled
with the sound of applause. The host gave a salute of
his own to his audience, spoke the traditional words he
always used to end his show, and then the screen was
filled with another commercial, which Alicia stared at
blankly without hearing a word. "Go easy on yourself," Ian had advised, Alicia thought with a wry sense
of black humor. She imagined he took his own advice
regularly...out of necessity, if last night's performance
was anything to go by.

Still, it was good advice as far as she was concerned for
the moment. If she kept on berating herself the way she
had this morning, she would go crazy! Why not let herself off the hook and place the blame squarely where it
belonged...on Ian Halsey's broad, strong shoulders. If
it hadn't been for him, she would have nothing to chas-

tise herself *for,* after all. She certainly hadn't set out to place herself in this ungodly position. And she had fought as well as she was able to prevent it. She ignored the still small voice in the back of her mind that pointed out that while Ian had precipitated events, she could still have salvaged her pride if she had been able to keep from responding to him. It was in all ways preferable to avoid accepting her own share of the blame when Ian presented such a satisfactory target.

Feeling much better than she had earlier, Alicia decided to use the rest of the day to clean her apartment. She could have gone into work, but she was reluctant to face anyone just yet. She told herself she needed more time to consolidate the facade she was about to adopt—that she was the same person she had been before Ian Halsey had appeared in her life and rocked the foundations of her self-respect.

By the time she entered her office the following morning, she had herself well under control and was able to parry the solicitous inquiries after her health with cool politeness. It was only when Brian Crossley appeared in the door to her office that her composure cracked a little. She eyed him warily as he entered the room and slouched down into the chair across from her desk.

"Good morning, Brian," she said with quiet calmness.

"Morning, Allie," Brian replied, his sharp eyes taking in the pallor of her face and the way she was nervously twisting a pencil in her fingers. "Are you recovered, or have you brought your germs into the office to infect the rest of us?" he said in his typical blunt fashion.

Alicia relaxed a little, a faint smile appearing to lighten her expression. "I think it was the other way around," she replied wryly. "Someone else brought the germs in, and I gathered them up and took them home with me.''

Brian shrugged. ''Hazards of the trade,'' he quipped unsympathetically. ''At any rate, it saved you from getting your tail chewed royally yesterday. I was in the mood to eat nails.''

Alicia raised her eyebrows inquiringly, waiting for Brian to bring up Ian's name. She was beyond doing so herself, though she was perfectly aware of where Brian was heading.

''Don't look so innocent, Allie,'' Brian said with a sardonic look in his eyes. ''You know damn well what I'm talking about. What got into you, anyway?'' The puzzled irritation was clear in his tone. ''You've never been like that before.''

''Like what?'' Alicia stalled, searching for some explanation to give Brian that would sound reasonable. She didn't know herself why she had baited Ian the way she had, and she wished to God she'd never given in to the strange compulsion to do so that he had elicited in her.

'Like what!'' Brian mocked her exasperatedly. ''Like some bitchy snob who's all claws and teeth and sneering superiority.'' He got up and paced to the window, his whole body expressing his irritation. ''I could have killed you,'' he informed her, his temper growing as he got into the discussion. ''Especially since I'd spent most of the day trying to talk Ian out of writing just the kind of book you would approve of and which would fall flat on the shelves and never make a dollar for him or for us.''

Startled, Alicia looked up at him in confusion. ''What?'' she asked in puzzled disbelief. ''What are you talking about, Brian?''

He came over to her desk and leaned on his hands,

thrusting his face at her to emphasize what he had to say. "I'm talking about the facts of life, my dear," he said harshly. "People like you have been getting at Ian ever since his first book came out. 'Why don't you write something *serious,* Mr. Halsey? You're capable of so much *more,* Mr. Halsey.'" Brian mocked the voice of a simpering socialite. Then he threw up his hands and walked back over to the window to stare gloomily out at the view. "It wouldn't be so bad if it were only a few people he meets casually, but his parents have been on his back as well."

"His parents?" Alicia interjected a little weakly, wondering why she had never thought of Ian as having parents. Had she thought he had just sprung up like a weed?

"Yeah, his dad's a professor of literature at one of the prestigious Ivy League colleges," Brian supplied absently, almost as though he were talking to himself. "Ian's apparently an embarrassment to him, writing the kind of stuff he does, and he wants him to try to write something worthy of the family." Brian snorted his disgust. "And his mom's the leading light of some literary society. It kills her soul that her author son hasn't written anything she and the other ladies can discuss genteelly around the tea table."

Alicia frowned, feeling an unwanted sympathy for Ian that she hastened to squelch. More likely his parents deserved the sympathy, she thought with hard cynicism. Not because of the subject matter of his books, but rather because of the sort of man Ian was.

Brian came back to her and perched on the side of her desk. "Why the hell can't people leave him alone?" he complained bleakly. "What's wrong with what he writes, anyway? *I* like it. Most of the people I know like it. It isn't porno, for God's sake!"

Alicia couldn't resist. "It isn't exactly material for children's bedtime stories either," she commented dryly.

Brian flashed her a look of irritation. "Neither are parts of the Bible," he snapped. "You want to ban that, too?"

"I didn't say I wanted to ban Ian Halsey's books," she snapped back at him.

"No, you just told him in no uncertain terms that what he does for a living stinks and implied along the way that he does, too!" Brian retorted. "How would you like it if someone did that to you?" Without waiting for an answer he continued. "I'd like to remind you, Alicia, that what Ian does pays a lot of the bills around here, including your salary. You want to turn down your next paycheck because some of it didn't come from enlightening, uplifting *literature* that meets your standards?" He fixed her with a grim look, hesitated, and then quietly hit her below the belt. "Or did Ben so thoroughly indoctrinate you into his way of thinking, you can't be objective anymore?"

Alicia jerked up her head, glaring at Brian with shocked anger. "That's uncalled-for, Brian," she said stiffly.

"Is it?" Brian didn't back down. "You didn't use to be so stiff-necked, Alicia. You used to have at least a partially open mind before Ben indoctrinated you." He gave a grimace of impatience when he saw the cold hostility on her face, but his tone was more reasonable when he continued. "Alicia, why do you think you haven't progressed more rapidly here?" he said more gently. "You've got a real flair for editing, but only with a certain type of material. Anything that offends your sensibilities throws you for a loop."

Alicia silently acknowledged Brian's criticism but

was unprepared to admit that there was anything wrong with her attitude, though for the first time in a long while she felt less sure of herself than she was willing to admit. She retreated into obstructive pride. "If you're not happy with my work, Brian—"

"Oh, for God's sake, Allie, if we weren't happy with your work, you wouldn't still be here! But don't you realize how you limit yourself? Don't you know how far you could go if you let down your hair a little?"

Feeling harassed and uncertain, telling herself she didn't need Brian forcing her into soul-searching on top of what Ian had already forced her into, Alicia stood up and walked nervously to the window, staring out without seeing any of the view. Brian didn't let up, however. He came up behind her and placed his hands on her shoulders, his voice gentle as he pressed his point.

"Allie, Allie," he said with muted impatience. "I'm not saying all of this to try to hurt you. Hell, we're friends, aren't we?" At Alicia's stiff nod he continued. "You're beautiful, warm, and giving, Allie. And you're intelligent as well. How did you ever get to be such a little prig?"

Alicia stiffened momentarily, then relaxed as her sense of humor acknowledged the justice of Brian's description. She tilted up her head over her shoulder to look at him, her eyes wryly humorous. She was wondering what Brian would have said if he could have seen her in Ian's arms two nights ago, when she had lost every vestige of priggishness she'd ever had. "I have my moments, Brian," she replied in a dry voice, permitting herself that much of a rejoinder while keeping her thoughts to herself.

Brian chuckled and gave her a little shake. "That will be the day," he mocked, clearly not believing her. Then he abruptly sobered again. "Seriously, Allie, when you first came to work here, you were a little prudish, but you weren't as tight as a clam. I can't help but think Ben wasn't good for you." The wary look in his eyes showed clearly that he knew he was treading on dangerous ground, but even Alicia's quick return to stiff hostility didn't deter him. "You didn't grow with him, Allie. He wrapped you up in an ivory tower where reality was seldom allowed to intrude, and I watched you get narrower and narrower." He held up a hand to stop the retort he could see coming. "A poet is supposed to *broaden* people's horizons, damn it, not shrink them! Why don't you go back and read Ben's poetry, Allie? If you've got any objectivity left at all where he's concerned, I think you'll see what I mean."

Alicia glared at him, struggling not to say something that would break their friendship into pieces that couldn't be repaired. But it was all she could do not to strike out in defense of her late husband *and* his poetry.

"Okay, okay." Brian backed away from the look in her eyes. "I won't say any more on that subject."

"Thank you very much!" Alicia snapped at him. "I'd appreciate it!"

Brian sighed and shook his head in resignation, but then his eyes grew sharp again as he returned to the subject he'd come to discuss. "Just cut out the needling where Ian's concerned, Allie. I've got my hands full convincing him to stay with what he's good at, and I don't need any interference." He turned away as though to go, then swung back, his expression hard. "And he *is* good at it, Allie. In fact, he's the best there is. He doesn't have a damn thing to be ashamed of where his work is concerned, and if you'd come out of your shell and unbend a little bit, you'd have to agree."

Alicia merely glared back at him, and with a snort of disgust Brian turned on his heels and left the room.

When he was gone, Alicia turned back to the window to stare out unseeingly, trying to get her jumbled thoughts and emotions under control so she could get back to work. But even when she was able to return to her desk and force herself to concentrate on what she was doing, Brian's words were lying at the back of her mind, tormenting her with the suggestion that there was a slight—a *very* slight—possibility that he was right.

Chapter Three

For the next several weeks Alicia dealt with the emotional shake-up Ian had instigated through the simple expedient of refusing to think about it. Whenever her thoughts threatened to drift in his direction, she used her not inconsiderable willpower to turn them to something else, working harder and longer and indulging in a round of after-work activities that gave her little time or energy for soul-searching.

She thanked God for the fact that Ian Halsey lived for most of the year on the other side of the country in South Lake Tahoe, California, only coming to New York when it was absolutely necessary. And she knew from overhearing office gossip among the secretaries that even if he should put in an appearance at Talton Publications, Brian Crossley was prepared to go out of his way to make sure Alicia didn't cross Ian's path. Her private thoughts were grimly satisfied upon hearing that tidbit as she reflected that Brian was no doubt unaware of the favor he was doing *her* in following such a course. He was, of course, protecting his author, but in this case it worked both ways.

Her dreams were the only irritant in the whole mess that she found hard to handle. If they had been constant rather than intermittent, she knew she wouldn't have been able to stand them, but her subconscious only played her up occasionally, giving her a chance to recuperate between occurrences. The ones that simply played back what had happened with Ian were disturbing enough, but when she woke up one morning with the realization that she had dreamed of Ian making love to her in an entirely new setting and with her full cooperation, she felt sick to her stomach.

It was only when the morning nausea reoccurred over a period of days that she began to wonder if it was brought about by her dreams, or if there might be some physical reason to account for it. She also began experiencing a tiredness that made her long for a nap after lunch, and it was only through sheer willpower that she could get through a long day. Once home, she would collapse on her bed for an hour or two of refreshing sleep before she could arouse herself to get up and tend to domestic chores or to go out with friends.

Strangely the one symptom that should have alerted her to what was the cause of her unusual physical behavior didn't concern her. True, she had always been regular with her monthly cycles, but since Ben's death, when she had gone off the pill, there had been an irregular episode or two that she attributed to being off the medication. If she thought of it at all, she merely thought this might be a reoccurrence of that irregularity.

It was at a weekend party at Howard and Samantha Talton's country residence that things came to a head. She had consented to go out of a desire to somehow make up to Howard for the night she had baited Ian. Not that Howard had given any indication that he held that night against her, but since Brian's little heart-to-heart talk about her editorial shortcomings, Alicia had felt a vague anxiety about her job. Her rational mind knew that Howard was not considering replacing her, but her emotional state had begun to exert a peculiar influence over her ability to reason objectively. There were times when she would find herself close to tears over the silliest things that in the past wouldn't have fazed her. Therefore she thought it wise to join the Taltons for the weekend if for no other reason than to reassure herself that she was simply being fancifully paranoid.

The Taltons had invited a number of people for the weekend, including a middle-aged doctor Alicia had met a few times before. He was a kindly man she found easy to confide in, but still she hesitated to bring up her health on a social occasion. She imagined doctors hated that sort of thing. Instead she intended to casually broach the subject of making an appointment with him when they got back to the city, but he precipitated things by remarking on her condition himself.

The two of them were seated on the patio, watching the Taltons' son and daughter play with their dog on the wide sweeping lawn one late afternoon while everyone else had gone off on an antique-hunting expedition to a nearby town. The children were squabbling irritably, when for the most part they were a good-natured pair, and Dr. Hill watched them with a professional eye.

"If they weren't normally such healthy kids, I'd say they were sickening for something," he commented lazily. "Usually they get along together so well, it makes me doubt the sibling rivalry theories of the psychiatrists."

Alicia smiled and raised a hand to lift her damp hair off her neck. "It's probably the heat," she said, stifling a yawn with her other hand. "This hot spell has knocked the pinions out of spring today. I hope it doesn't last. I'm not ready to bake on the streets of

New York when I haven't even put away my winter clothes yet.''

At her comment Dr. Hill turned his professional gaze her way, his discerning blue eyes studying her intently. ''You don't look as though you feel very well, Alicia,'' he said in a deceptively casual voice. ''Been having any little troubles you'd like to tell the good doctor about?''

His warm smile and evident interest encouraged her to reply honestly. ''As a matter of fact, I have,'' she said with a rueful shrug. ''I was going to see about making an appointment with you when we get back to town.''

His shaggy eyebrows rose in inquiry. ''You don't have a doctor of your own?'' he inquired mildly.

Alicia shook her head. ''I haven't needed one in so long, and my usual doctor retired,'' she said with a grimace, noting the disapproval in Dr. Hill's eyes. ''I know, I know.'' She protested what she foresaw coming. ''You doctors think regular checkups are one of the Ten Commandments, but some of us fallible lay people tend to let them slip when we're feeling well.'' She gave him a teasing, apologetic smile that made him smile back at her.

''You make us sound like we think we're gods,'' he said with wry self-mockery, then with a chuckle and a sly look he teased back. ''Of course, we *are*,'' he said in a confidential whisper, ''but we try to maintain an outward modesty at least some of the time so that we get invited to places like this for weekends.'' He spread his hands to indicate the lovely setting around them.

Alicia laughed, his humor putting her totally at ease. ''You mean you wouldn't get invited if people *knew* about your exalted state?'' she inquired innocently.

He adopted a sad expression and shook his head

dolefully. "No." He sighed. "It makes them nervous. They're afraid they'll break a commandment and get sent to a hospital for penance."

Alicia's laughter bubbled up as she shook her head at his teasing. He laughed with her but then returned to the subject with skillful persistence. "So what are these little troubles that are making you look pale and tired, Alicia?" he said with gentle concern. "Something female, or more general?"

Alicia shrugged one of her lovely shoulders that was bared by her sundress and already beginning to turn a peachy, glowing shade under the sun's rays. "I don't know," she replied, indicating her own puzzlement by a raised eyebrow. "I thought that was what gods were for...to tell us mortals what's wrong with us."

Her little barb was taken in good part by the doctor. He grinned self-effacingly and shook his head. "Even gods need a little information, Alicia," he protested. "Just give me a hint...please?"

His bantering tone contained an underlying seriousness that encouraged Alicia to confide in him, but just as she was about to do so Julie Talton's shrill childish voice was lifted in a howl of rage that drew both Alicia's and Dr. Hill's attention. The little girl followed her bellow of outrage at whatever her brother had done with a whopping smack to his head, at which point the boy had a fit of temper of his own and threatened retaliation.

Dr. Hill was on his feet in an instant, but before he could get to the children, Julie came running across the lawn to throw herself at Alicia in a burst of tears.

"There, there..." Alicia hugged the little girl and stroked the sweaty tendrils of dark curly hair away from the child's temples. "What's the matter, honey? Don't you feel well?"

Alicia's question was prompted by the heat she felt from Julie's skin and the red flush that lay across the rounded cheeks pressed against her bosom.

"No," Julie howled on a quaking sob. "I'm hot and I'm mad at Howie! He hit me with a stick!"

At that point Howie Talton came up to them with a ferocious scowl on his cherubic little face, his small fists clenched for battle. "I didn't hit her on purpose." He asserted his innocence manfully. "Pooky moved when I was getting ready to throw it for him, and Julie got in the way!" His glowering look said more plainly than words what he thought about a stupid girl who couldn't get out of the way of a thrown stick. "She said it wasn't an accident, but it was, and then she hit me!"

Howie sounded so indignantly offended, it was difficult for Alicia and Dr. Hill to suppress their smiles, but they managed, and after an amused glance at one another, Dr. Hill took charge. "It sounds like a case of accidental mayhem all the way around," he said gravely. "Why don't the two of you apologize to one another and shake hands?" The resentful look on both small faces and Julie's continued snuffling boded ill for a reconciliation. But then Howie's active curiosity got the better of him. "What's—mayhem?" he asked suspiciously, stumbling over the unfamiliar word.

For a second Dr. Hill looked disconcerted, then he rose to the occasion. "I believe 'damage' is close enough," he said with mild authority. Then, after a hesitant look at Howie's still glowering face, he added, "Do you know what that means?" he said uncertainly.

Howie looked mutinously stubborn. "Yes," he answered forcefully. "It means it hurt a lot when Julie hit me!"

Dr. Hill's eyes rolled toward the sky. Clearly he was stumped in his peacemaking efforts. Alicia stepped in to help. "Well, you both look like you could use a cold glass of lemonade," she offered with just the right touch of sympathetic firmness. "I'll take Julie in with me to get some while you stay here and talk to Dr. Hill, Howie." She lifted the little girl to her feet and took one of the small dirty hands in her own. 'Okay, Howie?" Alicia asked firmly.

The boy scuffed his foot for a moment, a scowl pulling his mouth down into a pout. Finally, however, he mumbled his agreement, and Alicia reached to ruffle his hair before she pulled Julie with her into the house. The little girl was stiff and unyielding at first, still sniffling and rubbing her eyes with a dirty fist, but then she relaxed and accompanied Alicia willingly, though her steps lagged and she seemed to have little energy.

In the bright, spotless modern kitchen Alicia helped Julie up onto a stool to wait while she got out a tray, glasses, and a pitcher of lemonade from the refrigerator. "Oh, this looks good," she chatted cheerfully in an effort to lift the child's lethargic gloom. "Are you thirsty, Julie?"

"Yes" was Julie's listless reply. "Can I have some now?"

"Sure," Alicia complied sympathetically, eyeing the little girl's flushed cheeks and fever-bright eyes with sudden concern. Julie's whole posture had changed from hot-tempered anger to slumping fatigue, and it seemed so unnatural when compared to the child's normal behavior that Alicia began to wonder what was wrong. "Here." She offered a cool glass of iced lemonade to Julie, who took it without any apparent enthusiasm. But when she lifted the glass to her lips, she drained almost half the contents in one gulp, leaving Alicia to blink in astonishment.

"My, you were thirsty, weren't you?" she murmured

in surprise and was about to turn away when Julie promptly spit up the liquid she'd just drunk all over the front of Alicia's dress. Ignoring the mess, Alicia hastened to hold the child until the spasms were over, then stroked away the tears that came when the girl was sufficiently recovered to be ashamed of what she'd done.

"Now, Julie, it's all right," Alicia soothed comfortingly. "You couldn't help it. I think you're sick, aren't you, honey?"

Julie nodded miserably, and then Alicia lifted her off the chair to carry her to the sink. "Let's get ourselves cleaned up just a little, baby, and then we'd better get you to bed and let Dr. Hill look at you, hmm?"

Thirty minutes later, after Alicia had bathed Julie and gotten her to bed to be looked at by Dr. Hill, the child's parents arrived, and it was another half hour before Alicia could get to the bathroom for a shower of her own. Later, at dinner, when Dr. Hill explained that it looked as though Julie had measles, all the guests agreed that it would be best if they left the household in peace. Howard and Samantha were visibly overwrought, never having had to go through such an illness with one of their children before, and everyone agreed that they didn't need guests at a time like that.

Alicia was offered a lift from a couple who lived near her, and it was only as she was about to leave that she remembered she and Dr. Hill had never finished their conversation about the state of her own health. He came up to her as she was about to go out the door, having determined that she would simply call him sometime during the next week to make an appointment, and his words reassured her that he would be an excellent doctor to have, if she hadn't already formed that opinion.

"I'm sorry we didn't get to finish our talk, Alicia,"

he said, focusing his complete attention on her. "You be sure and call me next week for that appointment, do you hear?"

"Yes, I will." Alicia responded with warm gratitude that even through the chaos of the last few hours he still remembered she needed him. He nodded, then turned to go back to his smaller patient.

The next week proved unusually busy, however, and it wasn't until the following week that she remembered to call for the appointment. Then Dr. Hill's schedule was full, and it was another week before she could get in. But, after she finally got there, she wished she could die after he had examined her and voiced his opinion.

"You're pregnant, Alicia," he said with a serious gravity that even through her stunned disbelief she realized was not the usual manner for a doctor to announce such a supposedly happy event.

Alicia swallowed, gazing at him with dumbstruck horror. "No ..." She almost moaned the word. "I can't be ... please ... I can't be!"

He gazed back at her with sorrow in his calm blue eyes. "I'm afraid you are, Alicia. And I'm sorrier than I can say."

She didn't take in the meaning of his words for a while. She was too numbed by the knowledge that she was pregnant with the child of a man she hated, a man whose seduction of her had changed her whole concept of herself.

Dr. Hill had to speak her name several times before she was able to focus her attention on him again. "If you want to have an abortion, Alicia, I think we'd better schedule it right away. You're too far along to wait much longer."

Alicia blinked at him, struggling hard to gather her

thoughts into some semblance of order. "Abortion?" she asked stupidly. "I don't understand...." Her mind was in chaos and she found herself wondering how Dr. Hill knew that she didn't want Ian Halsey's baby. Ben's, yes. But not Ian's. She had wanted for years to become pregnant while she had been married to Ben, but his otherworldly irresponsibility—no, not *irresponsibility,* she corrected her thoughts dazedly; absent-minded preoccupation perhaps—had necessitated that she work to provide for both of them. And when she was home, she had had to take care of all the responsibilities there, too, including keeping him fed and clothed properly. He had needed an exceptional amount of looking after, and there would have been no time or energy for a baby.

Dr. Hill was looking puzzled, and Alicia struggled to pay attention to him. "I thought you were unhappy about the baby because you knew there should probably be an abortion, Alicia," he said with hesitant gravity. And as she still looked at him uncomprehendingly, he went on. "Because of Julie's German measles... surely you knew that was what she had?"

"German measles?" Alicia knew she sounded stupid again, but she couldn't seem to get herself together enough to sound intelligent.

"Yes," Dr. Hill said gently. "You know they can cause birth defects in a fetus, don't you?"

Alicia closed her eyes and leaned weakly back in the chair, feeling mentally and emotionally bruised and battered, as though she had been struck by lightning. God, how much more could she stand? she wondered helplessly.

"Have you been ill at all since you were at the Taltons and Julie got sick?" Dr. Hill probed gently. "I mean, aside from the usual pregnancy symptoms?"

Still dazed, Alicia tried to search her mind for an answer. The morning sickness had all but disappeared, she knew that much, though she was still tired too often for comfort. She shook her head, not recalling anything other than that.

"No rash? Nothing of that nature?" Dr. Hill persisted.

Alicia stared at him with dawning horror. There *had* been a slight rash...almost no more than a pink flushing of her skin...earlier in the week, but it had only lasted a couple of days. She said as much and felt sick when she saw him shake his head grimly.

"Then I'm afraid you had German measles, Alicia," he said sadly. "They're often deceptively mild like that. At any rate, we have to assume you did. I have to advise you that I think it might be best if you don't carry this child to term."

For the first time in her life Alicia fainted. Everything suddenly seemed too much. Her stomach was boiling with nausea, a black nothingness obscured her vision, and she slipped out of consciousness before she even had time to realize she was going to faint. When she woke up, she was stretched out on Dr. Hill's examining table, and he was peering down at her with an anxious look on his kind face.

The brief retreat from reality seemed to have left in its wake a cold numbness that made Alicia feel as if she were disconnected from everything around her. The only emotion she was conscious of at all was an implacable hatred for Ian Halsey that sprang from so many different reasons, she was incapable of sorting them all out for the time being. But even her hatred was muted. It was a dim flame that simmered beneath nothingness, struggling to fill an empty shell.

She sat up and answered unemotionally when Dr.

Hill asked how she felt, assuring him that she was fine, just fine. And, indeed, she felt no pain; she just felt empty.

Apparently reassured by her calm manner, Dr. Hill made a suggestion. "Why don't you take off from work and rest for a couple of days before you make a decision about the baby, Alicia. There isn't much time, but I think we can wait at least that long. This has been a shock to you, and you must be sure of what you want to do. Give yourself time...."

"No." Alicia's denial was firm and assured. "I want the abortion. If you can check me into the hospital today, I'll make arrangements to be off work for however long is necessary."

Dr. Hill frowned, eyeing her with perceptive sympathy. "This is a big step, Alicia. Don't you think it would be better to wait until—"

"No." The flat word barred discussion. "I have no husband, Dr. Hill. No one to consult about this but myself. I have to make a living. It would be hard enough to take care of a healthy baby under the circumstances, much less one that was handicapped." *And much less one who might remind me of its father day in and day out...a father I hate.*

The doctor shook his head, then shrugged. "All right, Alicia. Sit here while I make the arrangements to get you admitted. I think you've made the right decision, but—" He stopped, gave her a pitying look, then left the room without expressing his opinion that she had made the right decision for the wrong reasons. It was only a hunch, after all, and Alicia's private reasoning was none of his business.

Chapter Four

For months after the abortion Alicia existed in a private hell that was unapparent to anyone except herself. Her friends and co-workers merely noted that she seemed slightly different from the old Alicia, and some of them, mainly Brian Crossley, were delighted with the change. His pleasure sprang from the fact that the new Alicia was harder, less idealistic, and more willing to take on work that formerly would have offended her. He would have been worried if he had known that her new attitude sprang from the fact that she simply didn't care about outward realities for the time being. She was too wrapped up in her own inner agony.

The guilt and uncertainty had started shortly after she had returned home from the hospital. The abortion had left her weaker than she expected, though later she realized that her weakness was more the result of emotional shock than any physical reason. She had taken off work for an entire week and spent most of it sitting in Central Park, staring sightlessly at the world around her. It was an unfortunate choice of a place to recuperate as it turned out, for the park was filled with young mothers or nurses escorting infants and children on daily excursions for exercise and fresh air.

Slowly Alicia had begun to watch the lively antics of

the various children that crossed her path, and the more she watched, the more uncertain she became that she had done the right thing. She began to torture herself with questions. Had she punished a child simply because she couldn't bear its father? Was it that certain that the baby would have been handicapped? And even if it had been, was that sufficient reason to dispose of it the way she had? If she had only taken Dr. Hill's advice and waited a few days before making her decision, might it have been different?

There were no answers...only questions...questions that were tearing her apart until she couldn't eat, couldn't sleep, and could barely function. Once back at the office, however, she was able to concentrate, at least superficially, on something other than her thoughts. After weeks of exerting her will to eat when she didn't want food, taking a mild sleeping pill Dr. Hill gave her to sleep when she couldn't sleep without it, and just getting through day after day of routine, mind-dulling activities, she began to become more normal.

But, there was something vital lacking in the new Alicia. Outwardly she was as calm and undisturbed as anyone else, but inwardly she was so depressed, she didn't much care whether she lived or died. Strangely enough it was Ian Halsey, the man who had precipitated her agonies of the past few months, who brought her out of her depression and focused her anger outward instead of inward upon herself.

Ian had a new book coming out, which meant he would be coming into the New York office for a round of consultations and advance publicity. Alicia dreaded his appearance so desperately, she was almost to the point of resigning her job in order to avoid seeing him. When anyone at the office brought up his name, it was all she could do to hide her inner distress, and she always managed to slip away before she could be drawn into any of the discussions.

She was still on tenterhooks, not knowing whether to take a vacation or take the drastic step of resigning, when Ian took the decision out of her hands. He came into the office two weeks early, and she almost ran into him one day as he and Brian were entering Brian's office. She acted instinctively, drawing back into an alcove before the two men saw her, shaking like a leaf and perspiring at the emotions that ran through her like wildfire at seeing that broad back and auburn hair again. When the men had disappeared, she fled to her office and shut the door, locking it behind her so that she would be undisturbed until she got herself under control.

Yet, after she had calmed down somewhat, she realized Ian's appearance had had the opposite effect to what she had expected on seeing him again. Instead of breaking down completely she was filled with the first real, forceful emotion she had had in so long, it shocked her to the core. The emotion was clean, healthy, outwardly directed anger—no, *rage!* Rage was in all ways a better description of the feeling that coursed through her, bringing her alive in a way she had forgotten was possible.

It was almost exhilarating to feel like this, she decided in an astonished burst of insight that brought the first genuine smile in weeks to her trembling mouth. It was a *good* feeling to be angry at someone besides herself for a change.

She paced the small room, her adrenaline soaring, her movements agitated and distracted. It wasn't enough to *feel,* she thought with bitter frustration. She wanted to act! She wanted to tear into Ian Halsey physically and punish him for all he had put her through so uncaringly, so casually. But, of course, physical punishment was impossible. He was so big, he would simply brush her off like a bothersome fly, and she would end up being the one who got punished... again!

So what *could* she do to make him pay? she wondered with frantic urgency. He wouldn't be there long, so whatever was to be done had to be done quickly. And it would have to be against his emotions... his ego... his self-satisfaction. Those were the only places he was vulnerable.

Alicia came to a stop before her window, staring at her reflection in the paned glass, searching for an answer with all her mind and will. And, finally, her mind began ticking over like a well-tuned computer as she looked at herself, and the answer began to materialize.

Why, she was beautiful! she realized with a sense of shock at becoming aware of the fact so unexpectedly. Her suffering of the past few months had defined the lovely bones of her face. Her eyes had a smoky, mysterious quality now that was sensuous and exciting and intriguing even to her own view. She had had no interest in a new hairstyle in so long, her wheat-colored streaked blond mane had grown out into a beautiful aureole around her face that was unconfined in its usual bun at the back of her head. She had been too distracted that morning to have the patience to confine it.

She knew her figure had changed after her pregnancy as well. She had always been well formed, but now her breasts were heavier, while her waist was tinier. Her clothes didn't fit the way they used to. Her blouses were almost strained at the buttons, the hips of her skirts molded in a way that made men turn to look at her when she walked down the street. She had been only vaguely aware of it, as she had no interest in men, but now she remembered the look in the male eyes that had followed her progress, and a tiny smile of satisfaction curved the full, gentle sweetness of her mouth.

Why, she had a weapon encased in her own body, she reflected with cool, dispassionate interest as she continued to gaze at herself. She felt no pleasure in her own beauty for itself, only for what it might make possible as concerned Ian Halsey. He was a lecherous, oversexed bachelor, after all, wasn't he? His exploits with women were legendary. Surely if she put her mind to it she could capture his interest sufficiently to gain his confidence. And once she had his confidence she could find some way to hurt him. It would be so much easier if she could make him love her, but since she doubted he was capable of such an emotion, she would settle for infatuation.

Hardly pausing to let the details of her half-formed plan pass through her mind, Alicia turned on her heels and headed purposefully toward the door of her office. Her sense of urgency was such, she was carried along by the sheer strength of it. There wasn't time to plan. It was time to act!

The hallway outside Brian's door was temporarily empty, and Alicia paused as she heard the voices coming from the room, quite shamelessly determined to eavesdrop. She needed anything she could use against Ian. and it was possible he might say something, anything, that could give her a wedge.

Brian was speaking, however, and he sounded upset and irritated. It was his normal manner around the office and meant nothing, but Alicia had never heard him use that tone to an author, especially a top author like Ian Halsey!

"Damn it, Ian, what can I say to change your mind?" Brian was saying in the tones of a wounded bull. "Don't you trust my judgment at all?"

Alicia strained to hear Ian's reply, but he spoke quietly, and she couldn't distinguish the words.

"Well, I won't work with you on it, Ian, and that's final," Brian replied in his most stubborn manner.

Alicia winced at the tone, knowing that it was a dangerous tack to take with an author as well known and profitable as Ian. Other publishing houses would snap him up in a moment, despite whatever terms were in the contract between Ian and Talton. Ian could most likely buy his way out of any contract. In any case, if he had a shrewd agent, there might not *be* any such terms.

Ian's quiet reply was indistinguishable to Alicia and she bit her lip in frustration. God, she hoped he wasn't telling Brian to go take a flying leap! If he left Talton, she wouldn't have any way of maintaining contact with him, and it was all she was living for at the moment! The threat of that happening galvanized her into action. She grasped the doorknob, took a deep breath, and opened the door with a flourish.

"Brian, I need—" Alicia stopped, adopting a look of complete surprise at seeing Ian Halsey seated in the chair across from Brian. "Oh, I'm sorry!" she said with innocent apology. "I didn't realize you weren't alone."

Brian's look of horrified consternation at seeing her would have made Alicia smile if she'd dared. Instead she pretended to misunderstand his frantic eye message that she get the hell out of his office and away from his most important author. She turned to look down at where Ian Halsey sat, a pleasant smile of apology on her lips. The smile faltered and died as she came face to face with the man who had turned her life inside out while he went on his Sybaritic way without a care in the world. She forgot her purpose at instigating this meeting momentarily, too caught up in the emotions he invoked to hide what she was feeling.

Ian's eyes widened with recognition, then narrowed when he saw the myriad feelings flash across Alicia's expressively beautiful face and come to rest in the cold hostility of her blue eyes. He got to his feet slowly and came to where she stood temporarily mesmerized. "Alicia," he murmured, his tone containing something more than a polite recognition that he remembered her.

Alicia stood frozen, hypnotized by the strength of will in Ian's eyes, by the cool appraisal he was giving her, coupled with an interest she shrank from. Brian broke into their total concentration on one another with an impatient exclamation.

"Damn it, Alicia, I can't talk to you now! Can't you see I'm busy?"

Alicia blinked, coming out of the spell Ian had cast, while Ian turned a lazy, purposeful smile on Brian. "Come now, Brian," he said with smooth humor. "Don't be rude. Perhaps what Alicia has to say can't wait."

Alicia stared at him with cautiousness, only now remembering what she had really gone in there for. Had she spoiled everything by showing him her feelings so clearly? Was he waiting for her to express verbally the hatred he must have been able to see in her eyes? She licked dry lips, trying to get her thoughts in order and to come up with something, *anything,* to rescue her plan. She cursed herself for being so precipitate and for being so vulnerable where Ian Halsey was concerned. She might have ruined everything!

"I—I can wait," she faltered, taking a fumbling step backward to the door. "I'm sorry to have interrupted you, Brian." She apologized to the older man without looking at him. She turned and reached a shaking hand for the doorknob when Ian's voice stopped her.

"Wait a moment, Alicia," he said with smooth firmness. She paused, keeping her eyes down in case there was any remnant of what she had felt earlier left for him to see. Ian turned to Brian then, his voice calmly cheerful. "It's almost lunchtime, Brian, and Alicia looks good enough to eat today. Why don't we take her out and make up to her for...uh...your rudeness."

Startled by his proposal, Alicia jerked her head up to stare at him disbelievingly. Brian was having trouble with the invitation, too, it was apparent. After his initial openmouthed astonishment had left him gaping, he recovered himself remarkably fast, however. "Oh, I don't think Alicia can get away, *can* you, Allie?" His thin smile didn't cover the unmistakable order behind his question. Alicia would have had to be a total dunce not to realize he didn't want her even considering accepting the invitation to lunch.

Ian's flashing golden eyes showed that he had heard Brian's silent order as well, and he lost no time making it clear that it carried no weight with him. Ian came to Alicia's side and put a hand on her shoulder, making her jerk under the unwanted touch. Ian cast a glance down at her, noting her reaction, but he was undeterred. "Oh, I think she *can,* Brian," he said with an unarguable order of his own in his tone. "But, of course, if *you* don't want to come...?"

Brian almost choked at that! He was around the corner of his desk and beside the two of them so speedily, Alicia could only gape at seeing him move so fast. "Very well, let's go!" Brian rapped out ungraciously, grabbing the doorknob and flinging the door open as if he'd like to take out his frustrations on the inanimate object, since he couldn't get his hands on either Ian or Alicia.

Giving her no time to even draw a breath, Ian put a hand at the small of Alicia's back and pushed her out the door after Brian, and when she unthinkingly glared up at him over her shoulder, she saw that he had a smug grin on his handsome face, along with a merry light in his eyes that made her grit her teeth and face forward again. For a moment he had seemed so charmingly likable, she had let slip the animosity she was determined to maintain as fuel for her campaign of revenge. She dared not let that happen, especially when she knew his charm was as practiced and hypocritical as everything else about him.

The two men didn't seem to think it necessary to give her a chance to do more than grab her coat from the rack by the door. She had to follow in their wake like the second-class citizen they no doubt considered her to be. Alicia ignored the fact that Ian, at least, was actually doing no such thing. He walked right beside her, glancing down at her from time to time with a speculative look that made her afraid that he could read her mind. She had to forcibly remind herself that while he might be aware of her hostility, he couldn't possibly know how she planned to act on it.

All the while they walked to a nearby restaurant Alicia's mind was working furiously on how she could repair the damage of that first revealing look she had given Ian, without seeming to behave unnaturally. Then her thoughts of his practiced charm returned to her and she had her answer. No doubt Ian Halsey thought he could charm *anyone,* even the birds in the trees, she thought disgustedly, and then with a little inner smile she determined she would let his own ego do her work for her. She would allow herself to thaw gradually under the warmth of that charm, giving the impression that he was simply irresistible, in spite of the good reasons she had to dislike him.

Alicia glanced up at his distinctive profile and allowed herself a small smile of anticipation. He would fall for it, she felt positive. The key thing was the timing. She mustn't thaw too quickly or too easily. The harder he had to work at winning her over, the more he would appreciate his seeming victory—assuming he *wanted* to win her over. The cold thought hit her, bringing a dart of alarm in its path. Her eyes mirrored that sudden anxiety just as Ian looked down at her, and she saw something move behind those golden eyes. Something remarkably close to regret and gentle tenderness?

Alicia dragged her eyes away from that look determinedly, telling herself she was imagining things. Regret and tenderness? Ha! He might have practiced projecting those emotions in order to further his own purposes, but as for actually feeling them? Not likely!

The thought stiffened her determination and she overrode her doubts about his interest in winning her over by remembering that he *had* insisted she lunch with them, hadn't he? And even if that was only a casual gesture, she could damn well build on it, even though she'd never had the slightest interest in acting the part of a femme fatale before. It was all a matter of limpid looks, suggestive body language, and playing up to his ego, surely? She'd seen enough women practicing the art to be able to copy their actions, she thought confidently, forgetting for the moment that her motivation was entirely different from those of the other women she had observed.

Brian started to steer them toward a noisy little Italian restaurant, hoping no doubt that conversation would be impossible under the usual cacophony of the place. But Ian merely shook his head at his editor and turned his steps in the direction of a quiet, elegant French restaurant where Alicia knew that if the patrons didn't speak, the atmosphere resembled that of a funeral parlor.

She hid a grin at Brian's comical concern when he saw where they were headed and avoided his eyes when he tried to send her another nonverbal message, pleading for her silence. If she could have, she would have reassured him that she had no intention of antagonizing Ian Halsey again, but since that was impossible, she had to let him suffer from his inner visions of the disaster he seemed certain was coming.

Once seated in the posh, funereal, and most importantly, *quiet* little restaurant, Alicia was amused to see that Brian deliberately placed himself between she and Ian as though determined to present a physical, if not a soundproof, buffer between the two of them. She smiled at him with innocent blandness when he glared down at her in warning, and then almost laughed out loud when he followed his look with a sharp little pinch of her forearm. She couldn't resist, though the pinch actually hadn't hurt. "Ouch!" she said in innocent, wounded tones, looking up at Brian wide-eyed.

He groaned in exasperation while Ian shot the two of them a sharp, penetrating look that boded ill for Brian if Ian learned what he'd done. Alicia let Brian suffer for the barest second before she murmured, "Excuse me. I bumped my ankle."

Ian didn't look as if he believed her, but Brian patted her arm in gratitude. "Careful, Allie," Brian said with expansive concern that barely hid the double meaning of his words. "You have such pretty little ankles, we wouldn't want them all bruised, would we?"

Alicia blinked for a moment in astonishment that
Brian Crossley had ever noticed her ankles before she
realized that he was actually couching another warning
in his playful words. She smiled sweetly at him then,
looking him straight in the eye. "Well, they are *my*
ankles, Brian," she teased him with the barest touch of
grimness in her tone. "If I want to bruise them, why
shouldn't I?"

Brian glared back and gritted out, "Because small in-
juries can lead to *big* trouble later on in life sometimes,
Allie," and then he caught himself and gave her a thin
smile. "But you're sensible enough to know that,
aren't you, my dear?"

Alicia gave him a demure nod, then glanced at Ian to
see how he was taking the barely muted exchange of
threats and warnings. Ian gave her a direct look of
amusement and self-confident masculinity that told her
he knew very well where Brian's concern lay, but that
he was man enough to handle anything she could dish
out. His arrogance grated on her nerves, and she
looked down at her plate, refusing to acknowledge
either his amusement or his cockiness.

The meal proceeded in a state of armed truce for a
while before Ian spoke to Alicia gently. "What sort of
books do you edit, Alicia?" he asked with genuine interest.

Before she could answer, Brian broke in to do so for
her. "Oh, Allie's tastes have always run to the highbrow stuff in the past, but lately she's coming out of
that. I don't know what's happened to her, but she's
matured considerably," he said with pleased satisfaction. "I don't have to worry so much about giving her
manuscripts that would have offended her just six
months ago."

Alicia almost choked on her food at that, and a

stealthy look at Ian didn't reassure her fears that he might attribute her change of attitude to what he had done to her. Of course, it was true, but she didn't want him to know it. She needed to retain at least a shred of her pride where he was concerned.

She raised wounded eyes to his to find him giving her another of those sad, gentle looks that were so compelling—until she remembered how false they were. But then, she also remembered she was supposed to make him believe he could wipe out what he'd done through sheer charm, and she let her eyes widen a little with uncertainty, as though she might be harboring just the tiniest inclination to admit she might have been wrong about him. She was gratified to see from his reaction that she must have been successful. His unusual eyes glowed with approval and encouragement of what he thought he saw.

Lowering her gaze at last, Alicia's thoughts were in direct contravention of what she'd tried to convey. The cad, she thought with bitter condemnation. How dare he *approve* of her! It was going to be so sweet when she was finally able to give him his comeuppance! She could hardly wait. Of course, she had to find some way to do that first, but at least she had made a beginning, and if there was any justice in the world, she would find a way to finish the job.

No other opportunity occurred for her to further her seeming capitulation to his charm at the luncheon, however. Brian dominated the conversation and determinedly kept it neutral—as uncontroversial as pablum. Before Alicia knew it, he was getting to his feet and dragging her up with him. She hadn't even finished her white-chocolate ice cream either, she thought resentfully as she tugged unsuccessfully at the grip Brian had on her arm.

"Time to get back to work," Brian was saying cheerfully, giving Ian no opportunity to remonstrate as he pushed Alicia in front of him away from the table. 'Come on, Ian," he said with brusque seriousness. "We haven't finished the conversation our charming Alicia interrupted," at which point he squeezed her arm warningly. "And I have a lot more to say to you on the subject."

Surprisingly, for Alicia knew by now that Ian Halsey was anything but the type of man to give in to anything he didn't want to do, he got to his feet and gave Brian a complacent smile. "Certainly, Brian," he agreed with uncharacteristic meekness. "In fact, I'm looking forward to it."

His manner seemed to disconcert Brian momentarily, and Alicia could understand the reaction. Ian's agreeableness smacked of danger far more strongly than would have his obstructiveness. But since Alicia didn't know what they'd been discussing in the first place, other than that whatever it was had Brian up in arms, she couldn't make a judgment of just how dangerous Ian was going to prove to be.

Back at the office, Ian gave her a warm smile as she took her leave of the two men, and once again she had to steel herself against an involuntary response to his appeal. It was easier to do once he was out of sight, however, and Alicia entered her own office with a scowl of annoyance on her face and vengeance in her heart.

She could barely settle down to work that afternoon for worrying over how she was going to make contact with Ian again. It had to be done so subtly that he didn't suspect she had maneuvered things. Perhaps she could manage to be innocently loitering in the hall when he came out of Brian's office? But the flaw there was that she hadn't a clue when he would leave. And she didn't dare prance around out in the hall at frequent intervals all afternoon in hopes of hitting it at the right moment. She might miss him.

Then her eye caught a manuscript she had been meaning to talk to Brian about, and an idea came to her. She could call Jennie, Brian's secretary, and ask her to call back when it looked like Brian and Ian's meeting was about over. If she made it sound urgent enough, chances were she could get there before Ian actually left. Brian always stood around in his doorway for prolonged farewells when he had a visitor.

She had her hand on the telephone to call Jennie when the door to her office burst open and Brian stood there glaring at her with gritted teeth and flames in his eyes. "Now you've done it," he snarled at her like a mad dog. "I hope you're satisfied!"

Taken aback by his fury, Alicia sunk into her chair defensively. "Done what?" she protested with feeble injury in her voice, wondering for a panic-stricken moment if there was any way at all Brian could have stumbled upon what was in her mind. But of course he couldn't have, she reassured herself as he stalked into her office and leaned on his knuckles on her desk.

"You've gotten your wish," he growled belligerently. "Ian Halsey is going to write a book *worthy* of himself," he sneered.

Alicia blinked up at him, disconcerted by his words and the tone he'd used. "Uh... what do you mean?" she asked cautiously.

"Just what I said. He's going to spend a whole year working on some damn book nobody will want to read just so he can show people like you and his damn snobbish parents he can do it!" Brian snorted in disgust and ran a distracted hand through his hair, all the while glaring down at her as if she were personally responsible for Ian's decision.

Alicia grappled for a defense. "But *I* didn't make him decide to do that," she protested. "What are you blaming me for?"

"You helped!" Brian shot an accusing finger at her. "Your whole attitude at that dinner awhile back screamed disapproval of what he does best!"

"But I don't mean anything to him," Alicia pointed out coldly. "It's not likely he would pay any attention to what I thought." She suppressed the uncomfortable remembrance that her baiting of Ian *had* provoked him considerably on that night, so while it was true that she didn't mean anything to him, she *had* been the catalyst to set him off on one sort of unaccustomed behavior at one time at least . . . if she could believe him when he had said he'd never had to force a woman before.

Brian came around the desk and hovered over her until she had to lean back away from his aggressive stance. "If that's true, then why is it he wants *you* to do the editing?" Brian accused.

"What?" Alicia yelped. "But you're his editor." For the moment she lost sight of what Ian's request could mean for her personally, and she reacted like someone accused of poaching on a dear friend's property.

Brian looked just a tiny bit disconcerted for a second, but then he recovered. "I wouldn't do it," he muttered tight-jawed.

"What do you mean you wouldn't do it?" Alicia asked incredulously. "You can't turn Ian Halsey down!"

Brian looked belligerently nasty. "I can and I have." And then he added with malicious satisfaction, "But you can't."

Alicia stared at him, resenting his attitude wholeheartedly until she remembered that this would give her the perfect opportunity to get closer to Ian and search for a vulnerable spot to hurt him. "I can if I want to," she said with sulky petulance, more because she knew Brian would expect her to protest than because she meant what she said.

As expected, Brian flew to the attack. "Then you'd better not want to," he threatened. "I want that book completed in record time."

Alicia shook her head in bewilderment. "I thought you didn't want the book done at all," she complained exasperatedly.

"I don't," he admitted more calmly. "But since he's determined to do it, and there's nothing I can do to stop it, I want it done and out of the way. When it turns out to be a flop, maybe that will convince him to stick to what he's good at."

Just for fun Alicia proposed the alternative, not really believing what she said. "But what if it doesn't turn out to be a flop?" she asked innocently. "What if he writes a blockbuster?"

Brian scowled, obviously unprepared to accept that it could happen. Then he shrugged and grinned as at a nasty joke. "Then you'll get a great deal of credit for it, won't you, my dear?"

It was Alicia's turn to scowl then, recognizing that Brian had turned the tables on her. It would look awfully fishy if she turned down this chance to further her career and espouse her often-stated principles at the same time...not that she had any intention of turning down this opportunity at all. Still, there was camouflage to be considered. Brian didn't have to know that she was actually eager to accept the assignment.

"I don't think he can write a decent book," she muttered coldly. "It will just be a waste of time."

Brian disagreed. "Oh, he can write a decent book, all

right,'' he said matter-of-factly, and then hastily added, ''Not that I think what he's been writing isn't decent. I've told you before he's the best there is.''

Alicia eyed him suspiciously. ''If you think he can write a different type of book, decent or not''—she waved a hand dismissingly at him—''then why do you object so to his trying something different?''

Brian looked at her pityingly. ''Alicia, what do you think we're in business for?'' he asked with gentle condescension. Before she could answer, he did it for her. ''Dollars and cents, that's what!'' He sounded exasperated again. ''Ian's present books sell like hotcakes. And I don't care what other type of book he writes, it won't sell like what he's been doing.''

Alicia looked at him in disgust, but he challenged her look with one of his own. ''Want to get into a discussion about your paycheck again, Allie?'' he taunted.

She glared at him, then calmed down. ''No,'' she said quietly.

''I thought not,'' he said with a great deal of satisfaction. Then he frowned at her. ''I thought you'd got over some of that snobbery of yours, Allie. Are you going back to being the prude again?''

Alicia didn't feel like telling him the real reason for her condescension toward Ian Halsey. It no longer had anything to do with the type of book he wrote. Indeed, she *had* mellowed. She no longer felt as superior as she had at one time toward Ian's brand of literature. And if she could have been completely honest with herself, which she wasn't prepared to do at present, she would have admitted that she had begun to derive a sneaking sort of admiration for his writing. She read his books as a matter of course because she worked for the publisher who put them out. But not until the last year had she begun to realize that Ian had an unusual talent that made even his most shallow books stand out from the ordinary.

Even the hint of such approbation for Ian Halsey made her so uncomfortable, however, that Alicia wouldn't acknowledge what she knew to be true. It interfered with her hatred for him, and nothing must be allowed to do that. It was all that gave her an interest in living for the present.

Now she answered Brian's question with a calm look. "You know better than that, Brian. I'm a lot different than I used to be." The faint hint of bitterness that accompanied her last statement went unnoticed by Brian.

"All right, then," he said with satisfaction. Then he got down to business. "How soon can you get everything cleared up here and be ready to leave?"

Alicia looked at him in astonishment. "Leave?" she asked stupidly.

Brian looked irritably cross. "Yes, leave!" he said impatiently.

"For where?" Alicia asked blankly.

"For California, of course," Brian said with exasperated asperity. Then he looked a little guilty as he realized that he hadn't told her all the details. "Oh, I guess I didn't tell you." He changed to mild wariness. "Ian wants you out there with him to work right along beside him."

"What!" Alicia's mutinous expression made Brian start for the door.

"Now, don't get on your high horse, Allie," he spoke rapidly as he started to make his escape. "I told you I want this book finished fast, and the best way to do that is for you to be on the spot. Maybe we can cut the time down to six months," he muttered to himself abstractedly.

"Brian Crossley, you stop right there!" Alicia was on her feet and across the room in record time. "You know we don't work like that! Have you lost your mind?" She glared up at him, her hands on her hips and mutiny clearly visible on her expressive face.

"We do this time," Brian countered grimly. "We've loaned you to Ian for this book. He'll even be paying your salary."

Alicia's voice strangled in her throat as she tried to express her outrage at this turn of events. She didn't want to be under Ian Halsey's authority in any way, even if it meant losing out on her chance to get even with him. And more to the point, she couldn't risk being closeted with him day after day in his own home, where there would be no escape from— From what? she asked herself in nervous panic. Of course, there was no danger he would be able to seduce her again. That was out of the question! It was just that she couldn't stand the thought of being around him for such a long time with no relief from his insufferable presence.

"I won't do it," Alicia threatened desperately.

"Yes, you will."

"You can't make me!" she gritted, fire in her eyes.

"You'll be out of a job if you don't!"

That stopped her. "You wouldn't."

"I would," he promised in his best I-mean-what-I-say manner.

"Brian, that stinks!"

"I know," he said imperturbably. Then he patted her absently on the shoulder and left her where she stood.

Chapter Five

Despite her anxiety over whether she was doing the right thing, Alicia had to admit to a surge of excitement as the plane landed at Reno, Nevada. After all, she'd never been west before, and if she got nothing else out of this fiasco, she would at least have broadened her geographical horizons. She wondered nervously whether Ian would pick her up himself or if he would expect her to catch a bus for South Lake Tahoe. She thought rather resentfully that with the amount of luggage she'd had to bring for a stay of several months, the least he could do was arrange for private transportation to his home rather than leave her to fend for herself.

But then he had been irritatingly vague about all the arrangements for this collaboration so far. She had made hasty arrangements to sublet her apartment under Brian's urging, then she had to put off the new tenants for a whole week and twiddle her thumbs at the office because Ian had taken his time about confirming things on his end. Just when she had been about to walk out on the whole venture, an envelope had appeared on her desk one afternoon containing a one-way ticket to Reno and a brief note. She thought back on the contents of that note sourly as she gathered up her hand luggage to disembark from the plane. All it had said was "See you on Tuesday. Ian."

Well, she was here now, she bolstered her courage feebly. And she had known all along it wouldn't be easy. But she had made up her mind to take the opportunity fate had provided to make Ian Halsey pay some long-overdue debts, and there was nothing to do but go through with it. She shouldn't complain if accomplishing her objective meant putting up with the man himself while she went about extracting justice.

Once inside the airport, Alicia looked around half-fearfully for Ian, but of course he wasn't there. She should have known he wouldn't have the common courtesy to meet her plane, she fumed underneath the relief she felt at having a slight reprieve before she had to face him again.

Then she was startled to hear her name called in a young, cheerful, feminine tone, and as she swung around to search for the speaker she couldn't believe her eyes when the only person she saw was one of the most gorgeous young creatures she'd ever laid eyes on. The girl had long straight blond hair, a healthy glowing tan, and a figure that would have made Hugh Hefner sit up and take notice!

"Mrs. Farr?" The husky tones must have caused many a young, or older, man's temperature to rise sharply, Alicia decided.

"Yes?" she responded tentatively, unable as yet to comprehend why this creature should know her name.

"Good," the girl said breathlessly, her full breasts rising and falling with the effort to catch her breath. "I've been running to get here so you wouldn't feel abandoned. I had a flat tire on the way, and it delayed me." She grabbed Alicia's overnight case and put a companionable hand on her shoulder as she steered

Alicia toward an exit. "Ian would have been proud of the way I changed that tire, though," she chattered on, still in that same breathless, entrancing little girl/siren voice. "Ten minutes flat! That's all it took!"

"Congratulations," Alicia said with a rather dry hopelessness in her voice that went over the girl's head. Alicia was feeling rather like she'd been geared up for a devastating plunge down an icy slope and instead had fallen with a disappointing plop before she'd gotten three feet. And she had thought she was going to infatuate Ian Halsey, had she? she thought with sour realism...when he had someone like this California snowbunny running around performing his errands and pleased as punch because she could report back to him that she had changed a tire in ten minutes!

"Thanks," the girl replied with unaffected pleasure. "I even had time to drop the tire off at a service station," she said with pleased self-congratulation. "We can pick it up on the way back. The guy said he didn't mind at all putting aside his other work when I told him how far I'd have to drive to get it back if he couldn't fix it right away."

Alicia reflected dryly that whoever the "guy" was would probably have volunteered to *roll* it back to South Lake Tahoe if this vision had asked him to. "That's wonderful." She masked her thoughts with an attempt at polite approbation. "By the way," she continued on a weak note, "who are you, and why are you picking me up?"

The girl swung her head to look at her in astonishment, her movement causing the silky blond hair to swirl enticingly. "Didn't Ian tell you?" she asked in surprise. "Oh, well, he's been busy lately," she added with cheerful unconcern, not waiting for Alicia to reply that Ian Halsey hadn't told her anything at all, much less that he had beauties like this one to do his bidding. "Uncle Ian's a friend of my dad's," she went on unconcernedly. "I've known him forever, so I guess you could say he's a friend of mine, too. He couldn't get away today because he's judging a ski race, so I said I'd come and get you. Do you ski?" Her tone made it sound as though any answer other than yes would be regarded as sacrilege.

Alicia felt privileged to be able to answer, "A little." And it was barely the truth. She had never had time to ski more than on an occasional weekend, and her snow plow was absolutely useless except on the easiest slopes.

"Oh, good." The girl beamed her approval. "We'll have to take you up and work with you until you're good enough to go with the rest of us. Ian's the greatest teacher in the world. He'll be glad to help you."

Alicia viewed that prospect with discreet alarm, but she said nothing, determining privately that she would find her own teacher. It might be too tempting to push Ian off a cliff if there was one available, and she had no intention of spending the rest of her life in prison because of him. She only wanted to dent him, not kill him!

"My name is Sandi, by the way," the girl offered as she pushed open the double doors that led outside. "And yours is Alicia, isn't it?" She looked charmingly apologetic for her presumption. "We don't go in much for last names out here. Do you mind if I call you Alicia?"

"Allie will be fine," Alicia replied with a touch of grimness. She felt unable to dislike this charmingly unaffected beauty despite every inclination to do so. She would much have preferred to hate her on sight, but as it was proving impossible to do so, she began to resign herself to accepting that God had been more than generous in handing out feminine attributes where Sandi was concerned than he need have been. Spreading the wealth around would have seemed to Alicia a far more generous course to take.

"Here's the van," Sandi informed her insouciantly as she swung open the door of a bright purple van and threw Alicia's hand luggage inside. "Oh, and here comes your other luggage." She waved at a young man who was hastening toward them, laden down with Alicia's two large cases, his smile as he focused his attention exclusively on Sandi as broad as a barn.

"Thanks." Sandi beamed at him, causing him to almost miss his footing on the curb.

"You're welcome" came the hoarse reply as the young man fumbled to get the cases inside the van while keeping his eyes fastened to Sandi's chest.

It was evident a tip wasn't wholly necessary, but Alicia extended one anyway, amused to see that the young fellow was barely aware that he had been given one. "Thank you," Alicia said quietly, though her words went unheard. Then she climbed awkwardly into the passenger seat of the van, threatening to split her narrow skirt on the steep steps, to wait calmly while Sandi exchanged good-byes with her admirer.

When at last the girl was seated in the driver's seat and gunning the motor with enthusiasm, Alicia ventured a question. "Do you know that fellow?" she asked, her voice rising with alarm as Sandi took off with a squeal of the tires.

"Who?" Sandi asked blankly, cutting in front of a taxi with dexterous aplomb and ignoring the sharp horn blast that announced the other driver's displeasure.

"The one who brought my luggage," Alicia gasped as Sandi swung into the far lane with frightening speed.

"Oh, him," Sandi said absently, concentrating on her driving. "No, he was just standing near where you got off the plane, and I told him your name and asked him if he would look for some luggage with your name tags on it and bring it out to the purple van. He was glad to do it."

"Of course he was," Alicia agreed with weak resignation, closing her eyes when Sandi ran through a yellow light with complete disregard for the fact that the driver to the left had started through a little early himself.

Alicia's stomach was churning by the time Sandi had collected the spare tire and got them out onto the highway heading south to the California side of Lake Tahoe. She had lived in New York for too many years to appreciate Sandi's freewheeling western style of driving, but as the trip progressed and the broad, straight highway unfolded before them, she forgot her apprehension as she gazed at the flat country beside the road, dotted with hillocks from time to time.

"It's prettier when we get up into the mountains," Sandi offered with her irrepressible cheerfulness. "You've never been here, have you?"

"No," Alicia replied. "I'm glad to have the chance to see this."

"Oh, wait until you see the lake," Sandi enthused. "It's the most beautiful blue you've ever seen, and it's even prettier in the winter when the snow's on the mountains, like now, than it is in the summer. At least I think so.

"You're so lucky to get to work for Ian," Sandi continued with fond affection. "He is absolutely the most wonderful man I've ever known. He's so kind and good"—she slid a blue-eyed glance over to Alicia and grinned companionably—"and handsome."

Alicia thought grimly that Ian Halsey was also undoubtedly the most successful conman in the history of the sex, if Sandi was anything to go by. The girl was obviously besotted with him, but Alicia wondered how Sandi would feel if she'd endured what she herself had at his hands. It would do no good to spell out her antipathy toward Ian to this fan, however, Alicia realized. And, in fact, it might defeat her whole purpose in coming here. She forced herself to smile reasonably normally and say, "Yes, he is, isn't he."

Fortunately as they began winding up into the mountains Sandi's conversation dwindled so that Alicia was free to view the scenery and calm her nerves for the forthcoming meeting with Ian. And if the view outside the van window was anything to go by, she thought there were certain to be other compensations on this trip other than getting even with a man she hated. She just might take Sandi up on the skiing invitation, for one thing. She'd always wanted to improve her ability, and this was the perfect opportunity.

She spotted a deer bounding up a hillside and gasped at its beauty. "Pretty, aren't they?" Sandi asked with a brief sideways flick of her blue eyes. "It's always a joy to get to see one."

"Yes," Alicia murmured, forgetting everything for the moment in the thrill of the beauty of nature at its finest all around her.

"My dad used to hunt." Sandi offered the information in a confidential tone as though she were telling a family secret. "But he doesn't anymore since the accident, and I'm so glad."

Alicia swung around to look at her and blinked. "You're glad?" she asked in puzzlement.

Sandi looked startled, then chuckled. "I mean I'm glad he doesn't hunt anymore, not about the accident.

Although if it hadn't been for the accident, we would never have come to live with Ian, and I wouldn't have missed that for the world. I just wish it could have happened some other way."

Intrigued, Alicia probed gently. "What sort of accident was it?"

"A fire," Sandi said with simple acceptance. "Dad used to own a garage where Ian got his cars fixed. They got to be great friends, and when the fire burned the garage down and there was no money to replace it even if Dad had been able to work that hard anymore, Ian brought us all to live with him."

Alicia didn't want to believe in Ian's generosity, so she searched for some other reason for his action. "Oh?" she said offhandedly. "How many are there in your family?"

"Just Dad, Mom, and me," Sandi said. "Dad takes care of the grounds and the cars. Mom cooks and cleans, and I help in whatever way I can when I'm not at school. Ian got me a scholarship and he insisted Dad and Mom put away what little equity they had in our old house for their retirement. We get room and board free, and Mom and Dad get a salary."

Alicia blinked at that, scowling just a little at her inability to fault Ian's conduct in the matter. She consoled herself with thinking he was probably a slave driver. Sandi apparently wasn't around enough to see it, and in any case, she was obviously so infatuated with Ian, she would excuse him anything.

As they wound down into the basin that held Lake Tahoe, Alicia became fascinated again with the scenery, catching glimpses of the blue water through the trees before it was finally revealed in all its loveliness. "Oh, Sandi, it *is* beautiful," she exclaimed to her companion when she got her first unobstructed look at the body of water.

"Of course it is," Sandi agreed complacently. "Ian has a sailboat we go out on in the summer. Do you sail?"

Alicia sighed, having to confess that she didn't. She was beginning to think she was ill suited for the life in this part of the country, since she'd never had much of an opportunity to be athletic before.

"That's all right," Sandi soothed comfortingly. "We'll teach you that, too."

With an amused smile Alicia said, "I *am* here to work, you know."

"Sure, I know." Sandi shrugged. "But anyone who works for Ian has plenty of time to enjoy life, too. He doesn't believe in work and no play, and he's always generous with everything he owns."

Tiring of hearing Ian's virtues extolled, Alicia elected to interpret the remark negatively. She decided grimly that if Ian's version of play included forcibly seducing any female who didn't worship at his altar, he was in for a shock when he discovered Alicia's *own* version of play for the time being. It was, after all, going to be pure pleasure to set him on his ear for a change.

They were in South Lake Tahoe itself now, and Alicia craned her neck interestedly at seeing the casinos lining the streets of the town. She could almost have predicted Sandi's next question. "Do you gamble, Allie?"

With a helpless laugh at having to disappoint her young companion once again, she shook her head. "No, I'm afraid not. I've never had the money or the opportunity to indulge in it before."

With a gleam of humor in her blue eyes Alicia gave

Sandi a smile and spoke simultaneously as the girl offered, "We'll teach you that, too."

They both laughed, and Sandi gave a little moue of self-mockery. "I guess I *have* been coming on pretty strong, haven't I?"

"Not at all," Alicia said graciously, warming to the girl further. "I appreciate your generosity. It's just that I'm beginning to feel a little inadequate for the life out here."

Sandi smiled broadly. "I imagine it's different from New York, but I'm sure you'll like it. I wouldn't live anywhere else, myself."

Then they were south of the town, and Sandi was pulling off of the main road to follow a winding street leading ever closer to the lake. Alicia began to tense up as she sensed they were nearing Ian's home. She hoped he would still be off skiing somewhere in order to allow her a little time to settle in and gather her resources before she came face to face with him.

When Sandi finally pulled into a long winding driveway, Alicia gave a little gasp of astonishment. Ian's house was half-chalet, half-ranch, constructed in the most unusual style she'd ever seen before. She wondered how one woman, Sandi's mother, could manage to keep it clean and cared for, and she mentally reaffirmed her image of Ian as a slave driver if he expected such a feat from his housekeeper.

There was a three-car garage, and the drive was neatly cleared of all traces of the snow that blanketed the grounds and the surrounding area and succeeded in setting off the beautiful home to advantage.

Sandi pulled up before the front door, which opened upon their arrival, framing a tall, statuesque blond woman whose bosom immediately identified her as Sandi's mother. Alicia climbed awkwardly down from the van as the woman came toward them. Sandi was already out and sliding open the van's rear door to get at Alicia's luggage.

"Hello," the woman greeted Alicia in a warm, cheerful voice reminiscent of Sandi's husky tones. "I'm Ingrid Johnson. Come in out of the cold. Sandi and my husband will bring your bags."

Alicia couldn't help but smile at the friendliness of the greeting as she shook the hand the woman extended, then accompanied her into the house. The short entranceway floor was of shining wood covered by a long strip of Oriental rug in glowing colors. A living room with floor-to-ceiling windows that bathed the room in light was equally welcoming, especially since there was a fire going in a huge stone fireplace that took up nearly all of one wall.

When Ingrid Johnson steered her to a sectional sofa patterned in bright autumn colors and fronted by a large coffee table upon which rested a tray of coffee and cookies, then seated herself beside Alicia to pour, it was clear to Alicia that Sandi and her parents did regard Ian's home as their own. She had to fight against the softening this recognition brought, as she was still determined to regard Ian in the worst possible light.

"We're so glad you're here," Ingrid was saying as she handed Alicia a cup of steaming coffee. "Ian has wanted to do this book for so long, and he says you're the perfect person to help him."

Alicia almost choked on her sip of coffee. There was no trace of anything other than complete approval in Ingrid's voice, but Alicia couldn't help but believe that if Ian really had said something like that about herself, then he must have meant it in a much more uncomplimentary way than Ingrid had taken it.

She permitted herself an inner gloat as she answered.

"I'm looking forward to it myself," she said with complete truthfulness, though not for the reasons she was implying. A gleam of an idea was forming in her head that needed some refining before she put it into action.

"Ian is rather nervous about doing this book," Ingrid said confidentially. And at Alicia's doubtful look—she couldn't imagine Ian Halsey being nervous about anything at all—Ingrid chuckled. "Oh, I know he's successful and wealthy and handsome and charming and all those other adjectives that sound so wonderful, but everyone has inner doubts about *something,* don't they?" A fond, affectionate look came into her blue eyes. "I'm sure he has nothing to worry about, he's so talented, but I do hope this book goes well for him, simply because *he* wants it to so much."

"Does he?" Alicia said thoughtfully, her ideas gaining force. "I wonder why?"

Ingrid Johnson snorted, her expression taking on a look of disapproval. "Oh, I expect because it will please those parents of his so much, for one thing," she said crossly. "They're always on him about making them proud of him, as though they didn't have enough to be proud of as it is!" She sounded indignant as she turned her blue gaze on Alicia. "Why, if I had a son as wonderful as Ian, I'd consider myself the most fortunate of women. I wouldn't always be after him to do more, for heaven's sake!"

"Ummm..." Alicia said placatingly. "Parents can be difficult, I suppose. And it's...uh...commendable of Ian to want to please them."

"Humph!" Ingrid Johnson said with a shrug of one statuesque shoulder. "If you ask me, he'd do better to forget about pleasing *them* and get on with his own life. It's about time he had a rest and found himself a wife, so he can get on with starting a family!"

Alicia's face whitened at the words and her hand rattled the cup of coffee in its saucer. She set it down hastily. "I wonder if I might go to my room now, Mrs. Johnson," she said in a strained voice. "I'm rather tired, and I—"

Ingrid Johnson jumped to her feet at once, her face a study in chagrin. "Oh, of course you are, and here I've been bending your ear when you probably need a nap. It's a long flight from New York, and I'm sure you've been very busy lately, getting ready to come out here."

Alicia smiled wanly, hastening to reassure the woman that she had enjoyed the coffee and the talk immensely. Then she followed Ingrid down a long hallway, glancing almost incuriously at the huge dining room on one side, a closed door that might be to Ian's study off to the other, until finally they were at the back of the house where the bedrooms were.

Ingrid chattered as they walked with every bit as much cheerful enthusiasm as her daughter had on the ride from Reno. "Ian will be back shortly before dinner," she informed Alicia. "That should give you time to settle in and rest a bit. I hope you like your bedroom. Ian said he thought it would suit you perfectly, and I must say, since meeting you, I think he's right."

At that she swung open a door leading into a bedroom, and Alicia stopped on the threshold, catching her breath on a gasp as Ingrid's words took on meaning. The room resembled a boudoir for a Scandinavian ice maiden. It was decorated in clear blues and white, and the four-poster bed even had a pristine white canopy to match the stark white coverlet. There was a chaise longue covered in an ice-blue velvet on a white frame, and a dainty white desk that looked like it couldn't support more than one stack of paper.

Resentment boiled in Alicia as she realized that Ian

saw her as an icy cold virgin with no warmth in her veins at all. And just how had he come to that conclusion, she thought furiously, when he had seen how her own apartment was decorated and had felt her passion in his arms on that long-ago night! The remembrance of that night only increased her anger as she followed Ingrid slowly into the room.

"This is his mother's room when she comes to visit," Ingrid said apologetically, as though she felt it necessary to amend any idea Alicia might have that her own resentment of Ian's mother would spill over onto Alicia. "I think it's a beautiful room," she said admiringly. "Perhaps because I'm of Scandinavian stock, and I like its simplicity." She turned back to look at Alicia then, perhaps expecting confirmation that the room was lovely, and then looked disconcerted when she saw the fire in Alicia's eyes.

"But if you don't like it"—she faltered—"we can always move you to another bedroom." She gave Alicia the benefit of a wise scrutiny from her clear blue eyes. "As a matter of fact, though I thought the room suited you when I first saw you, I'm beginning to think that though you look very cool on the surface, some brighter colors might suit your personality better."

Her wry words, spoken in an almost teasing vein, drew an equally wry smile from Alicia. "No, this will be fine," she said a little grimly. "If Ian thinks this room suits me, we wouldn't want him to lose faith in his judgment, would we?"

A delighted chuckle escaped Ingrid's generous breast. "Oh, Alicia, I think I'm going to like you very much," she said, giving Alicia a quick hug, which, surprisingly, Alicia didn't mind at all, though she'd never appreciated intimate touches from strangers before. Warmly affectionate in private with loved ones, she was nevertheless reserved with people until she got to know them.

"Seriously, though," Ingrid went on with a doubtful look, "if you won't be comfortable in here, there's another bedroom where I'm sure you would be."

Alicia shook her head and walked over to the chaise longue and dropped her purse onto it, that small action denoting her intention to stay. "I wouldn't dream of it," she said in a flat tone. Then realizing she might have hurt Ingrid's feelings, she turned a warm smile toward the other woman. "Thanks, anyway, Ingrid." Changing the subject, she asked, "What time is dinner? And can I help you prepare it?"

Ingrid looked shocked at such a suggestion. "Of course you can't!" she answered indignantly. "The kitchen and the house are my job. You have your own!" And then she gave a broad smile to take the sting out of her words. "You won't have time to help me while you're here if I know Ian when he's working on a book, and I don't need help anyway."

Moving toward the door, Ingrid closed the subject. "Dinner's at seven. I'll look in on you in case you over-sleep."

Then she was gone, and Alicia was left to survey her domain on her own. She turned slowly to look at the virginal room, her mouth tightly grim, her hand clenched where it rested on her hip. Well, she thought grimly, perhaps it was best if Ian Halsey saw her like this. She had pretty well reached the conclusion that her idea of infatuating Ian was the wrong way to go about things anyway. A man like him must have women falling all over him. Indeed, she had witnessed the phenomenon herself the night at the restaurant when she had baited him so unwisely. So why had she thought he would be interested in her that way now?

she wondered fumingly, failing to acknowledge the slight disappointment the thought invoked.

No, it would be better to pursue the other idea that had been swimming around in her head lately . . . that of hurting Ian's professional ego rather than his male one. So he was sensitive about this book, was he? she thought with spiteful pleasure as she pulled off the woolen jacket that matched her skirt. And he wanted it to be successful, did he? Well, she must be all the help she could be to him, then, she reflected, a slow smile curving her mouth in anticipation. And if it didn't turn out to be quite the sort of help he had in mind, well . . . those were the breaks of the game.

Chapter Six

After a brief rest, Alicia ventured cautiously out of her room shortly before seven. She could hear distant voices coming from a room on the other side of the dining room as she passed it, and she assumed that it was the kitchen. The living room was empty, however, when she entered it, and she took a deep breath to fill her lungs, only then realizing she had ceased to breathe in expectation of coming face to face with Ian.

This won't do, she told herself with a chiding grimness. She mustn't start off giving the impression that she was nervous of him in any way. She wanted to give the impression of being calm, cool, collected, and competent. It was essential that Ian respect her professional ability if she was to accomplish what she intended.

She moved closer to the blazing fire, enjoying the warmth and intimacy it provided the room. Idly perusing the mantel, she was somewhat annoyed to see that there were no writing mementos there...no indication that Ian was a world-famous author with a right to show off his fame. Instead there was a sailing trophy and a skiing trophy, and various wooden carvings of wild- and sea life, all excellently done. Alicia would have much preferred to be able to sneer at Ian's ego over his writing than to find that he seemed much more interested in the outdoor life. She consoled herself with the thought that his study was probably papered with framed bookcovers.

A noise behind her made her swing around to confront a large homely man who nevertheless had the kindest pair of brown eyes she'd ever seen. As he moved toward her with an outstretched hand she saw that he limped noticeably and deduced that this was Mr. Johnson.

"Alicia?" he inquired with a gentle smile as he approached. "I'm Borg Johnson."

Alicia responded to his gentle warmth with a smile of her own, liking him immediately. "It's good to meet you, Mr. Johnson," she said warmly.

"Call me Borg," he invited with casual ease. "Can I get you a drink?" he asked as he released her hand and moved toward a concealed bar.

"Some wine if you have it," Alicia responded.

"White or red?" he asked with all the aplomb of an accomplished host, though he looked as though a mountain cabin would suit him much more easily.

"White," Alicia said, moving to the sofa to seat herself. When Borg joined her, a glass of wine looking incongruous in his huge hand, he seated himself beside her with complete naturalness, inquiring about her trip out.

They were exchanging small talk with all the ease of lifelong friends, and Alicia was completely relaxed, when the voice she had been expecting but had temporarily forgotten existed spoke behind her.

"Ah, Alicia," Ian said with warm welcome as he came up behind the sofa. "It's good to see you. How was your trip?"

Alicia froze for the barest instant before she looked up over her shoulder to see Ian leaning with both hands on the sofa back, his eyes taking her in with a hint of amusement lurking in their depths. "The trip was fine," she said somewhat stiffly, and then belatedly, "Hello, Mr. Halsey."

The gleam of amusement deepened at her formality, and out of the corner of her eye Alicia saw that Borg Johnson looked astonished at hearing her use of Ian's last name. But all Ian said was, "Ian, Alicia," in a murmur that nevertheless forbade protest.

Ian came around the sofa then to stand with his legs spread apart in a casual stance before the fireplace. "Dinner about ready?" Borg inquired calmly, sipping his wine and stretching out his long legs with a grimace that bespoke the discomfort his bad leg must afford him.

"In a few minutes," Ian answered, never taking his eyes from Alicia. She withstood his intent scrutiny as long as she could before dropping her own while she took a sip of wine. She couldn't fathom the meaning behind Ian's eyes, but she felt unaccountably irritated and nervous. He seemed to be laughing at her in a gentle way that scraped her nerves. He was the last man on earth she could bear being a source of amusement for.

"Who won the race?" Borg kept the conversation going, though he didn't seem to be aware of the undercurrents Alicia could feel swirling around her like waves in a deep sea.

"The Barber twins." Ian laughed, the corners of his eyes crinkling with amusement. 'Was there ever any doubt?"

Borg snorted. "No, I guess not. If those boys would put their energies into something besides skiing, they'd conquer the world!"

"Don't look for that anytime soon," Ian commented dryly as he moved toward the bar. Alicia found herself watching him furtively, dismayed to note how attractive he looked in a well-worn shirt of wool plaid and an old pair of cords. Didn't the man *ever* look anything but self-assured and disgustingly attractive? she wondered irritably.

Ian had barely poured himself a scotch and soda before Ingrid and Sandi appeared in the doorway to announce dinner. Then all of them trooped into the large dining room to seat themselves around the table like one big happy family, laughing and joking and teasing one another in an infectious manner that had Alicia smiling in spite of her nervousness about Ian.

She found herself placed beside Sandi on one side of the table, while Mr. and Mrs. Johnson sat across from them. Ian, of course, had the place of honor at the head of the table. The meal consisted of Swedish meatballs on egg noodles, a green salad, and homemade bread that was still warm from the oven. Alicia had no trouble complimenting Ingrid on the food, and surprisingly little trouble eating it, though she had expected to be so nervous that she wouldn't eat a bite.

But the warm family atmosphere and the fact that Ian didn't address her directly once during the meal helped her to forget her inner battle stance for a brief time. She even forgot to view the natural manner between Ian and the Johnsons in a jaundiced light. He was so obviously fond of the family that she had no justification for thinking he was exploiting them, and she granted him one small bonus for having the good sense to appreciate their worth.

At the end of an excellent dessert of wine, fruit, and cheese, however, she tensed as Sandi jumped up from her chair and went behind Ian to give him a giant hug and to place a kiss on his temple. Sandi's generous bosom was pressed against Ian in an intimate way, and Alicia thought he would have had to be a saint not to be affected by such temptation...and there was no question in her mind that Ian Halsey bore no resemblance to a saint.

"Thanks for letting me have the Porsche tonight, Ian," Sandi was saying with a warm smile. "Buck will be in seventh heaven."

"Just so the two of you don't end up there literally," Borg Johnson said with a snort, seemingly completely unmoved by the fact that his daughter was hanging all over Ian in a manner that would have given most fathers heart failure. "You tell him to keep the speed down, his hands on the wheel, and his eyes on the road," he ordered good-naturedly.

"Ah, Dad," Sandi teased impishly, moving away from Ian to give her father a kiss on the cheek. "That doesn't sound like any fun at all!"

"Fun's not everything," Borg replied with a fond swat on Sandi's shapely bottom. "Just remember what I said and come home in one piece."

Ian was grinning as he watched the byplay between Sandi and Borg, and then he turned his golden gaze on Alicia, his teasing look indicating that he knew very well what she thought about Sandi's exuberant affection. Alicia gave him a cool look that was meant to be off-putting, but it had no effect. Ian simply grinned wider.

Ingrid got up to begin clearing the table, and Alicia automatically stood up to help her. Ingrid gave her a motherly scowl and a gentle swat on the wrist. "Stop that!" she said in a scolding voice. "I've already told you I don't need any help."

Alicia was about to protest, but Ingrid gave her a look that shut off her words before they could be uttered. Alicia caught a glimpse of Ian's amused grin and his uplifted eyebrow and desisted quietly, picking up her half-filled glass of wine and making a move toward the living room. She was desperately hoping Borg would accompany her and Ian there so she wouldn't be left alone with him quite yet, but the older man disappointed her. He stood up and gave a huge stretch, then started toward the kitchen. "I'm going to check the oil in that Porsche," he said lazily as Sandi fell in step beside him. "Seems to me it's been using a lot lately."

As Alicia moved into the hallway on her way to the living room, she felt Ian come up behind her and then the warm touch of his hand on her elbow. "Let's go into the study, Alicia," he suggested with lazy assurance. "I'm sure you're anxious to see where you're going to be working for the next few months."

Alicia had stiffened slightly at his touch, but he seemed unaffected by her action, though he had to have felt it. She stiffened even more when he leaned his tawny head down close to hers and whispered, "By the way, that's a lovely dress. It suits you."

As the dress she had on was an ice-blue creation that echoed the colors in her bedroom, Alicia felt a surge of anger run through her. She fought it down and smiled coolly up at Ian, shaken a little by the warm approval in his arresting eyes. "Thank you," she said stiffly, and left it at that.

The broad smile that greeted her prim expression of thanks made her even angrier, but she was determined not to show it. Ian opened the door she had earlier decided might be his study and ushered her into a room that caught at her heart immediately, though she tried not to let it.

The small fireplace in the room was blazing cheerfully and casting intimate shadows that joined with the soft light of a lamp on the desk. The fireplace was fronted by a deep, comfortable sofa in dark leather and two leather chairs that looked so inviting, Alicia knew they were for comfort rather than show. Ian's huge mahogany desk was cluttered with papers and books, and the plush chair behind it looked well used. The walls of the room not taken up by windows or the fireplace were lined with bookshelves occupied by hundreds of books that looked read.

Alicia's eyes must have shown how much she liked the room, for Ian's chuckle sounded well pleased. "I'm glad you like it," he said complacently. "You'll be spending a lot of time in here, and I'd hate to think you didn't like the decor."

Alicia swung around to face him with a denial on her lips, but then she realized it would be useless to lie. He'd already seen on her face what she thought of the room. "I'm—I'm sure I'll be very happy here," she muttered resentfully and then had to bear the brunt of another of Ian's broad smiles of amusement.

"Now, Alicia, don't tell lies," he chided her gently. "We both know you have no intention of being happy here."

Startled by his words, Alicia raised widened blue eyes to his. Before she could speak, however, he guided her to the sofa and pushed her down among the cushions. Then he sat down beside her, turning his body so that he could look straight into her eyes.

Alicia swallowed under the onslaught of the tender warmth she saw in the dancing brown lights of his eyes, trying to remember that such emotions weren't real where Ian was concerned. He was merely a practiced charmer, she reminded herself weakly.

"I knew you wouldn't want to come and work with me, Alicia," Ian murmured as his eyes roamed her face. "I told Brian to use anything he had to to get you here."

Alicia swallowed again, turning her head to break the awful fascination of Ian's look. "Why?" she asked on a strangled note. "Why me?"

Ian shrugged as he lifted a casual hand to twine one of Alicia's curls around a finger. She jerked her head away, though for the barest second she had wanted to lean against his hand and let him run his fingers through her hair. That thought made her jump to her feet and approach the fireplace with her back to Ian. Damn him! she thought with helpless anger. Even knowing what she did about him, it was going to be harder than she thought not to fall prey to his totally false appeal.

She heard Ian give a deep sigh before he spoke. "You're the type of editor I need for this book, Alicia," he said in a slightly weary voice.

Alicia swung around to fix him with a glare. "You mean it's going to be *heavy*, meaningful wisdom?" she asked sarcastically. "Something a highbrow like myself can relate to?" Then she stopped, startled by the resentment she felt that Ian viewed her that way. What was the matter with her anyway? she asked herself furiously. What did she care how he viewed her?

She was dismayed when she saw the sudden interested, speculative look that sprang into Ian's eyes at her words, and she searched desperately for something to say that would undo the damage. "I...uh...what's the book about anyway?" She struggled for a normal tone of voice. "Brian didn't seem to know."

A boyish grin lightened Ian's rugged features. "Oh, he knew, all right," he chuckled. "He just doesn't like to think about it, much less talk about it."

Alicia's wry look and slight smile acknowledged the truth of that statement. "No doubt," she said dryly. "He isn't exactly happy about your change of subject matter." And then she cocked a shapely eyebrow at him. "What *is* the subject matter?" she asked curiously.

Ian's expression grew bland and unrevealing, but he watched her closely as he answered. "It's a psychological study of a woman," he said softly. "A woman who buries her potential out of some misguided notion of what's really important in life."

Alicia stopped the pacing she had begun out of her nervousness and stared at Ian in stunned amazement. "*You're* going to do a study...a psychological study of a woman?" she asked incredulously, unthinking of the inherent insult in her question.

Ian's face grew hard and purposeful, reminding Alicia all at once of the night he had brought her home: his anger, his determination, the sheer male aggressiveness he embodied. He had been so different on the two occasions she had seen him since then, she had almost forgotten how hard he could be, how dangerous.

"I'm aware you think I'm completely unqualified to tackle something like that," he said with hard sarcasm in his flat tone. And then he seemed to catch himself, and his expression returned to blandness. "That's where you'll be such a big help to me, Alicia," he said in a smooth tone that somehow made her uneasily suspicious. She had an instinctive reaction of mistrust from his statement, though *why* she had that reaction was unclear to her.

Ian got to his feet and came to take Alicia's shoulders in his hands, holding her firmly when she would have pulled away, ignoring the caution that sprang into her eyes. "But, first, we have something more personal to get out of the way, Alicia," he said on a sincere note that matched the straightforward look in his eyes. "You wouldn't accept my apology the night I ran roughshod over your feelings. Will you accept it now?''

If anything could have been said to reawaken Alicia to her purpose here, Ian's words rammed it home to her with a vengeance. So he considered that he had merely ran roughshod over her feelings? she thought bitterly. How typical of his sense of values. Blatant seduction and a resulting abortion were merely bad manners, to be wiped out with an apology. She looked back at him with cold hostility.

"And *are* you sorry, Ian?'' she asked flatly, letting none of the hatred she felt at that instant leak through into her tone.

To her surprise, Ian seemed to consider the question seriously, and when he answered, there was a disconcerting honesty behind his reply. "Yes and no,'' he admitted, giving her a searching glance that shook her with its implacability. "I'm sorry if I hurt you, yes,'' he went on in the same vein. "But I'll be damned if I can say honestly that I regret what I felt when you finally let go and began to make love with me.''

Alicia froze at the deepening huskiness in his tone and the blaze that sprang up behind his eyes. She felt her arms begin to tingle where Ian held her, and a weakening warmth spread through her stomach at the demanding look in his eyes. Then he was pulling her toward him with slow, inexorable strength, and she was paralyzed by his dominance. His hands slid down to her waist and molded her against him, and as his mouth closed over hers, she gave a half-strangled moan, as she was powerless to prevent what was happening. It was as though Ian held her will hostage for the moment through sheer physical magnetism, and there was nothing she could do to break the spell.

His mouth was warmly explorative and then firmly

demanding as he forced her lips apart and thrust his tongue inside her mouth to take possession of the sweet moisture within. Alicia shuddered at the invasion, wanting desperately to be able to stop him from inciting the response she felt instantaneously, but she was caught between the need to let her body rule her and the need to let her head hold sway.

Her warring emotions were evident in her clenched hands as they rested on Ian's shoulders, refusing to clutch the firm muscles that she could feel bunching as he gathered her more closely against him. An instant later she knew she should have pushed him away rather than stay frozen with indecisiveness when she felt the arousal in his thighs.

God, she couldn't let this happen, she thought with weak helplessness as she fought her own arousal, an arousal she would have sworn Ian Halsey couldn't invoke again. But the sensations of his hands sliding over her were so delicious; his body was so warm and hard and yet yielding, inviting her to sink into his flesh.

"Alicia..." he murmured as he released her mouth to slide his lips down her throat. "I can't stop wanting you. God, you make me go crazy to have you!"

His words broke the spell he had invoked with his touch. *Wanting... having...* The words jarred her with their selfishness and gave her the impetus to fight her own desires. "Let me go," she gasped, pushing against him with renewed strength. "Let me go, Ian!" she repeated when he didn't immediately release her.

The urgency in her tone got through to him finally, and he raised his head to look at her, his eyes softly glazed with passion. "Why, Alicia?" he murmured tenderly. "Don't tell me you aren't wanting me, too, because your body says differently."

Alicia stared at him, hating him for knowing that

truth, and hating him even more because he could instigate the basis for that truth in the first place. "I don't care what my body wants," Alicia spat at him. "It means nothing except that I'm a human being with physical needs. I don't have to give in to them, and neither do you!"

Ian frowned at her words, an exasperated impatience coming into his eyes. "Why the hell shouldn't you give in to them?" he said with puzzled asperity. "They're as natural as breathing."

Alicia closed her eyes, confirmed once again in her opinion that Ian had no moral character to speak of. In a clipped, cold voice she spelled out for him why she had no intention of giving in to her physical nature. "Because I don't love you," she answered with cold precision. "And you don't love me. Because I believe in love...and in marriage...and in babies...." She was half-hysterical by now, the mention of babies bringing back all her pain in having destroyed one. "Do you ever think of babies, Ian?" she almost ranted at him, her eyes clearly showing the pain she felt. "Did it ever once occur to you that giving in to physical needs has consequences and that sometimes the consequences aren't pretty at all?"

Ian's puzzlement was growing at her hysterical behavior and he gripped her hard, as if he could dampen that hysteria through sheer force. "What are you talking about, Alicia?" he demanded with a shake.

Alicia gulped down a sob, realizing she had said too much and shown too much to this man she meant to exact revenge from. He mustn't learn at this stage just how much reason she had to hate him.

A burst of inspiration saved her. "Merely that you might consider the consequences of your actions once in a while, Ian," she said with cold deliberation. "I don't happen to use birth control."

Ian looked shocked for a moment, then frighteningly determined. "Alicia, did anything happen the last time?" he asked bluntly, maintaining his grip on her with bruising force in his agitation.

For a moment Alicia was panic-stricken before she realized that she was under no obligation to tell Ian Halsey the truth. Neither did she have to lie. "Do you see a child with me, Ian?" she asked sarcastically, spreading her hands out as best she could under his grip.

He stared at her hard, looking as though he wanted to beat the truth out of her, which only increased her returning control over her emotions. She was beginning to get herself in hand now, though her eyes still glimmered with tears and she felt as though she might collapse when Ian finally let her go.

Whether Ian would have pursued the matter or not, Alicia was not to know. A knock on the door preceding Ingrid's entry with a tray of coffee saved her from any further probing, and as Ian released his hold on her, she sank gratefully into a chair to give her time to get control over her trembling legs before she made her escape. She was exceedingly grateful when Ingrid sat down on the sofa to pour out the coffee rather than leaving the two of them alone. "I thought you two might be ready for this," the woman said with cheerful unconcern for the thick atmosphere in the room. "Sit down, Ian, you look tired."

And, indeed, he did look tired, Alicia thought as she glanced up at him from beneath her lashes. He suddenly looked as though the weight of the world had descended upon his shoulders, and she felt a great deal of satisfaction at seeing his carefree irresponsibility replaced for once with the cares every other human being had to withstand.

"Are you two going to start work tomorrow?" Ingrid

chattered on. "Or are you going to give Alicia a chance to get familiar with the area and perhaps recuperate from her trip a little before you start your slave driving, Ian?"

Ian looked distracted, as though his mind wasn't on his reply when he answered. "By all means, Alicia can have all the time she wants before we start work," he said on an absent note.

At Ingrid's inquiring look Alicia forced a smile and a cheerful answer. "A day or two might be nice," she agreed, since that was what Ingrid obviously expected. Then she got to her feet, waving away the coffee Ingrid was offering her. "In fact, if you don't mind, Ian, I think I'd like to have an early night now. I'm more tired than I realized."

The searching, forceful look Ian gave her made her want to back toward the door, but Alicia controlled the urge and stood where she was, waiting quietly for a reply. "Yes, of course" it finally came. "Go on to bed, Alicia. We'll see you in the morning."

Alicia hoped she was imagining the promise—or threat—she thought she heard in Ian's tone. She nodded her head, gave Ingrid a warm smile, and left the room after saying quiet good nights to the two of them. When she reached the dubious safety of her bedroom, she sagged onto the pristine white coverlet and bowed her head in her hands, knowing that if she was ever to accomplish her goal here, there must be no more incidents of the kind that had happened tonight. Ian Halsey was far too formidable an opponent to allow him any advantage whatsoever...and her own unexpected weakness toward his brand of seduction was all the advantage he would need to destroy not only her goals, but also what little self-respect she had left.

Chapter Seven

Surprisingly the next two days turned out to be far more pleasant than Alicia had expected them to be, chiefly because Ian was absent from the scene. When she emerged from her room on the morning after their confrontation in the study, it was to find that he had left town unexpectedly. Ingrid, though unaware of where he had gone, was unperturbed.

"He does that sometimes," she said unconcernedly. "He's probably off doing research somewhere for the book or for some other one he has in mind. I suppose that since the two of you weren't going to start work for a couple of days, he decided to use the time profitably some other way. He has that look."

"That look?" Alicia inquired in puzzlement.

"His working look." Ingrid laughed fondly. "When Ian is in one of his working moods, he goes at it with total concentration. It's the same when he plays. Whatever he does, he does it wholeheartedly."

For some reason the information made Alicia feel uneasy, but since there seemed no real basis for her feeling, she pushed it aside in favor of enjoying the whirlwind entertainment schedule the Johnsons set in motion for her benefit.

On the first day Sandi took her for a drive around the

area, ending up at one of the numerous ski slopes that ringed the lake. Despite Alicia's half-hearted protests, she soon found herself aboard a ski lift, being hoisted toward the top of an alarmingly steep-looking mountain while she wondered if Sandi had forgotten the fact that Alicia was a novice skier.

As things turned out, however, she had little to worry about and a great deal to enjoy. Sandi directed her to the gentle slopes and then set out to provide the instruction Alicia needed. The girl turned out to be an excellent teacher, and Alicia found herself to have more aptitude for the sport than she had earlier supposed. Added to that, the scenery was superb, and the two of them developed a companionableness that alleviated a loneliness Alicia hadn't even been aware she suffered from. Her concentration on Ben during his life, and her absorption in her grief over his death, and then the troubles Ian had left in his wake had kept her apart from friendships she now knew she needed.

They returned to Ian's home, tired but in excellent humor, to find a hot meal awaiting them, and then Alicia was greeted with the news that Ingrid, Borg, and Sandi wanted to make a night of it at the casinos.

"But I don't know how to gamble," Alicia informed them with a touch of apprehension. "And I can't afford to lose very much money," she added frankly.

Borg was stolidly unperturbed. "Don't worry," he said with a glint in his kind brown eyes. "We have a system."

While Ingrid and Sandi were laughing at that, Alicia gave a groan and rolled her eyes. "I've heard about people's gambling systems," she said dubiously. "They swear by them all the way to the poorhouse."

Borg shook his huge, shaggy head in denial. "Not *this* system," he said confidently. "All it consists of is setting aside a certain amount of money to gamble with and walking out the door when it's gone.''

Alicia joined in Ingrid's and Sandi's laughter then. "Oh, well, by all means, then, I'm ready to try *that*! I only hope you all weren't planning on a long evening. With the amount of money in my purse at this moment, I think about twenty minutes ought to take care of it...if I pull the nickel slot machine arms very slowly!"

They were all in a festive mood when they entered one of the larger casinos later that evening, and for a while Alicia was content to watch the others and the various people who filled the huge gambling room.

Borg had seated himself at a two-dollar blackjack table and was steadily building his supply of chips through patient, skillful play. Ingrid was enjoying herself at her favorite quarter slot machine, and Sandi headed for the crap table, where she was soon whooping uninhibitedly as she threw the dice while men all around her contented themselves with watching her jouncing body language and forgot all about why they were there themselves!

Alicia strolled up and down the corridors, trying to decide where she wanted to lose her own money, when she spotted a poker machine with a comfortable-looking stool in front of it and elected to try her luck there. Her legs were tired from the skiing and she had played poker with her father when she was younger, so she at least felt she might have some chance of influencing the fates.

Alicia won some money, then lost it, and when she had reached the limit she had set for herself, she slipped from the stool and went to join Borg, feeling poorer but wiser.

Borg had accumulated a respectable pile of chips, and

when she joined him, he obligingly taught her some of the tricks of playing blackjack until he started losing himself, at which point he collected the remainder of his winnings and got up from the table.

Alicia teased him. "I thought you were supposed to leave after you'd lost *all* your gambling money," she complained. "I took your advice and lost all of mine before I quit."

Borg grinned down at her from his impressive height and shook his head. "Sorry about that," he said with no real sign of repentance. "I should have gone into more detail about my system, but now you know from experience, and that's always a better way to learn."

Alicia agreed with him wholeheartedly, hiding her private thoughts behind a warm smile as she related his words to her personal experiences with Ian Halsey. The thought of him, and the fact that she had obviously *not* learned her lessons well enough where he was concerned, judging by her physical response to him the night before, dampened her spirits somewhat, but she was determined not to spoil the evening for the others. Still, she was relieved when Borg rounded up the remaining members of the Johnson family and they headed for home.

Early the next morning Sandi took Alicia skiing again, this time on a different, slightly more difficult slope, and by the time the day was over, Alicia felt rather proud of herself at the progress she'd made on skis. Sandi shared her pride, rightfully so as her teacher, and remarked as they left the slope that she couldn't wait for Ian to see how well she was doing.

"Oh...uh...well, perhaps we'd better work a little longer before I show off for him," Alicia responded a little grimly, inwardly determining that any playtime with Ian was going to be kept at the barest minimum.

Sandi protested. "But I have to go back to school in a few days," she said spiritedly, "and I want him to see what we've accomplished."

Alicia shrugged, unmoved by Sandi's desire to gain Ian's approval. "He doesn't know how bad I was to start with," she pointed out reasonably. "So anything we show him at this stage isn't going to impress him very much."

To her surprise, Sandi stopped short and looked at her in bewilderment. "Oh, but I thought—" Then she broke off her words, her expression eloquent with puzzlement. "You don't really seem to know Ian very well at all, do you?" she asked with a curious tilt to her shining blond head.

Alicia faced her with raised eyebrows, wondering how to answer that. In truth, she didn't know all that much about Ian, though she felt in some ways, due to their disastrous acquaintance so far, that she might know a great deal more about him than Sandi did. She hedged her answer. "We haven't known one another very long, no," she said quietly, keeping her voice neutral.

"Funny," Sandi said musingly, giving Alicia another of those puzzled looks. "I could have sworn—" But then she seemed to think better of whatever she'd been about to say and changed the subject, rather too abruptly to sound natural. "I have a date with Buck tonight, and he's going to be disappointed when he finds out we can't have the Porsche."

Puzzled in her turn, Alicia nevertheless went along with the change of subject. "Why can't you?" she asked. "Surely Ian wouldn't mind."

Sandi looked shocked. "Oh, he probably wouldn't," she agreed, "but I wouldn't dream of taking it without asking first . . . even if Dad would let me."

Alicia smiled at Sandi then, liking the integrity of the girl . . . indeed of her whole family. "What do you study at school, Sandi?" she asked easily, feeling curious about what would appeal to a young woman with Sandi's obvious physical attributes.

"Medicine," Sandi answered with a casual shrug. "I intend to be a plastic surgeon."

It was Alicia's turn to stop and look at her companion in surprise. The girl looked like a perfect candidate for a Playboy bunny, but here it seemed she had brains as well as beauty. She smiled at her own prejudice and gave Sandi an approving look. "Good for you," she praised sincerely. "When do you finish?"

"I start my internship next year," Sandi replied with unconscious pride and eagerness. "I'm in the top ten percent of my class."

Alicia was delighted for the girl, reflecting that she was a perfect example of the case for not allowing appearances to deceive one about a person's capacities.

That evening the Johnsons had something to do of their own, and since Sandi had a date, Alicia was left on her own. She decided to explore Ian's study with the idea of familiarizing herself with the room she would spend a great deal of time in over the next few months. She really hadn't done more than gain an overall impression the night Ian had taken her there.

A fire burned in the grate when she entered, and Alicia thought rather wryly that no doubt the Johnsons took pains to take good care of Ian, even to the extent of keeping his study warm in case he should arrive back unexpectedly. He was a very lucky man in a lot of ways, and she wondered if he ever realized the fact, or if he just went on about his life, taking everything for granted. It would be like him to do so, she reflected bitterly as she stood in the center of the delightful room and turned slowly around to look at its interior.

She moved to the desk and spotted a smaller table behind it with a modern typewriter in one corner. A little surprised that Ian hadn't invested in a word processor, which would have been a great help to him, considering the volume of work he turned out, she touched the keys gingerly, shrinking a little at the impression of warmth they provided, almost as though Ian had just used the machine. The fleeting impression of pleasure she received made her draw her hand away hastily, dismayed at the betraying feeling. She tightened her mouth and determined once again to hold firm against whatever innate power he had to make people—herself included—ignore his shortcomings when confronted with the power of his personality.

Turning, she glanced over his desk and spotted a picture in a gold frame on one corner amidst all the disorder he apparently favored. Curious, she leaned over to pick it up and found herself staring at a family portrait of a much younger Ian and his mother and father. She recognized his mother at once. Ian bore a strong resemblance to her . . . except that where his eyes were a golden brown and his hair was auburn, legacies from his father, his mother was a blond blue-eyed prim-looking woman whose frozen stare made Alicia uncomfortable. She knew instinctively that if the woman were actually in the room with her, Alicia would start to check to see if her slip was showing or her hair was mussed. . . . Ian's mother was *that* sort of woman.

She shifted her gaze to Ian's father and decided she would be equally uncomfortable with him, but for a different reason. The man had that otherworldly, preoccupied expression that betold a typical absentminded professor. In fact, he reminded her of—

As her thoughts exploded inside her, Alicia almost threw the picture back down upon the desk. Her breath was coming hard and fast, her eyes wide with incredulity. Ian's father reminded her of Ben, of all people! A Ben stripped of her love for him and revealed in all his selfish exclusion of everything except what interested *him*.

Alicia hugged herself against a sudden chill, alarmed and amazed at the thoughts that had taken hold of her. Why was she thinking of Ben like that? she wondered almost frantically. Hadn't he been the best thing that ever happened to her? Wasn't he the wonderful, gentle genius she had always admired and loved and given her whole life to?

She came out from behind the desk and paced distractedly. The phrase *given her whole life to* rang in her mind with distressing emphasis. She didn't like the resentment she was feeling as whole series of memories drifted through her mind. Ben accepting her every sacrifice without so much as acknowledging that she *was* sacrificing. He had been so caught up in his own little world that he hadn't even been aware of how hard she had to work both at the office and at home to keep them solvent and to provide a pleasant atmosphere where he could concentrate on his work.

Ben digging into their meager savings to take little trips for research, never even asking if she'd like to go along...not that she could have. Her vacations had been spent painting the apartment to save money or scouring secondhand shops for furnishings at a cut-rate price. Even his reaction when she had once, in a fit of yearning she hadn't been able to control, brought up the subject of having a child. He had looked up at her distractedly, seemingly puzzled that such a thought could occur to her, and had made some vague comment about what a distraction a child would be. Then he had gone back to reading some weighty tome that no doubt only such an exalted mind as his could have fathomed.

Alicia stopped her pacing, feeling ashamed of the bitter condemnation she had just experienced at that point in her reminiscences. What had got into her? she wondered angrily. Ben *had* been a genius, even if the world had never seen fit to acknowledge that genius. But she had. And she had made up her mind before she ever married him that it was her duty to protect that genius... to keep cares and troubles away from Ben so he could concentrate on exploiting that genius. She had admired his mind, which was so above her own, even though she had never been regarded as stupid, and she had felt it her duty to protect Ben, since his intellect was so far superior to everyone else's.

Unbidden, Brian Crossley's words to her of several months back came into her mind. "A poet is supposed to broaden people's horizons," he had said. And she had thought Ben was doing that. She had drunk in the words of his poetry, struggling to find the meaning behind them when they seemed obscure. Was it possible she had been wrong all those years? Had Ben perhaps been only the selfish, self-preoccupied man Ian's father resembled, with no real capacity for communicating? And had Alicia, so admiring of intellectualism all her life, been fooled into worshiping at his altar with no real justification for such behavior?

Feeling weak and betrayed, Alicia sank into one of the chairs before the fireplace, staring into the flames unseeingly and feeling as shaken as though someone had told her the sun wasn't coming up the next morning. Where were all these thoughts coming from? she wondered with helpless bitterness. Was it the atmosphere in Ian's study? The picture of his parents? The scathing denouncement she remembered him expressing of how she treasured Ben's memory the night she had met Ian for the first time?

Her thoughts were broken off as the door to the study swung open and the man himself stood regarding her from the doorway, his presence immediately dominating everything around him. He looked unutterably tired, but even in his fatigue he exuded a sense of energetic power that made Alicia shrink back into her chair.

"Ah, Alicia," he said with dry weariness as he came into the room and shut the door behind him. "What are you doing in here all alone? Soaking up atmosphere to help me with my book?"

There was a faint tinge of mockery in his words that made Alicia uneasy. But he couldn't know what she planned to do about his book, could he? she reassured herself with false courage.

"Uh—the—the Johnsons went out, and Sandi had a date. It just seemed more comfortable in here," she replied faintly, wishing she could have chosen a less intimate way of describing his room.

She disliked the fact that her words seemed to please him, though his pleasure was tainted with the mockery she had heard in his voice. "Good," he said with casual ease as he moved to drop down onto the sofa and lean his head back in a restful pose. "I'm glad you like it in here. In fact, I'm glad you *are* here. There's something I want you to listen to." Then he smiled as he saw her regarding him with puzzled unease. "But, first, would you mind fixing me a drink? It's been a long day, and I'm tired, or I'd get it myself."

Surprised a little at his way of putting the request—it was so unlike Ben, she thought fleetingly; he would have taken it for granted, and rightly so, that she would

have a drink in his hand before he had to ask—she got to her feet and went to the small bar in one corner of the room. "What will you have?" she asked with soft huskiness, dismayed at the almost submissive note in her voice.

"Scotch and soda with a little ice." Ian cocked his head back to smile at her warmly. "Why don't you have one yourself? You look tired and depressed."

Startled by his perceptiveness, Alicia shot him a brief glance before she complied with his suggestion. Normally she didn't drink anything so hard, but if she and Ian were to have some kind of interview, perhaps it would be as well to fortify herself against these first moments of working together alone.

She brought the drinks back to where Ian was seated, taking care to make sure their hands didn't touch when she handed him his. Then she went back to the chair and seated herself, taking a long gulp of the drink she held and avoiding looking at Ian.

"Actually, what I want you to listen to has nothing to do with the book you and I are going to work on together. I had another idea for a book set in the early days of this country. The hero and heroine are Indians." Ian sounded so calmly impersonal that Alicia found herself relaxing. He had a pleasant deeply masculine voice, and his attitude seemed so professional, she automatically adopted a frame of mind she employed in her work.

Ian outlined the story for her, which, although along the lines of the books he normally wrote, had the twist of being set in a time and locale he usually didn't deal with. Most of his earlier stories had taken place either near the sea or in Europe. And then, too, his characters were non-European, which Alicia considered an interesting switch.

"I want your opinion of a scene I just dictated to-day," Ian was saying with casual disinterest as he pulled a small dictating machine out of his pocket. He handed it to her, asking if she knew how to operate it. Upon learning that she did, he said, "Turn it down low. I know what I've said, and I'll be able to hear enough to recall it. I'd rather see its effect on you so that I can tell if I've got what I was striving for." He smiled lazily then, his eyes warm with amusement and something Alicia couldn't define. "Besides, the nature of the scene is such that you might rather not share it with me." He paused and then added with quiet meaning, "Verbally."

Alicia shrugged, puzzled by his words but unsuspecting of what was to come. Ian leaned back against the sofa, his long legs stretched out, his eyes half-closed as he watched her, one arm behind his head for support, the other stretched out along his thigh. Alicia turned her attention to the machine she held, and after a moment or two of adjustment, she heard Ian dictating in a soft, sensuous voice that made a shiver go down her spine. It reminded her of the tone he had used when he'd made love to her.

The scene consisted of an Indian man and woman at the end of a day of travel together, getting ready for sleep. Ian provided both the man's and the woman's thoughts, and he did it so well, Alicia unconsciously slipped into the story as though she were attending a theater presentation, visualizing the light of the camp fire, the huddled form of the Indian woman as she sat before it, and the man as he squatted before her.

"Why are you afraid, little one?" the man was ask-ing—in Ian's tones, with Ian's inflection of gentle hu-mor and tenderness. "We will be man and wife soon enough. What harm is there if we anticipate the event by a few days? I have watched your form long enough. You have the grace of the deer, and its shyness as well. And yet when you move, I see the sensuousness of the big cats, and my loins swell to possess you. I do not wish to wait any longer to take what is mine.''

After a momentary sense of dismay at the nature of the scene she was listening to, Alicia conquered her misgivings and tried to adopt a professional attitude. But the flickering warmth of the real fire in the fireplace echoed the scene Ian had dictated, and his presence impinged on her consciousness far too strongly for her to be able to forget that he was seated a mere few feet from her, lounging on the sofa in masculine comfort, his body providing a vivid mold for her to place around the Indian man's in the scene.

However wary she was, the low, sensuous tones of Ian's voice on the recorder wove her again into the spell of the story, the flickering light from the fire in the room providing an effective atmosphere to enhance its telling.

The young woman in the story was both impelled to submit to her future husband's seduction by her own burgeoning sexuality and fearful of venturing into this new area of male/female relations that she knew nothing about. The man's whispering encouragement was so tender, so understanding, and yet so forceful as he began to stroke her skin erotically that Alicia became fascinated with the age-old tale of the chase, wondering when and if the girl would submit under the skillful coaxing of her man, and whether he would force her if she should finally decide to refuse him.

As she listened Alicia was unaware that her eyes had found Ian's and that the two of them were communicating nonverbally in tandem with the story. Her mind was with the couple Ian was portraying, but her body was responding to the piercing demand in Ian's eyes, the taut sensuality she could detect in his physique. His gaze caressed her as the Indian man in the tale caressed his lover, coaxing, enticing, disturbing her into responding against her cautious instincts. Ian's voice on the machine was as low and intimate as if he were speaking directly to Alicia, adding its part to the process of arousal she was undergoing.

She forgot where she was and *became* the young Indian woman while the man on the tape became Ian. Her lips parted slightly as her breathing rate increased, and she let her lids droop over the sensuous softening glow in her eyes. Even her posture relaxed into a submissive softening, her clenched fists gradually opening until her hands lay palm up in her lap, relaxing their hold on the machine to let it lie passively, spilling the charm of Ian's voice into the room where it wrapped itself around her mind and body until she was completely under its spell.

The seduction was almost complete now. Ian's words were erotically explicit as he described the scene, but they failed to shock or disturb Alicia. Perhaps because the words were tape-recorded instead of being actually spoken to her, Alicia heard only the beautiful description of love at its most erotic rather than experiencing any shame at their detail. And they were beautiful. When she had read his earlier books, she hadn't thought of his love scenes as oeing tender and sensitive. Perhaps they hadn't been, but this one was. And she felt something inside her open up to that portrayal of love as being right and good and wonderfully exciting. When the man in the story took his lover with gentle passion, Alicia felt the ecstasy he imparted to his wife-to-be. She felt the sharp pain of intrusion, then the warmth of possession building up into a fierce desire for unity, for oneness with this man, for fulfillment...the fulfillment of giving and taking and becoming one flesh.

She wanted to close her eyes at the moment of completion, but Ian's gaze held her fast, willing her to share with him what she was experiencing, and it was as though the two of them shared that moment every bit as completely as the two in the story did. Alicia was shaken by the intimacy Ian insisted upon, feeling a part of her slip into his keeping from which she was afraid she would never get it back.

And then it was over. The tape fell silent, and Ian and Alicia sat for a long moment staring at one another while the spell it had cast died away. Then Ian's smile warmed her as he asked, softly, "What did you think of it?"

His voice—not the voice on the tape, but his real voice—shocked her into reality again. She sat up with a jerk, swallowing the little moan of disappointment she felt at having the episode come to an end, and clutching the tape recorder in her hands as though she would like to throw it at him. But her control held. She took a shaky breath and forced herself to reply calmly. "It...it was very effective. You're a true master at that sort of thing, Ian," she said with a hint of bitterness in her voice and a cold look in her blue eyes.

"You don't think it needs any revision, then?" Ian inquired with a hint of lazy amusement underlying his innocent blandness.

Alicia forced herself to shrug uncaringly, then got to her feet. "I'm not an expert at this sort of writing," she said flatly. "And it's not what I'm here for. You would do better to discuss it with Brian." She made a move toward the door, anxious to escape Ian's presence and to go to her room, where she could overcome the trembling in her limbs and the languorousness she still felt as a result of the story...and Ian's domination of her during the telling of that story.

But he was on his feet and blocking her way before she could reach the door. He didn't touch her to keep her where she was. He didn't have to. His eyes held her as forcefully as they had while she had been under their spell earlier. "I think you could become an expert at this...uh...sort of story," Ian said softly. "Don't you ever feel the need to tackle something new? Wouldn't you like to expand your horizons, venture into new paths, open yourself to new...experiences? Professionally, of course," he added dryly.

Alicia was aware that Ian's words had a double meaning...that he was asking something much more personal than was apparent on the surface. But she couldn't deal with those implications. She was having to fight with all her will to remember her purpose in going there. Her animosity toward Ian was threatening to slip away from her, and she clutched at it frantically, only too well aware of the danger of veering from her purpose in favor of submitting to his brand of seduction.

"No," she said with cool implacability. "I'm happy as I am." She would have brushed past him, but he put out a hand to enclose her upper arm, his warm touch sparking off a jolt of awareness in Alicia that almost panicked her.

"Are you?" Ian inquired musingly as he watched the emotions warring in her expression. "I don't think so, Alicia. There's so much inside you that you won't let out. Don't you get tired of expending all the energy you have to to keep a lid on what you really feel?"

With a strangled gasp of desperation Alicia jerked away from him and fled toward the door. "You don't know what you're talking about!'' she cried as she went.

Ian's voice stopped her on the threshold. ''Alicia!'' he said with firm authority, not moving toward her, but compelling her to listen. ''I think I do know . . . far more than you give me credit for.'' He paused, and then more calmly he finished. ''And if you ever want my help in exploring what I'm talking about, say the word. You'll find me a willing ally in getting to the bottom of who Alicia Farr really is.''

Alicia gave him one last, slightly wild look of fear and bewildered anger before she left the room and retreated to her bedroom, where she lay awake into the small hours of the morning, reliving what had happened and desperately holding on to the purpose that had become her all-encompassing obsession — to make Ian Halsey pay for changing her into a stranger, a woman with depths of passion that frightened her, capable of actions that repelled her.

Chapter Eight

After breakfast the next morning, Alicia joined Ian in his study, her manner cool and professional, the walls she had erected against him the night before firmly in place. She was determined he was never going to undermine her defenses again and her remote indifference toward him was meant to spell out how their relationship was to be conducted henceforth.

She was a little disconcerted when it became evident that Ian's attitude reflected her own. There were no warm, lazy, amused looks now, no teasing intimacy, nothing, in fact, but a brusque professionalism and concentration on the work at hand that left her feeling strangely bereft and a little depressed.

"Here's the first chapter," Ian said, placing the sheets on a small table he had evidently brought in after she'd left his presence the night before. "And a red pencil," he added in a dry, remote voice that spelled out his expectation that she would be using it liberally. "I'll be at the typewriter working on the next one if you have any questions."

That simply did Ian spell out how they were to conduct their working sessions in the days to come. Alicia took a deep breath, watching as Ian moved with masculine grace to seat himself before his typewriter, his manner indicating he had already forgotten she was in the room with him. She found herself resenting that manner, but she buried her resentment underneath the excited, fearful anticipation she also felt at last embarking on her plan to destroy Ian Halsey's complacency in himself.

Seating herself at the small table, she drew the pages he had written toward her with trembling hands, eager, and at the same time almost afraid, to begin the task she'd set herself. On one level what she was about to do violated all the professional ethics she had developed over a period of years. She had always been sensitive toward the authors' work she edited, trying to maintain a balance between objective, guiding criticism and sympathy for what they were trying to get across. It was sometimes a difficult role to play, requiring tact when she honestly felt authors needed steering toward a different mode of expression, yet without destroying their motivation or disturbing the delicate egos that often went along with their creativity.

Now, however, she planned to deliberately set out to subvert an author, and the guidance she intended to offer would have little to do with improving the quality of his work and everything to do with revenge. She hoped this book of Ian's wouldn't prove to be good enough to give her many qualms over her actions, but even if she found that it had promise, her purpose was firm. She would do everything she could to destroy whatever good qualities the work might possibly have and replace them with mediocre shallowness. It only remained to be seen how extensive her sabotage would have to be, and given her opinion of Ian Halsey and his work to date, she thought there shouldn't be too much effort required on her part.

With a last, glittering glance of dislike at Ian's broad

back, Alicia set to work. Normally she would have discussed the book in detail with him before she even read a page, but since he seemed in no mood to talk at all, and she was set on her purpose in any case, she decided it made little difference whether she knew what he intended, other than his general description of the book as a psychological profile of a woman.

The first chapter was a delicate portrait of a female child growing up in a marginal neighborhood where she was exposed to extravagant wealth on one hand and desperate poverty on the other. The girl fell somewhere in the middle, and toward the end of the chapter it became clear that, to her, it was a very unsatisfactory place to be. She was a person of extremes in her own character and had a highly developed taste for power, so that she would have preferred either the impetus of poverty or the advantages of wealth rather than floating between the two in what she considered a state of limbo.

At first Alicia became so caught up in Ian's mastery of the language that she forgot to read the chapter objectively. And that fact disturbed her when she realized what had happened. Grimly she began to reread the chapter, searching for seemingly legitimate criticisms to make, whether they existed or not. It disturbed her even more when she found none, unless she challenged Ian in a purely subjective fashion regarding the whole character of the girl in the story, an area where she was on very shaky ground indeed.

Alicia glanced up at Ian, noting that he was pounding away steadily at the typewriter with none of the pauses for thought that might indicate he was having difficulty finding his way through the story. The fact brought a frown of resentment to Alicia's smooth forehead and a grimace of disgust to her generous mouth. She should have been glad that he was working so quickly. After all, the sooner he finished, the sooner she would be able to leave there with her purpose accomplished. On the other hand she didn't like the image he projected of professional competence...the surety of where he was going displayed even in the set of his shoulders.

She turned back to the pages in front of her, biting her lip as she worried at the problem of how to attack them. Perhaps it *was* going to be necessary to have a talk with Ian, find out how he planned to develop this character, find a basis for disturbing that sureness he embodied, which grated on her nerves and undermined her own confidence in succeeding at her task.

At last, impatient at the impasse she faced and unwilling to disturb Ian for the moment when he seemed so completely oblivious to her, Alicia stood up and crossed the room to go in search of Ingrid and some coffee. She had reached the door before Ian spoke. "Bring me some, too, will you?"

Startled, Alicia swung around to face him, reaching up a nervous hand to brush away a strand of her hair from her cheek. "What?"

Ian barely glanced up from his work, continuing to type as he spoke to her. "Some coffee. .that's where you're going, isn't it?"

His voice was brusque and slightly impatient, irritating Alicia out of all proportion to what seemed called for, perhaps because his tone was so different from what she was used to hearing from him...perhaps because the fact that he kept right on typing was further indication that he knew exactly where he was going. "Black or white, master?" she snapped out unthinkingly, her hand on her jean-clad hip, her head tilted mutinously.

Ian didn't even seem to hear the insulting description she imparted to him. "Ingrid knows," he muttered, returning to his work as though Alicia didn't exist.

Alicia glared at him, opened her mouth for a retort, then closed it again as she swung out of the room. But her scowl must have looked ominous when she entered the kitchen, because Ingrid looked at her askance. "My goodness," the woman tutted chidingly. "Are you and Ian having a fight? You look as though you've either been in the ring recently or are contemplating getting there as soon as possible."

Unthinkingly Alicia spoke her mind. "Who can fight with a man who's so engrossed in his own little world, he doesn't know you exist?" she ground out through her teeth. Then, at Ingrid's knowing chuckle, Alicia wished she'd kept a guard on her tongue. "What are you laughing at?" she muttered with half-muted resentment.

Ingrid wiped flour off her hands, the result of kneading another of her loaves of homemade bread, and came to put a motherly arm across Alicia's shoulders. "Not at you, sweetheart," she said comfortingly, her eyes twinkling blue lights. "At least not maliciously. I'm just always amused when I see the game of love being played out so predictably by every new couple that gets entangled in its coils. No one ever seems to learn the shortcuts."

Alicia stared at Ingrid as though she'd gone crazy. "What are you talking about, Ingrid?" she asked with injured exasperation. "There's nothing like that between Ian and me."

Ingrid gazed back unperturbed, her wise, kindly eyes mischievous. "No?" she asked innocently. "Then what was that scene all about in the study the other night? When I walked in, you could have cut the atmosphere with a knife."

Alicia squirmed inwardly and drew away from Ingrid to cross to the sink and stare out the window with concentrated interest. "That was just...just some personal differences we had to get out of the way before we could work together," she answered with a vague motion of her hand.

"Ummm..." Ingrid made a dry sound that denoted doubt. "If you say so," she said lightly. "In that case, I guess I don't need to tell you, since you obviously wouldn't be interested, that although Ian might exclude his loved ones while he's working, he more than makes up for his neglect when he's not."

Unthinkingly Alicia accepted the bait. She swung around and eyed the other woman with glaring interest. "How do you know?" she asked sarcastically. "How many times has Ian been in love, anyway?"

Ingrid affected astonishment. "Ian?" she questioned incredulously. "Why, Ian has never been in *love* that I can recall." She adopted a musing stare for a second, then added thoughtfully, "Of course, he hasn't been a monk either."

Since this description of Ian Halsey fitted with how she viewed the man, Alicia responded with satisfaction. "Ha!" she gloated. "I'll just bet he hasn't! Judging by his reputation, I doubt if a monastery would even allow him within its gates for a visit!"

Ingrid shook her golden head impatiently, clucking with indignation. "Oh, Alicia," she scolded in tart defense of her employer and friend. "You don't honestly believe all that garbage about Ian, do you? You, of all people, ought to know it was just made up to sell books!"

Alicia was unconvinced. "*All* of it?" she asked sarcastically. "You've just said yourself that he hasn't been a monk."

Ingrid shrugged, moving to the counter to get down cups and saucers, though Alicia hadn't as yet expressed any desire for coffee. "Of course he hasn't," she said with placid indifference. "He's a red-blooded male with all the normal desires of any other male. But he's also something of a romantic. He's never played games with the real thing. I've always believed that when he finds the right woman, he'll settle down and devote himself to her exclusively."

"We must not be talking about the same man," Alicia retorted, irritated by Ingrid's defense of Ian. "I've heard him say himself that a man like that would be utterly boring. Poetry, undying love, and fidelity are not his style."

Ingrid turned and smiled sweetly at her over her shoulder. "How do you know?" she asked with innocent blandness. "I thought there was nothing like that between the two of you?"

Alicia flushed at the gentle barb. "There isn't," she asserted stoutly. "I don't know how you ever got the idea there was."

Ingrid's skeptical look and noncommittal "Hmmm..." were not reassuring. "I guess I just got carried away by the vibrations you two put out when you're together," she said offhandedly.

Alicia deemed it time to change the subject. "I came to get some coffee," she said, unnecessarily so, since Ingrid was already placing two cups and saucers and a pot of coffee onto a tray.

"Yes," Ingrid agreed wryly. "I thought it was about time for some. Ian takes it black, by the way."

She handed the tray to a mutinous Alicia, who stared down at it as though she'd like to bring the whole thing down on Ian's head. Instead, she took the tray into her own hands and turned on her heels to return to the study, her mood spoiling for a fight with the real source of her animosity.

Ian was still pounding away at his typewriter and he didn't look up when Alicia set the tray down with a thump and a rattle of crockery on his desk. "I want to talk to you, Ian." Alicia interrupted his concentration on a grim note. "I can't do anything with that chapter until I know where you're going." She poured his coffee with a vigorous splash and carried it to his side, almost exploding when she realized he hadn't heard a word she'd said.

"Ian!" she almost yelled at him. "Will you stop that and listen to me, damn it?"

Ian broke off typing, turning an irritated glance up at her. Spotting the cup of coffee in her hands, he reached up and took it from her, bringing it to his mouth for a huge gulp. "What *is* it, Alicia?" he asked irritably as he viewed her aggressive stance and scowling face with disfavor.

"I *said* I want to talk to you," she replied, enunciating the words slowly and distinctly. "I can*not* do anything with that book when you give it to me piecemeal unless I know where you're going with it." Her eyes sparkling with hostility, Alicia said with cold determination, "You'll just have to break off what you're doing for a while and fill me in."

Ian cocked an arrogant eyebrow at her, returning her coldness look for look. "I can't do that," he announced firmly.

Alicia, puzzled and further irritated, demanded, "Why not?"

Ian shrugged. "Because I don't *know* where I'm going," he replied dryly.

His words enraged her for some reason. "You do so!" she accused him heatedly.

Again the raised eyebrow emphasized his arrogance. "Do I?" he asked sarcastically. "How kind of you to inform me of the fact."

Alicia stiffened at his tone. With a sharp gesture at the typewriter she said, "If you don't know where you're going, you're sure in a hell of a hurry to get there. What are you doing, then, typing out the alphabet over and over?"

The dangerous light in Ian's tawny eyes told her she had gone too far, and Alicia backed up a step, biting her lip in consternation as she saw the same look on his face she had seen that long-ago night in New York, when she had angered him beyond the point of caution. This time, however, at seeing her obvious trepidation, Ian's expression quickly reverted to mere irritation, and Alicia had the odd impression that the irritation was self-directed.

"Alicia," he spoke with patient firmness, "you might as well get used to doing things *my* way from the start. You will get the chapters when I'm ready to give them to you and not before. If *I* feel like it, we will discuss them at the end of the day." And then, as Alicia stiffened again at his arrogant laying down of the law, he gentled his tone. "I'm sorry if you find you have time on your hands doing it this way, but there's plenty of entertainment available here any time you feel like taking advantage of it. Why don't you go skiing *now*, as a matter of fact? It doesn't look as though I'll have anything for you until tomorrow, beyond what I've already given you."

Alicia was outraged at his suggestion. Ian had voiced it as though he wanted to get rid of her and to be left in peace, and such a blow to her self-esteem had her choking on a suitable reply. But when she saw him watching her with a sort of wary, tender amusement, she clamped down on her inclination to pummel him with her fists and took a deep breath. Her blue eyes spat ice at him when she was able to speak, but her tone was sweetly reasonable.

"Why, what a good idea, Ian!" she purred at him silkily. "Aren't I lucky to have such a peachy job! I'll be the envy of everyone at Talton when they find out working for you is more play than work!"

The enigmatic look that greeted her baiting might have given her cause for worry if she'd been in a mood for caution. Even Ian's murmured "Don't be too sure, Alicia. There'll come a time when you'll have to work harder than you ever have in your life" didn't dent the reckless fury that spurred her onward.

"I'll just go find Sandi and get on with the 'fun' part of my job," Alicia continued in that same sweet, reasonable tone, moving toward the door of the room with a spring in her step that was meant to convey cheerful energy, but which sprang from an anger that filled her with electricity. "See you later, Ian." She smiled back at him from the doorway, batting her eyes at him in a flirtatious manner that cost her a great deal to accomplish.

"Good-bye, Alicia," Ian drawled in a dry tone that told her he wasn't in the least fooled by her manner, and then he turned back to his typewriter and was banging on the keys before she even got the door closed behind her.

As Alicia stomped to her room to change into ski clothes she was filled with a rage that was all-consuming. So she was supposed to cool her heels and await the lord and master's pleasure to begin her work, was she? she thought furiously as she pulled off her blouse in favor of a warm sweater. She wasn't *needed* yet, and Mr. Ian Halsey would let her know when she was, would he? she continued as she stepped into a warm pair of ski pants. Well, Mr. Ian Halsey was in for a surprise if he thought his dicta would bother *her*! He was going to find out that she had a capacity for play that could match his own. And she was going to put it into operation beginning now.

Chapter Nine

And so began another transformation in Alicia's behavior instigated by Ian Halsey. Sandi proved a willing ally in Alicia's search for amusement, though the younger girl seemed somewhat puzzled by her new friend's almost frantic desire to keep herself occupied during every spare moment when she wasn't required to be at Ian's bidding.

The days began to develop a pattern. Skiing in the mornings, when Alicia increased her skill at the sport steadily, then lunch and a short rest before Sandi bore her off to join friends in whatever endeavor they had concocted for the afternoon, then back to the house for dinner. The evenings belonged to Ian, and every day, after the evening meal, Alicia would join him in the study for what was supposed to be a critique of his writing efforts during the day.

Alicia had found her own method for coping with this particular thorn in her side as well, however. Usually she collected the pages Ian had finished that day before she went to her room to change for dinner, read them between taking her shower and dressing, and without making any effort to critique what she'd read, she merely made polite noises when Ian discussed his work with her after dinner. She had decided that in the interest of not tipping her hand to him, she would wait until the book was all but finished before ripping it apart. And she was longing to rip it apart, because its content was beginning to disturb her profoundly, adding to her desire to fill her days with frantic activity in order to blot out her thoughts.

Ian had confessed to her that he was basing the book on his mother, a woman so caught up in establishing a position for herself in life, she had let slip all her opportunities for obtaining anything worthwhile in the process. Lacking any real talent for gaining prominence on her own, Ian's mother had buried herself in the task of pushing her husband toward success. And Ian's father, a selfish, preoccupied man of some, though limited, talents himself, had responded by allowing his wife to take care of the social necessities and academic politics that were required to get ahead while he concentrated on burying himself ever further in his own world of obscure literature.

As a result, Ian had lacked any warmth in his growing-up years at home, though he had received a portion of it from a neighboring family whose life-style was the exact antithesis of his own family's. Alicia realized then why Ian was so fond of the Johnsons. From his descriptions of his early neighbors, it was clear that they were just the sort of warm, loving people as the family that now made their home with Ian, and that he was drawn toward the environment they automatically created through some deep desire for the loving family life he had missed out on as a boy.

These revelations tore Alicia apart when she allowed herself time to think about them. Indeed, her emotions were roiling with conflict after every evening of sitting listening to Ian quietly and calmly discuss his innermost feelings without giving the slightest sign that they caused him any distress.

She had to fight the pity she felt for the young boy he had been. Against her will she had to fight the admiration she felt for Ian when he discussed such painful memories without self-pity, but rather with the detachment of an author probing into the characters he was creating while somehow remaining apart from them. And she had to fight to maintain her motivation for continuing to plot to destroy his creation.

By the end of the first week Alicia was practically reeling from the weight of her inner conflicts, her face pale and wan, her eyes bright with the tiredness she felt as a result of sleepless nights and activity-filled days. And underneath all of her conscious confusion there was the growing resentment she felt at the inner certainty that Ian was speaking to her on some other level than what seemed obvious. She knew he equated her with his mother in some fashion. Why else had he put her in his mother's room, saying to Ingrid that he thought it suited her perfectly? And the thought was becoming increasingly unbearable the more she learned about the woman who had borne a son and then practically ignored him through all the years when he needed her so desperately. And yet she didn't know why she should feel so hurt that Ian saw her that way...why his feelings toward her should matter at all.

One night, when Ian had grown quiet after explaining to her the background for a certain scene he had written that day, Alicia could stand it no longer. "What do you think your mother should have done with her life, Ian?" she burst out jaggedly as she got to her feet to stare into the flames of the fire burning so cheerfully, wanting its warmth to dispel the chill she felt at hearing once again how bleak had been his boyhood.

She felt his eyes on her as he paused momentarily before replying with a question instead of an answer. "What do *you* think she should have done, Alicia?" he said quietly, something in his tone causing her to swing around to face him.

"Me?" she asked in surprise. "What does it matter what I think?"

He didn't answer, merely awaiting a reply, his eyes basking her in a glow as enigmatic as the expression on his handsome face. Alicia fidgeted under that look, beginning to pace back and forth with agitated steps. Then she stopped and actually considered her answer, speaking thoughtfully, though her attention was still taken up far too much by the man who watched her.

"I suppose," she began hesitantly, "that I think if she wasn't suited for a career of some kind, she could at least have provided you and your father with love." She raised her head to look at Ian defensively. "Don't you?"

Ian's slow grin had the effect of both irritating and captivating her. "Of course." He shrugged offhandedly. "But then, I'm prejudiced on the subject." His glance was oddly piercing as he pinioned her with it. "Is that what *you* would have done?"

Without thinking, Alicia shot him an impatient glance. "Of course!" she responded as though it were self-evident. "I love children!"

Ian's skeptical, enigmatic glance infuriated her suddenly, helped along by the discussion of children, which brought back her own pain at having lost his. Facing him with stiffened posture, and hostility radiating from her blue eyes, Alicia continued scathingly. "What's the matter, Ian? Is that so difficult to believe?

Do you want to equate me with your mother? Is that it? Is that why you gave me that refrigerated closet for a bedroom?''

The moment the words left her, she wished she could take them back, but it was too late now, and Alicia maintained her control in the face of Ian's sudden interest. "Is that how you think of that room?" he asked quizzically.

"Is that how you think of *me*?" she challenged him bravely.

Ian's whole manner was curiously guarded, yet tense, as though he were poised for something to happen...something he had been waiting for. "Well"— he shrugged offhandedly—"there are certain resemblances.''

"Such as what?" Alicia demanded in fury.

Ian watched her through half-closed eyes, then spoke in a flat voice. "Do you remember the first time we met, Alicia?"

"How could I forget it?" she responded with instantaneous contempt.

He ignored her reference to the latter part of the evening they'd spent together months earlier. "Are you aware that everything you said to me that night was a repetition of things I'd been hearing from my mother ever since I started writing?"

Alicia stared at him disbelievingly, compelled to refute any identification whatsoever with his mother. "I don't believe that," she asserted in a low, forceful voice.

"Oh? Why not?" Ian responded with a raised eyebrow and irony in his voice.

"Because—" Alicia sputtered helplessly for a moment, searching for an answer. "Because I don't think your mother has the sensitivity to object to the things I object to in your writing!" she finally answered with heat.

Ian smiled cynically. "Touché!" he murmured quietly. "But then, my mother is very good at mouthing the right words, even if she doesn't understand very much with her heart."

Alicia was stunned at his words, taking them as criticism directed at herself rather than at Ian's mother... or at the very least, at his seeming to think of them as identical twins. Her hurt goaded her into a lapse of rationality. "Just who did you take to bed that night in my apartment, Ian?" she gasped out in a strangled voice.

Instantly Ian's subdued tenseness became very apparent. The muscles in his legs and arms bunched as he got up from the sofa to stand in front of Alicia. "What do you mean by that?" he asked with quiet dangerousness.

"You know what I meant!" Alicia cried out, too distraught to take heed of the danger Ian represented. "Were you punishing me or your mother? Or were you looking for the love she denied...."

With lightning speed Ian reached out to grasp her shoulders, giving her a shake that jarred her teeth. Then he was hauling her against him with a rough strength she was helpless to combat. "Shut up, Alicia!" he grated out between clenched teeth. "You don't know what you're talking about, and I'll be damned if I'll let you practice any amateur psychology on me!" He gathered masses of her hair in his hand at the back of her head and pulled until she had to lift her face to his, while with his other hand he took hold of her chin in a hurting grip. "You're right about my intention to punish you that night, Alicia," he said with soft menace, holding her eyes with his own and exerting his will over her. "And you're right that your having used my mother's words to score off me precipitated the *desire* to punish you!" His eyes searched her face with a scathing interest that made her want to flinch away from him. "But I knew who it was I held in my arms that night, just as I know who I'm holding now. And what I felt then...and now...doesn't bear the slightest resemblance to what I feel for my mother, I assure you." He brought his mouth to within a fraction of an inch of her own, holding her easily as Alicia tried to pull her head away. "But if you need proof of the fact..." he murmured an instant before he caught her lips in a bruising kiss that brought a moan of pain from within her throat.

After hearing that moan, Ian softened his grip on her and tempered his kiss into a forceful, and painless, assault that soon had Alicia sagging against him in weak reaction to the relief she felt at this indication that Ian was in control of himself and wasn't going to force himself on her as he had that night in her apartment. But her relief soon changed to alarm as she began to feel the same disturbing effect on her senses he seemed always able to arouse, regardless of how she felt about him in her mind.

Tensing to fight not only him but herself, Alicia brought her hands up to his shoulders to push against him, but Ian chose that moment to deepen the kiss, bringing forth an entirely different sort of moan that encouraged his actions rather than discouraged them. Alicia hated herself for that and hated Ian even more for bringing it about, but now he was intent on building upon what she had inadvertently disclosed, waging an all-out war on her senses that was devastating in its effectiveness.

Alicia felt him lift her into his arms and deposit her

onto the sofa, following her down until they lay side by side, body against body, on the soft cushions. She was trembling with her efforts to hold firm against the instantaneous warmth that flooded her at feeling the hard maleness of him against her, but her muffled protest was smothered by his mouth again as he took her lips in a sensuous kiss that robbed her of breath.

When at last he released her mouth to slide his lips down her throat to its pulsating hollow, Alicia was weak with the desire he had aroused and helpless to prevent his hands from roaming over the sensitive areas of her body only he seemed to have the key to ignite.

"Ian..." she moaned weakly, meaning to tell him to stop but finding her protest ending in a gasp when his hand found her breast. She gasped again when he roughly shoved aside her blouse and substituted his mouth for his hand, nuzzling gently, then using his tongue to elicit delicious sensations of stabbing arousal that galvanized Alicia into striving for protection from his seduction.

"Ian, please..." she panted as she pushed ineffectually against him, succeeding only in disturbing the both of them more with the friction. "Please don't do this to me, Ian," she groaned helplessly as he placed a hand under her to lift her against him more closely.

"Stop me, then," he ground out huskily, roughly, as he moved to her other breast to wreak havoc there.

"I can't, Ian," Alicia said in pitifully weak and despairing admission. "You know I can't!"

Ian ceased his assault on her breast momentarily to lift his head and use the weapon of his mouth against her own, teasing her for agonizing seconds before her lips parted to allow him entry, her body arching under his to emphasize the submission her mouth had spelled out clearly. Ian took advantage of that submission immediately, shifting his body to lie more fully atop hers and pressing her down into the cushions until she ached to remove the barriers of their clothing and take him inside her in total fulfillment.

Ian drew back only slightly, teasing her mouth as he asked for verbal as well as physical submission. "Why can't you, Alicia?" he murmured into her mouth. "Why can't you stop me?" His golden eyes were slumberous as they raked her face. "Tell me," he goaded her sensuously, then prevented her from doing so momentarily as he kissed her deeply again.

His eyes asked the question again when the kiss was over, and Alicia stared up at him in wretched, subjugated helplessness. "I don't know, Ian," she whispered on a shuddering breath. "You take me over when you do this. I don't want it to happen, but I—"

"You forget everything but what I make you feel?" Ian murmured in a soft, indulgently sensuous voice.

Alicia nodded with the barest movement of her head, closing her eyes against the face that was so exultant at his victory. "You forget about love...marriage...babies?" Ian goaded her further.

Alicia's eyes flew open at that and she stared up at Ian in shocked surprise. "No!" she gasped out in protest, stiffening against the body that threatened to engulf her own.

"No?" Ian said with mocking gentleness. "When were you going to remember all those things, then? In the morning...after your body had had all it wanted?"

With a hurt cry Alicia struck out at Ian's mocking face, but he captured her hands and held them above her head, stilling her struggles through the use of his superior strength. Alicia's eyes filled with tears as she looked at him with renewed hate shimmering beneath the moisture. "Oh, God, I hate you, Ian Halsey!" she stuttered out on a sob. "You are the cruelest man I've ever met! What pleasure do you get out of hurting me like this?"

Her words wiped the mockery from Ian's face, and it was replaced by a simmering anger of his own. "Exactly what have I hurt, Alicia?" he demanded on a hard note. "Since you're not in love with me, it must be your pride, right?" He smiled without humor. "I think you should remember that pride usually goes before a fall!"

Alicia was crying openly now, and she turned her face away from Ian as she mumbled brokenly, "Damn you! I hate you, Ian!"

A frown of hard exasperation crossed Ian's handsome features as he released her and sat up with a jerk. "Damn *you*, Alicia!" he echoed her words. "I hate myself when I let you provoke me into something like this!" He got to his feet and stared down at her, still with that unyieldingness in his face despite his words. "I don't know how Ben Farr stood it," he continued, sarcasm dripping from his voice. "That's another way in which you're like my mother. You must have driven your husband to desperation with your smothering desire for his success! Did you protect him from the world, Alicia?" he asked with contempt. "So that he could concentrate on his intellectual gibberish?"

Bewildered and further angered by Ian's unexpected attack on how she had conducted her marriage, Alicia struck back in self-defense. "It wasn't like that!" she cried out through her tears, struggling to sit up so that she wouldn't feel at such a disadvantage with Ian glowering down at her like an overpowering ogre. "I loved Ben! I didn't want to protect him, I wanted to share with him! *He* was the one who shut *me* out!"

The instant the words left her mouth, Alicia froze into shocked disbelief that she had actually said them... or even thought of them! Her eyes wide, her lips apart, she stared at Ian's suddenly interested expression with horrified dismay, wishing with all her heart that she hadn't spoken such a devastating insight in his presence, under his instigation!

"Oh, yes?" Ian prodded her, moving to pull her up to stand in front of him and holding her where she stood. "Tell me about your marriage, Alicia," he ordered in a tight, hard voice that allowed no reprieve. "Didn't you want him to succeed?"

Alicia shook her head with frustrated bewilderment, still suffering from the shock of facing the fact that her marriage hadn't been as sweetly fulfilling as she had told herself it was all these years. "Of course I wanted him to succeed!" she admitted with tight anger. "But for *him*, not for me! I have my own career!"

Ian tightened his grip when she would have pulled away from him. "You didn't want to bask in his glory?" he goaded with cynical disbelief. "You didn't trail around after him, granting his every wish, because he was the great genius and you could fulfill yourself through him?"

Alicia glared up at him with all her hurt anger displayed in the vivid blue of her shimmering eyes. "I took care of him because it was the only way he could survive!" she shouted at Ian. "He expected it, and I couldn't do anything about it." She panted with the strength of her emotions. "And I don't know any more whether he was a genius or not. I never understood his poetry. I still don't."

With the sound of her own devastating revelations dying away in her ears, Alicia broke down then, sobbing with the agony of release, feeling weak with shock at realizing how frustrating her life with Ben had actually been. Why had she never faced it before? she wondered blankly as Ian gathered her to him to comfort her, holding her in the strength of his arms against the warm firmness of his body. But he wasn't finished with her yet.

"And what about children, Alicia?" he asked more gently, but still with that note of determination in his voice to get at the truth. "Why did you never have children with Ben?" he pressed.

"I wanted them," Alicia sobbed against his shoulder. "But Ben was such a child himself, I had nothing left to give a child ... and he didn't want any...."

Remembered disappointment was eloquent in her voice, and Alicia subsided into another round of weeping that left her drained and she leaned against Ian as if she had no more strength to hold herself upright. He stroked her hair as she sobbed and murmured meaningless comfort that Alicia didn't hear as words, but merely as sounds that made her feel protected and cherished. But as her sobs died away and she was able to think again, Ian's talk of children echoed in her mind and brought her back to reality. Suddenly she was incensed at his superior attitude toward her and how she'd lived her life when he had reason for such guilt of his own!

Pulling away from him, she stared up at him wildly and voiced what she was feeling. "How *dare* you question me about my marriage," she said with utter contempt. "You've never even cared enough about anyone but yourself to attempt marriage!" She jerked out of his arms and began to back away from him. "And how dare you question me about children after what you did!" she said hysterically, forgetting for the moment that she didn't intend to let him know what he had done ... not yet.

Ian's puzzled, startled look changed to grimness.

"What *did* I do, Alicia?" he asked with quiet forcefulness, starting toward her purposefully.

Alicia backed away faster, eluding him when he would have captured her again, fearful now of what she had almost revealed. "Leave me alone!" she said with the desperation she was feeling coming through in her voice. "Just leave me alone, Ian Halsey!" She reached the door and swung it open, pausing in her flight when she saw that Ian had stopped his pursuit. "I'm here to edit your book and that's all!" she flung at him wildly. "From now on don't touch me, don't question me, don't even talk to me about anything except your work!" She uttered her final threat in tones that echoed her conviction. "Or I'll leave here and say to hell with the whole thing! Do you understand?"

Ian faced her with sadness in his face, and something else that frightened Alicia... something that made her doubt she would ever tell Ian about the child they both had lost.

After a moment, he gave her the assurance she was asking for... or at least part of it. "I won't touch you again, Alicia," he said, sounding undefeated, though he was capitulating to her wishes. "Not until the day you come to me and ask me to." And his eyes were unrelenting as he tacked on a last stipulation. "And not even then, unless you admit you feel more for me than hatred."

Alicia stared at him with the certainty in her eyes that that day would never come, and then she stepped through the doorway and closed the door behind her with quiet finality.

Chapter Ten

Alicia awoke the next morning after a night of leaden sleep, feeling as though there were stones weighting her eyelids and her muscles, so that she could hardly drag herself out of bed. She caught the haggard expression on her face in the mirror and decided she couldn't let Ian see the results of his despicable behavior of the night before and derive any satisfaction from further humiliating her.

With that in mind she slipped to the kitchen to find Ingrid and impart the news that she was feeling unwell and meant to spend the day in her room. Ingrid was immediately sympathetic, shooing her away and saying she would bring tea and toast to her room in a few moments. Alicia didn't even have the strength to protest, though she doubted if she could get anything past the lump that seemed to have settled permanently in her throat.

Back in her room, she settled into a chair placed close to a window and stared out at the blinding whiteness of new snow that had fallen during the night, wondering how she was going to find the courage and the sheer willpower to stick things out until she could accomplish the purpose that had brought her there.

One part of her was almost resigned to the fact that as long as she stayed anywhere near Ian Halsey, she was letting herself in for one shock after another as he peeled layer after layer away from the entity she had always known as Alicia Farr. But another part of her rebelled with stubborn persistence at letting Ian mold her into a person she didn't know. Or did she? she wondered with idle speculation as her eyes followed a group of children hauling a sled to a nearby hill.

Was Ian molding her, or simply releasing her? She pursued the thought with determined doggedness. Surely everything she was doing that seemed so strangely out of character sprang from a part of her that was truly her? No one could *force* reactions from someone that weren't essentially a part of that person's character, could they?

She felt a sense of tired, wry bewilderment that at the age of thirty, she was coming to know a side of herself she must have buried away all those years under layers of supposed civilized respectability. She sensed that she was at one of the crisis points in her life that she had read about but had never thought to apply to herself, and the realization brought with it a sense of fearful challenge ... even excitement.

Perhaps she could get some good out of all these experiences Ian Halsey was forcing upon her if she viewed them positively, she reflected as she got to her feet to pace aimlessly around the room. All it required was adopting a new point of view, surely, and the willingness to change, if she thought the change was for the better.

Seating herself on one side of her unmade bed, Alicia propped her chin on her fist and contemplated what it was she wanted out of life. For years there had been only Ben and what *he* wanted. Then, when he died, there had been a period of blank grief, when she permitted no thought of anything but getting from one day to the next and when she had no goals other than a weak desire to survive.

A dawning restlessness seized her as Alicia contemplated the person she had been ... surely a rather spineless, unmotivated drifter who had let others define her life for her rather than seizing it in her own hands and steering it in a direction she chose for herself. What a very unsatisfactory picture that made, she thought with frowning disapproval, almost as though the old Alicia was a stranger she had no real affinity toward.

But it was not enough to chastise the old Alicia, she knew as she got to her feet to begin to pace again. She had to define what it was she *did* want. Where was she going with all this new insight and a burgeoning restlessness that warred with her fatigue? The only clear goal she had at the moment was to get even with Ian Halsey, which might not be very civilized, but which was the only thing she could contemplate with any anticipation for the time being.

Ingrid knocked on the door, disturbing Alicia's concentration and reminding her that she was supposed to be ill. She crossed to the chaise longue and stretched out before she called for Ingrid to come in.

The older woman tutted when she saw Alicia lying there in nothing but a thin negligee. "You'll catch a cold like that," she scolded like a mother hen as she came into the room, bearing a tray. She placed the tray in Alicia's hands, and while Alicia was contemplating her meager breakfast with an air of gloom, Ingrid crossed to the bed to snatch up a blanket. "Here, put this around you if you're not going to stay in bed, where you belong," she instructed Alicia reprovingly.

"You're just like Ian. Neither one of you have the sense God gave you!"

Alicia frowned at the comparison, scowling up at Ingrid like a petulant child. "I do, too, have sense," she muttered mutinously. "I just don't feel cold."

Ingrid surveyed her with firm concentration before bending down to feel her forehead, muttering something about a temperature.

"I don't have a temperature," Alicia protested, backing away from Ingrid's hand to no avail. "I just don't feel well."

Ingrid straightened and there was a wicked gleam in her blue eyes as she looked at Alicia with satisfaction. "Well, whatever you have, it must be catching," she announced with calm speculation, "because Ian's not feeling well either."

Alicia's reaction to the news was cautious. "Oh?" she asked with casual unconcern. "What's the matter with him?" Inwardly she was feeling a spiteful sense of satisfaction that Ian hadn't escaped unscathed from his actions of the night before. Even if he'd only caught the flu, she considered it just punishment that for a change he wasn't filled with the electric energy he exuded so forcefully.

"I don't know," Ingrid said with casual blandness as she went to the bed to straighten the covers. "But he must be coming down with something, because he's as grouchy as a hibernating bear who's been awakened before the spring. It seemed to get worse when he found out you were ill."

Alicia gave a betraying start before she caught herself up. "No doubt he can't stand for one of his employees to take sick time," she muttered resentfully.

Ingrid disagreed. "Not so," she pronounced with cheerful energy as she plumped a pillow within an inch of its life. "He's always been the soul of a beneficent employer, fairly oozing sympathy when one of us got sick."

"Yes, but that's you and your family," Alicia said unthinkingly. "He *loves* the three of you."

Ingrid turned to look at her consideringly. "Yes, I think he does," she agreed with musing thoughtfulness. "But men behave differently toward each loved one in their lives. I've always suspected Ian would take falling in love with a woman rather hard. He hasn't had any practice at it, you see, and it's tending to make him grouchy."

Her words failed to register with Alicia momentarily, and when they did, she sat up with a jerk, almost spilling her tray, and stared at Ingrid as though she'd seen a ghost. "What did you say?" she asked breathlessly.

"You heard me," Ingrid replied without turning a hair. "I think Ian's in love."

Alicia turned away from the smug satisfaction she saw in Ingrid's face and collapsed against the back of the chaise longue. Swallowing down the tight lump in her throat, she ventured the question trembling on her tongue. "Who do you think he's in love with?" she asked hesitantly, dreading the answer without knowing why.

Ingrid's reply was casually unconcerned. "How should I know?" she said with disgusting cheerfulness. "He doesn't take me into his confidence. I'm not even sure if he knows he's finally fallen yet himself."

She bustled back over to Alicia, beaming down at her with kindness, but seeming to ignore the pale pallor that had chased away Alicia's normal peachy complexion. She reached down to tuck the blanket more securely around Alicia's stiff form. "Ah, well," she said with a sly smile. "I suppose we'll be put out of our suspense before too much longer. Once Ian discovers what has happened to him, you can be sure he'll act on it. It's not in his nature to be passive."

Alicia controlled the scowl of agreement threatening to reveal her feelings while she silently agreed whole-heartedly with Ingrid that Ian Halsey was the very opposite of passive.

Ingrid left the room with the cheerful admonition for Alicia to call her if she needed anything, and Alicia settled back to resume the contemplations the woman had interrupted earlier. But her mind wouldn't seem to turn to anything but speculation as to who it was Ian loved... if he really was capable of such an emotion, she thought scathingly.

But there grew in Alicia's mind a gnawing, irritating discomfort at the thought that Ian might love someone. Alicia was aware of the discomfort without being able to pinpoint its source... not until she had a flashing image of Ian in another woman's arms. The image slashed through her with an intensity that brought a small gasp of agonized denial from her lips. There was no escaping the realization that she was jealous.

"Oh, good God, no!" Alicia whispered disbelievingly. It couldn't be true! There was absolutely no basis for jealousy in the sort of relationship she had with Ian. She hated the man! She despised him! She planned to hurt him in the only way available to her. What possible reason could she have for feeling jealous at the thought that he might love another woman?

Before she could deal with the implications her thoughts were leading to, the man himself appeared at her door, hardly bothering to knock before he entered the room, his expression indeed as cross as though he were suffering at the very least from indigestion.

He crossed the room to where Alicia lay huddling protectively beneath her covers to regard her with a scowl of disapproval.

"What's the matter with you?" he asked with no sign of sympathy.

"What do you care?" Alicia flared back at him coldly. "I've got all the chapters you've done so far here in my room and I plan to work on them later, if that's what's worrying you."

Ian seemed to grit his teeth against an equally heated reply then. Closing his eyes for a moment as though to gather his control, he made a visible effort to relax. When he looked at her again, there was a sort of bleak resignation in his eyes. He sat down wearily on the end of the chaise longue, causing Alicia to draw her legs up hastily out of his way. Her glare faded, however, as Ian leaned his head in his hands in a gesture of tired dispiritedness that was so unlike him, and Alicia felt a small stab of alarm. Perhaps he really was ill?

That impression was dispelled an instant later when he raised his head to stare at her with grim determination. "All right, Alicia," he said doggedly. "I guess I have to apologize again."

Since his tone didn't sound especially apologetic, Alicia viewed his peacemaking effort dubiously. "I guess you do," she answered unrelentingly. "Go ahead."

For a moment she thought her words would provoke him into another act of violence, but then, after a staring contest between the two of them that lasted a full minute, he began to relax and a slow grin dispelled the taut anger of his features. "Why the hell do you get to me the way you do?" he asked on a note of self-mockery. "You're hardly bigger than an overgrown adolescent and yet you have the power to turn me into a stranger to myself."

"*I* turn *you* into a stranger?" she sputtered indignantly. "Surely it's the other way around!"

Ian's features relaxed even more as he leaned on one arm and began to fiddle with the blanket that covered Alicia's legs. "Hmmm..." he said with speculative interest. "Do you mean I have that effect on you, too?"

"God! Do you ever!" Alicia muttered half beneath her breath, her expression indicative of disgust.

Ian let that pass. "I thought you weren't going to talk to me anymore," he said with innocent inquiry. "Does this mean I'm forgiven?"

Instantly Alicia stiffened into glaring dislike. "What do you mean, forgiven?" she stormed at him. "You haven't even apologized yet!"

Ian shrugged one shoulder dismissingly. "Okay," he said with maddening agreeableness. "I apologize." And then he spoiled it by adding, "But if you don't mind, I'd like to know for sure what it is I'm apologizing *for*."

Alicia couldn't believe him! "If you don't know that, then I don't accept your apology!" she gritted at him.

Ian sighed, giving no sign that her attitude worried him. "Let me think about it," he said. "Could it be that I made you admit you're physically human? So human you're capable of letting your body rule your head?" He moved on quickly to another speculation, ignoring Alicia's white-faced dislike of his dragging her pride through the dust once again. "Or are you angry because I made you admit that your marriage to Ben wasn't all sweetness and light?"

He watched the anger building up in Alicia with imperturbable dispassion. "No"—he shook his head with an attitude of surety that he was right—"I don't think it could be either of those things. I shouldn't have to apologize for bringing to light what was already there waiting to be discovered, whether you like the discovery or not." And then he looked down to where his hand rested on the blanket, avoiding her furious gaze. "But I suppose I should apologize for misjudging you." He looked up at her again, noting her puzzled expression at this new tack he was taking. "And I do apologize, Alicia. You're nothing like I thought you were, and even if you were, it's not my place to judge you."

His admission took her off guard, dissipating her anger and filling her instead with an uneasy softening toward him that disturbed her almost more than her earlier anger for him had. She fought to maintain that anger. "You're right, you *don't* have a right to judge me," she came back at him with grim determination. "You're far from perfect yourself, you know."

"I know," he admitted in a soft voice that brought goose bumps to her bare arms. "But I'm less perfect with you than with anyone else I've ever met. Did you realize that?"

Unwillingly Alicia met his eyes, softening further at their expression of amused self-mockery coupled with gentle teasing. "No—I didn't," she faltered, struggling to maintain her enmity. "And I can't think why that should be so. I only baited you a little. I was in a bad mood that night. I certainly didn't deserve—" She broke off, avoiding his eyes as she veered away from dangerous territory.

"Alicia..." Ian said her name caressingly. "Believe me, I'm sorrier than I can say that I hurt you so badly. I was in a bad mood that night, too. I'd just had one of those conversations with my mother where she spouted all the nonsense she's always on at me about, and when you did the same thing, I'd had all I could take. But that doesn't excuse what I did, I know." He reached up to trail his fingers down Alicia's bare arm, leaving trails of warmth in their path.

Desperately Alicia sought to dispel the inroads he was making on her need to keep her distance from him. "You said you wouldn't touch me," she reminded him with nervous asperity. And when he withdrew his hand, giving her a rueful, knowing smile as he did so, she pressed on to regain some of the ground she'd lost. "And I don't admit that what I said was nonsense." And then honesty compelled her to admit, "Though I don't feel as...as strongly as I did before about what you write."

"Don't you?" Ian asked with dry interest. "Why is that, I wonder?"

Alicia glanced at him nervously, licking dry lips before she replied. She was beginning to react to his nearness in a way that was becoming disgustingly predictable, and she only hoped he would leave before she gave in to the desire to touch him that was beginning to make itself noticeable with the moistness of her palms. "I—" She faltered in her explanation, wishing she had never brought things to the point where one was needed. "I suppose I'm a little more...uh...open now," she struggled on. "Brian says I used to be an...uh...intellectual snob and a—a prude."

She winced at seeing the grin this information brought to Ian's rugged face. "And now you're not?" he said gently.

"Well, at least I'm *trying* not to be," she said with defensive resentment. She gave him a flashing look of dislike. "You taught me that I hadn't any reason to feel superior to anybody," she finished.

Ian frowned at that. "I wasn't trying to teach you any such thing," he said with firm straightforwardness.

"And it isn't true. You're a hell of a woman, Alicia Farr," he said with a touch of resentment of his own. "You're certainly not *ordinary,* at any rate, as I've learned to my cost."

"Why should it cost you anything?" she replied coolly. "I mean nothing to you."

Her words focused Ian's attention on her in a way she wished she hadn't provoked. "Don't you?" he asked, indicating that he was asking the question of himself more than of her. "If that's true, then why do I find myself doing things I never even contemplated before?" he mused, watching Alicia and making her feel uneasy. His next words made her even more uneasy. "And why am I having trouble sleeping at night? And why am I suddenly thinking about marriage and babies and all the rest of the domestic bliss scene when I never have before?"

Alicia shifted nervously beneath the look in his eyes and the almost casual questioning in his voice. "Possibly because I've brought those subjects up to you," she suggested as calmly as she could manage. "I may have stirred your conscience a little ... I don't know...."

"My conscience has never hurt before, that's true," Ian agreed with her dryly. "It's never had to. All the women I've ever been involved with before you knew exactly what they were doing and they were definitely practicing birth control."

Alicia started at his mention of a subject that strained her equilibrium to its utmost. "I wouldn't have touched them if they hadn't," Ian went on with firm decisiveness. "Because I wasn't in love with any of them and I have definite views about how to raise children. And I don't approve of abortion," he added softly, watching her closely and noting that the color had suddenly drained from her face. Her reaction seemed to set off some savagery in him that took her completely by surprise. It was always beneath the surface with Ian, but it was also always so utterly unexpected when it happened that Alicia couldn't seem to adjust to the fact that it was there.

"I've been wondering ever since the night you arrived here whether you shared my views on abortion, Alicia," Ian said with hard purpose, capturing her wrist in his hand when she made an instinctive gesture of denial. "I've been wondering if perhaps there was an unwanted result of that night we made love...unwanted on your part, that is," he said cuttingly. "*Did* anything happen as a result of that night, Alicia?" he persisted, exerting his will in the fashion she found so hard to resist. "Did you become pregnant? And did you get rid of the child?"

Alicia cried out as Ian exerted enough pressure on her wrist to bring pain, but her cry was equally a result of the inner pain she was suffering. "Answer me, Alicia!" Ian demanded without letup, his face displaying a pain of his own along with an anger that sparked her own fury.

"Yes!" she snarled at him, uncaring that he flinched away from the answer he had demanded. "Yes! Yes! Yes!" She hit out at him with her other hand only to have him capture that one, too. "Damn you, Ian Halsey!" she grated out from the depths of her agony. "You came into my life and ruined it, do you know that? I didn't ask you to seduce me, and I didn't ask for the child you left me with! What right have *you* to be angry about what I did? I had no choice!"

Ian's face was terrible to look at, but Alicia forced herself not to turn away. "You could have told me," he said with deadly quietness. "You could have let me have a say in whether or not you destroyed our child. I wouldn't have permitted it if I had known, and I'll never forgive you for doing it!''

Alicia gave a half-hysterical laugh. '' *You* won't forgive *me*?'' she asked incredulously, her limbs beginning to tremble in the grip of her emotions. ''That's funny, Ian . . . .'' She began to laugh in earnest, her hysteria taking over. ''Oh, that's *very* funny!'' she said between gasps of laughter.

Ian's slap brought an abrupt end to her hysterical laughter, and Alicia's head snapped back with the force of it. She stared at him with the bruised look of a child who's been punished unjustly. To his credit Ian looked ashamed of the force with which he'd hit her, acknowledging that it sprang more from a desire to hurt her as he'd been hurt than from a desire to quell her hysteria. ''I'm sorry,'' he said stiffly, getting up from the chaise longue to stand over her like some dark avenging angel. ''I shouldn't have hit you so hard.'' He turned away from her then, starting toward the door.

Alicia watched the straight, proud set of his shoulders as he moved . . . the tautness in his whole body that spelled out the control he was exerting over his emotions.

''I'll leave here as soon as possible, Ian,'' she said with determined emphasis. ''I won't force my disgusting presence on you any longer than is necessary—''

Ian swung around to stare at her with a violence in his face that made her words die in her throat. ''The hell you will!'' he said with a suppressed violence that made her shrink back against the chaise longue. ''You're not going anywhere until I've decided what to do about this. You owe me something, Alicia Farr,'' he promised threateningly. ''And you're going to stay put until I decide how to make you pay.''

He slammed the door behind him when he left, and

the sound made Alicia jerk in reaction. She sat staring after him for long moments before she was able to relax her body and contemplate the position she'd got herself into. She had never imagined that Ian would feel so strongly about a child of his. But it was evident that her action in destroying the seed he had planted so casually—an action that she had no intention of telling him was due to the almost certain possibility that her bout of German measles had damaged the fetus—had provoked an implacable hatred on his part that was ironic to contemplate when she had thought she had all the justification for such an emotion against him!

His condemnation nevertheless evoked all the old doubts as to whether she had done the right thing, making her agonize once again over her precipitateness in making her decision to have an abortion. She considered his suggestion that she could have told him about what had happened laughable, in light of her state of mind at the time. He was the last one she would have consulted, had she considered consulting anyone at all!

Dry-eyed, Alicia got up from the chaise longue and began to dress with automatic movements. She wasn't certain what she was going to do, but she found the idea of waiting to see what Ian decided in the way of punishment unbearable. It was ironic how their positions had changed in the space of a few short moments...moments in which a revelation had been made that she couldn't take back...and did not wish to.

Let Ian bear some of the pain she had had to endure alone all these months, she decided with a dull lack of satisfaction at the prospect. There was no longer any need to use his book as a means of inflicting her own brand of punishment. She had inadvertently found a much more effective weapon. If she had known beforehand how effective that weapon could turn out to be, she knew she wouldn't have had sufficient enmity in her heart to use it. But since it had been used accidentally, in a moment of unthinking rage and hurt, there was an ironic sense of justice being served about the whole matter.

Yet, as she began to pack her things into a suitcase, tears rolling unheeded down her pale cheeks, she found herself wishing that justice didn't always have to be served so hurtfully...so unmercifully...so finally.

Chapter Eleven

To her dismayed surprise Alicia found Brian Crossley waiting for her at the airport in New York. As she gazed at him over the heads of the crowd she couldn't fathom how he had known of her arrival. Upon emerging from her room at Ian's home, and finding that he had left the house immediately after leaving her room, she had taken advantage of the situation to ask Borg Johnson to drive her to the airport in Reno. She had glossed over her reason for leaving, saying there was an unexpected emergency in New York that she had to see to, and implying that she would return when it was over. Her shame at the deception was buried beneath all the other emotions she was having to cope with, and she knew it was just one more thing she would have to learn to bear as a result of her unhappy relationship with Ian Halsey.

Brian's look was typically exasperated when she finally made her way to him, but at seeing the strained tension in her face and the sad defeat in her eyes, he had smothered his natural inclinations and caught her up in a gruff hug. After releasing her at last, he held her away from him and sighed with a shake of his head. "Damn it, Allie, what have you done now?" he asked with no real condemnation but with simple frustration.

Alicia smiled wanly, acknowledging their basic incompatibility, but grateful for their incongruous friendship nonetheless. She needed someone at that moment who cared about her, regardless of whether the friendship included approval. "In a word, Brian, I blew it," she said tiredly, straining for humor and not bringing it off very well.

"What do you mean you blew it," Brian responded in puzzlement, taking her arm and guiding her toward the baggage claim area. "Ian didn't say anything about any real problems when he called. He didn't sound very happy, but he wasn't as mad as I've seen him get before."

"Ian called you?" Alicia responded warily. "Why? What did he say?" Suddenly her tiredness was dispelled by a return of the tense caution Ian was so good at inspiring.

"He said to pick you up!" Brian said impatiently. "What did you expect him to say?" He didn't wait for a reply, and Alicia couldn't have given him one if he had. She was too surprised at the speed with which Ian had learned she'd left, and his unexpected reaction to the news. "He'll be mailing the final chapters of his book in a couple of weeks, along with the ones you left behind," Brian went on disapprovingly. "Why the hell did you leave them behind anyway? I would have liked to read them." Back to normal, he glared down at her in typical Brian fashion. "And for that matter, why did you come back before the job was done? You were supposed to stay there and keep Ian's nose to the grindstone in order to get this book out of the way."

Alicia responded to each of his questions absently. "Why do you want to read the book, Brian? You won't like it," she predicted flatly. "And you don't have to worry about Ian's wasting any time in finishing it, because at the speed he writes, it won't even take six months to finish."

Then, realizing she would have to provide an explanation for her precipitate return, and not having thought up one that would sound convincing, she tried for weak humor instead, not really caring if it fell flat or not. "I came home because I missed the bright lights, Brian," she said with dry irony. "You know how I am about keeping up with my social life. California was just too tame."

Brian, unappreciative of her frivolous reply to his question, snorted disbelievingly. "Sure," he said with exaggerated sarcasm, "and tomorrow they're going to send the Statue of Liberty back to France." He was opening his mouth to voice his question again when Alicia's patience gave out. She faced him with an expression on her face that he had never seen before and which left him gaping awkwardly like a fish out of water. "Drop it, Brian!" Alicia said with flat unemotionalism that was nevertheless highly convincing; she meant what she said. "I don't want to discuss it...not now...not ever."

After a moment of conflicting emotions warring for dominance, Brian mastered his offended dignity, if not his curiosity. "Very well," he said with a stiff formality that would have been comical if Alicia had been in the mood to laugh. "It couldn't have been much, since Ian still wants you to edit his book."

Alicia stopped in her tracks, eyeing Brian with astonished disbelief. Fortunately his attention was directed elsewhere as he searched out the particular baggage claim area where Alicia's bags should come in, and by the time he returned his attention to her, Alicia was under control. "Ian wants me to edit the book," she said with more calm than she felt, wondering desperately what game Ian was playing by making such a decision.

"That's what I said," Brian replied, looking suspiciously puzzled. "You knew that, didn't you?"

His question alerted Alicia to the need for concealment with renewed fervor. She had no intention of giving Brian anything to get his teeth into. "Sure, Brian," she responded in an emotionless voice. "I knew that." And only then did she realize that she wasn't totally surprised. Ian was not the sort of man to give up easily when he had set his mind toward something, and since the book was the one sure way to enable him to keep in contact with her, of course he would use it to do so . . . until he decided what method of punishment was suitable for a woman who had dared to destroy something of his . . . particularly his own flesh and blood. It never occurred to him that she had already received more punishment than he could inflict, no matter how hard he tried . . . a punishment consisting of guilt, doubt, and regret that would stay with her for the rest of her life.

"I got you a hotel room for tonight," Brian said, interrupting her thoughts as he seated her in a chair to wait until the luggage arrived on the carousel nearby. "And I talked to the people in your apartment. They're willing to leave by the end of the week if you'll waive keeping their deposit."

Alicia forced herself to return to the realities at hand, giving Brian a smile of gratitude for the trouble he'd taken on her behalf. "Thank you, Brian," she murmured. "I'll talk to them tomorrow."

Making an effort to seem normal, Alicia then encouraged Brian to fill her in on what had taken place at the office while she'd been absent, and the two of them made small talk until Brian deposited her at a small hotel near the office for the night.

Later, as she lay in the small barren room, feeling lonelier than she'd ever felt in her life before, Alicia's thoughts returned briefly to her reflections about what she was going to do with the rest of her life. But she was too tired to deal with such a weighty matter for the time being, and she merely made a mental note to do some serious thinking on the subject before too much more time had passed. She was not getting any younger, and the prospects stretching before her if she went on as she had been were bleaker than she cared to contemplate.

During the next two weeks, however, Alicia found very little time for such thinking. She was too busy getting back into the routine at the office, moving back to her apartment and finding that her erstwhile tenants' standard of housekeeping had left her with a great deal of work to be accomplished, and generally settling down again into a life that while not very exciting, at least had the advantage of being comfortably steady.

The arrival of a complete first draft of Ian's manuscript on her desk one morning was therefore jarring when she had at last begun to regain some of her customary equilibrium. She contemplated the package in front of her for long moments, filled with a sense of dread at the task she faced. Reading such an intimate portrait of Ian's mother, and having to cope with the resulting pity she felt for him, would, she knew, thrust her back into the sort of emotional turmoil Ian Halsey had instigated from the first moment she'd ever laid eyes on him.

There was a note from Ian on top of the pages she withdrew from the envelope, and Alicia picked it up gingerly, wondering what he could have found to say to her that would in the least resemble polite communication, considering the bitter contempt he held her in. A wry smile curved her mouth when at last she found the courage to read the words.

"Here it is. Do your damnedest. We aren't finished yet. Ian."

Well, at least it was brief, she thought with a sigh of resignation. Now what was she going to do with it...and with the implicit threat contained in the last sentence?

Finding that she was incapable of dealing for the moment with Ian's intrusion into her life again, Alicia set the manuscript aside and concentrated on her other tasks until the end of the day. Since it was Friday, she knew she had the whole weekend in which to reach the decisions she had been putting off, and which were suddenly demanding her attention to the exclusion of all else. There would be time to deal with Ian's manuscript on Monday, when she returned to the office...if she decided to deal with it at all.

Alicia spent the next two days entirely alone, delving into her own psyche with painful thoroughness, refusing to let anything distract her from the task of determining who she was and where she was going. By Sunday evening she was mentally and physically exhausted, but she nevertheless felt reasonably content with the conclusions she'd reached.

She had determined that she had no reason to castigate herself about her career. She liked her work...she always had. She had no inclination to try something new but rather a new determination to succeed at what she was already doing. Ironically Ian Halsey deserved the credit for making that success more possible than it had ever been in the past. He—not Ben—had succeeded in opening her mind and heart to the worth of other types of literature than what she had always considered to be suitable for publication. She could even smile now when she contemplated her past snobbish prudery, wondering how she had ever justified setting herself up as the infallible arbiter of suitability. Surely the point of literature was communication, and each book spoke to its reader in a different way. Who was she to interfere in that process? Her job was merely to facilitate the smoothness of it.

She had decided also to put her life with Ben into perspective and then to leave it where it belonged—in the past. Certainly she now realized that their marriage had not been as perfect as she had always thought. But who was to blame for that? Only herself. She had accepted Ben as he was... or at least as she had *thought* he was. Upon rereading his poetry, as Brian had suggested months ago, she found it disappointingly mediocre and shallow, now that her perception was stripped of all the illusions she had built around her husband. Ben had considered himself a genius, and she had accepted his own evaluation of himself without question. Now she realized her objectivity had been sadly lacking, clouded as it was by her faith in the man she loved... her loyalty toward the institution of marriage itself and what was required of the participants.

She still felt an aching fondness for her memory of Ben, refusing to regret the years she'd spent with him. She had not been actively unhappy, after all. In fact, there had been good times, far more than bad. Those selfsame illusions had made them possible, and it was only now, through hindsight, that she realized so much more was possible between a man and a wife than she and Ben had experienced.

Ian Halsey was responsible for that revelation, too, she thought with ironic admission. His lovemaking, even without love, had shown her that what she had known with Ben was a very weak approximation of what was possible in a relationship. His determined probing into her innermost consciousness had taught her the value of examining her real feelings instead of living on the shallow surface of life. And the seed of life he had planted inside her had taught her the value of life itself, but only after she had taken the enormous step of destroying that seed.

Regardless of the pain Ian Halsey had inspired throughout their relationship, Alicia now faced the fact that it was only through such pain that she had been shaken out of her stultifying routine and been forced to grow as a person. And surely that was ultimately constructive. The process might have been agonizing, but if she built on the result, wouldn't she be the better for it? And didn't she owe Ian Halsey something for having been the catalyst that sparked off the emergence of a new Alicia Farr?

Resignedly she decided that she did. Instead of using Ian's book as an instrument of revenge, she would put forth her best efforts to make it a success, thereby repaying him for turning her life around, if not for depriving him of his child. She considered they were already quits in that area. She had suffered as much, if not more, than he had or could because the baby had been a part of her own body, and she had made the decision to get rid of it. Nothing would ever completely ease the feelings that that decision had set off, but in time she supposed she would learn to live more comfortably with them.

Meanwhile, besides the new direction she intended her career to take, there was the question of her private life to consider. She wanted other children. She wanted the intimacy and stability of marriage again. It was time she came out of her self-imposed shell and began to search for a mate who wanted the same things she did...a mate who was very different from what Ben had been and much more like—

At that point in her soul-searching Alicia almost retreated from the knowledge she had been trying to bury in her subconscious. She didn't want to have to face up to the additional pain that was inherent in it. But in keeping with her newfound determination to delve deeply into herself rather than skirting the edges, she forced herself to face squarely the fact that Ian Halsey had somehow succeeded in making her love him, despite all the flaws in his character she was agonizingly aware of.

There was no possibility of their ever getting together, of course. Not now—not when Ian was filled with hatred and contempt for her. Her love was just one more thing she would have to overcome and set aside while she got on with her life. She reflected that it was most likely just as well that Ian would never return her love—that there was no chance they would ever marry. In his own way, Ian was just as unlikely a mate for her as Ben had been. His underlying savagery unnerved her. His cruelty had the power to hurt her in a way no one else could and which was awesome to contemplate on a lifetime basis. It would be too high a price to pay for his laughter, his gentle teasing, the passion he could inspire in her at will, and the uncomfortable facility he had for reaching into her soul and bringing its contents into the light.

No, Alicia determined as she got ready for bed that Sunday night, feeling drained but somehow at peace. There must be someone out there who was somewhere in between the conflicting characters of Ben and Ian. Someone who would add to her life without dominating it. Someone who would be willing to share love on an equal basis without robbing her of her will and making her into a puppet, as Ben and Ian had done in their own differing ways. And starting tomorrow she would begin her search to find that someone. Suddenly she had no more time to waste.

Chapter Twelve

A few weeks later Alicia walked into Brian's office and deposited a manuscript in the middle of his desk. "What's this?" he asked with a lazy lack of curiosity. He was suffering from his annual case of spring fever, a fact that was evidenced by the magazine featuring distant paradise islands he now clutched to his chest. Every year he threatened to go away, and every year he managed to put off the trip until his spring fever was replaced by his usual energy.

Alicia seated herself on the edge of his desk, swinging a shapely leg as she grinned down at him. "Ian's book," she said succinctly. "It's ready to go to press."

"Oh?" Brian raised a lackadaisical eyebrow, trying to hide the curiosity Alicia knew was eating him alive. She had evaded his hints for weeks now, keeping Ian's book strictly to herself. The process of editing it had been far too delicate to risk discussion with someone of Brian's admitted jaundiced viewpoint. "Is it any good?" he asked, his tone indicating that he didn't expect her response to be positive.

"It's the best thing he's ever done," Alicia replied with quiet conviction. And then, at seeing Brian's patent skepticism, she shrugged. "Don't take my word for it. Read it yourself." She got up from her perch, making no attempt to convince Brian further. She knew the book would do that.

"When I get time," Brian muttered, eyeing the pages with barely concealed greed, though he was determined not to appear too eager. His pride had been ruffled by Alicia's refusal to let him see the manuscript before this.

Alicia hid a knowing smile. "Well, don't take too long," she replied with dry casualness. "The schedule has already been set up, and I want you to handle things with Ian from now on."

She didn't have long to wait for Brian's expected reaction. "You've got to be kidding!" he protested on a note of astonishment. "You've worked your tail off on this book and you want me to step in at the last moment and garner all the glory?"

"What glory?" Alicia responded with innocent blandness. "You think the book is going to fall flat on its face, remember?"

Brian scowled, not wanting to admit he might have been wrong but convinced by Alicia's attitude that that was probably the case. "But you don't," he pointed out logically. "So why are you handing it to me on a silver platter?"

Alicia paused on her way to the door. "Ian and I don't work very well together, Brian," she said with reasonable calm. "At least not face to face." Which was true. They hadn't even spoken together since before Alicia had left California, all their exchanges about the book having been conducted by mail. It had taken longer that way, but it had suited Alicia—and apparently Ian—to keep contact to a minimum. The arrangement had worked surprisingly well, each of them having a facility with words on paper that they had never managed to duplicate verbally . . . at least not with one another.

"Come on, Alicia." Brian was scowling suspiciously. "That can't be true. I've spoken with Ian from time to time during the past few weeks, and he had nothing but praise for the work you were doing for him. He said you were better than I am, as a matter of fact," Brian confessed with a growl of mock jealousy.

Alicia, though more pleased than she would ever reveal at Ian's praise, kept her expression unrevealing. "I didn't do that much, Brian," she said wryly. "Ian's not an author who needs much editing."

Brian's sly smile belied the slightly shamefaced look in his eyes. "Oh. You found that out, did you?" he said a little uncomfortably.

Laughing, Alicia couldn't resist teasing him. "I certainly did, and it opened my eyes to what a complete fraud you are, Brian Crossley. Here, all this time, I thought you were solely responsible for Ian Halsey's success, and it turns out you were riding his coattails."

Brian's look of outrage made her relent. "All right, all right, I'm only teasing." She soothed his ruffled feathers. "Ian's good, but he isn't perfect. And you were the one who discovered him, after all."

Brian subsided under her flattery, but he still looked slightly ruffled, and Alicia decided to ice the cake. "I would appreciate your looking over the manuscript as soon as possible, Brian," she said, coaxing him. "I'm new at this...at working with Ian, I mean," she added hastily after seeing Brian's surprise at her statement, "and I'd like your stamp of approval. You're so much more familiar with his style." She didn't add that Ian's style in this particular book was a great deal more complicated than was his usual wont, and that she was looking forward to Brian's surprise when he found that out.

Brian harumphed a little, but when Alicia left him,

she knew she had managed to restore his ego to its usual health, and she knew also that he was probably already buried in the pages of Ian's book with all the formidable concentration he was capable of. Her smile was a little strained when she got back to her office, however, as she faced the fact that the totally engrossing task of editing Ian's book was now over and that there would be no further reason for communicating with him, even through the means of the businesslike letters they had exchanged during its progress.

Well, she reflected as she seated herself behind her desk and leaned back in weary relaxation, she had known she would reach this point sooner or later, and there was nothing to be gained by letting herself become depressed by it. As for shepherding Ian through the next stages of publication and publicity, there was no question of her becoming involved. She was simply incapable of the close contact they would necessitate, and Brian was better at that sort of thing than she was anyway.

So it was over, she thought, straining for brisk acceptance and coming up with sad inevitability instead. But the book was something. She and Ian's collaboration had forged something excitingly worthwhile, despite their personal differences, and she was proud of her own small contribution to what she knew would be an outstanding success on the literary market. Brian had been wrong when he had thought the book wouldn't sell. It would; and more so, it would establish Ian's reputation solidly as an author capable of succeeding with any kind of literature he chose to turn his hand to.

Alicia's secret pride in Ian had grown by leaps and bounds as she had worked on the book. And her love had grown right along with that pride, though she tried to bury it through a round of socializing and dating that had so far proven more tiring than satisfying. She viewed each new man who came into her life with hopeful expectation, wanting to experience at least an approximation of the excitement and interest Ian could provide. Each time, however, she had been doomed to disappointment. One kiss, and Alicia was forced to realize that each succeeding man was not the right one. But that didn't mean she was giving up, though she was beginning to suspect she might have to settle for a great deal less than she had planned on if she was ever to have the chance at the satisfying family life she craved so greatly.

Now she turned to her work to ease the dull ache of disappointment that pressed so persistently against her heart, quelling the dissatisfaction she felt at the words she read that weren't Ian's, determined she wasn't going to let him spoil her satisfaction for her profession.

She had managed to reach a point of relative quietude when Brian came bounding into her office, excitement beaming all over his craggy face. "Damn it, Allie, you've done it!" he cried as he pulled her up from her chair to give her an exuberant hug.

Astonished at this uncharacteristic display of emotion on Brian's part, Alicia leaned away from him to eye him suspiciously. "Have you been drinking?" she asked witheringly.

"Hell, no, I've been reading!" Brian replied, undisturbed by her attitude. "And I've been talking to Ian." He let her go to pace excitedly around the office, ignoring her perplexed stare. "I never thought he would come up with something like this," Brian said with a chuckle and a disbelieving tone in his voice. "I mean, I knew he could!" He continued his conversation with himself as though Alicia weren't in the room. "I just didn't think he would.'' He faced her then, satisfaction evident in his expression. "And he has! We're going to have a best-seller on our hands, Allie, did you know that?''

Alicia nodded, aware that Brian really didn't expect a reply. He was too caught up in his own excitement and he wanted only an audience. "We've got a lot of work to do publicizing the book, of course,'' Brian went on, running a hand through his unruly hair and adopting an abstracted expression that Alicia knew meant his mind was running at full speed. "I know you haven't done much in this line before, Alicia''—he finally turned his attention back to her—"but I'll help, and—''

Alicia stiffened, cutting him off in midsentence. "What are you talking about, Brian?'' she asked ominously. "I don't want anything to do with the publicizing of this book. My job is over!''

She felt like crying when she saw what she termed Brian's stubborn expression spread over his face. "Now, Allie,'' he began in a firm tone, before Alicia cut him off again.

"Don't 'now, Allie,' me, Brian Crossley,'' she threatened, feeling desperately depleted of the strength she needed to fight this battle. "I've done my part. It's your turn now and you'd better get used to the idea.''

Brian folded his arms and adopted a belligerent stance. "Tell that to Ian, Allie,'' he pronounced with heavy sarcasm. "I told him you wanted me to handle things from now on, and he flatly refused to consider it.''

Alicia flinched at the words, realizing that she should have known Ian hadn't given up on his idea of punishing her. He had merely been biding his time. "Brian, please...'' She changed her tone to one of pleading appeal. "I can't do this. You've got to help me get out of this.''

Brian frowned, his air of belligerent aggressiveness fading to one of concern. "It's not that hard, Allie," he said soothingly. "And I've said I'll help you. It just takes learning the ropes."

Alicia shook her head, realizing she was going to have to take Brian into her confidence, at least partially, if she was going to obtain his help. "It's not the work, Brian," she said, pleading. "It's Ian. I can't be around him, don't you understand?"

Brian stared at her speculatively before he spoke with slow emphasis. "No, I don't think I do, Allie. What are you trying to tell me?"

Alicia looked at him in despair, hating to spell it all out for him, but desperate enough to do just that. "I'm in love with Ian, Brian," she said with quiet force. "And he doesn't love me. In fact, he hates me. *Now* do you see why I can't work with him any longer?"

For a moment Brian looked astonished, and then his astonishment changed to discomfort. "Yeah, I see, Allie," he said with a sympathy that grated on her nerves. "At least, I see why you don't *want* to work with Ian," he went on more slowly, "though I don't understand how you fell in love with him when you never even used to like him—nor do I see why he hates you," he finished more briskly. "But that's beside the point. I'd help you if I could, Allie, but I'm afraid there's no way you're going to be able to get out of this. Ian left me in no doubt that it's you or nothing."

Alicia looked up at him with weary puzzlement. "What do you mean nothing?" she asked in a tired voice.

"He said he'd withdraw the book if you refuse to work with him," Brian informed her uncomfortably.

Alicia sat down, feeling as though she'd gone through this scene before. Blackmail was beginning to be a very effective weapon in Ian's arsenal. "Can he do that?" she asked resignedly.

"Yes." Brian avoided her eyes when she looked up at him in disgust. "We could take him to court, I guess," he admitted with a martyred sense of fairness, "but in my opinion we'd be cutting off our noses to save our face."

Alicia understood what he meant. If it came to that, Ian would never work with Talton Publications again, and her own name would be mud from then on. She gathered her courage, her anger at Ian's blackmail giving her the incentive to face what she must.

"Very well," she said with hard determination in her voice. "If that's what Ian wants, that's what he'll get— this time." She realized Brian couldn't know that after this once, it was likely Ian would never want to use her services again. He would have accomplished whatever it was he had in mind to punish her and would have no further use for her . . . ever.

Brian beamed with satisfaction, then tried to hide that satisfaction when he encountered Alicia's hard look of disgust. "Uh—fine." Brian faltered weakly, then took a deep breath as he dropped his next bombshell. "He, uh—Ian, that is," he stalled briefly, "wants you to come out to California again." As was his habit, he started for the door rather than face Alicia's expected wrath at his announcement. But Alicia didn't even raise her voice this time.

"No, Brian," she said with quiet certainty. "I'm not going to California or anywhere else. If Ian wants to work with me, he can come here. Otherwise I don't care what happens. He can withdraw his book and you can take him to court, or whatever. I just don't care."

Brian stopped, opened his mouth to protest, then closed it again when he saw the expression on Alicia's face. He lifted his shoulders in a helpless gesture of resignation, then left the room with a worried shake of his head and a concerned expression that failed to move Alicia in the slightest. She had had as much as she could take of being pushed around for Ian Halsey's personal pleasure, and though she might have to give in to a certain extent, she didn't have to let him have his way completely ... even if it meant she had to wash dishes for a living for the rest of her life.

Chapter Thirteen

Alicia shifted her weight from one tired foot to the other, taking a sip of champagne and trying to avoid looking at the other side of the smoke-filled room where Ian was being besieged by yet another glamorous creature who clung to him, flirted with him, flattered him, and no doubt hoped to take him home with her to her bed for the evening. She had no idea whether Ian ever actually acted on any of the numerous invitations he must receive from the women he captivated so easily, but it made no real difference whether he did or not. Alicia's persistent jealousy was the same regardless, for her active imagination had convinced her that he couldn't possibly resist all the temptations that were being thrown at him night and day.

Alicia sighed and thanked heaven that this was the last night of a two-week ordeal that resembled nothing so much as a masochistic experience in a torture chamber. She had no choice but to attend these functions with Ian, of course. The masochism came in when she couldn't stop herself from watching him lap up the attention every female from the age of twenty to seventy gave him. Even that was nothing, however, compared to the fact that Ian *knew* what he was doing to her. She had caught him time and again viewing her misery with a cool satisfaction that made her sick at heart.

But then Ian was proving to be a master at torture in every form imaginable, she thought bitterly as she watched him lean down to give his present admirer a light kiss. Every word he said to her was calculated to hurt, every look he turned her way contemptuous. He was extracting his pound of flesh with effortless ease, and Alicia had not yet found the strength to deny him his satisfaction. In time she would. She realized that through the haze of pain she moved in these days and gained hope from the realization. It was the only thing that had enabled her to get through this debilitating experience. But she was not at that point yet, and she glanced down at her watch with dreary gloom to see that it would be at least another hour before Ian would be ready to leave and she could end this present agony combined of pleasure and pain. The pleasure sprang from being near Ian... the pain from knowing that his hatred of her hadn't diminished.

"Excuse me," a pleasant male voice brought her attention back to the immediate surroundings. 'Aren't you Alicia Farr?"

She looked up to find herself facing an attractive younger man who was eyeing her with obvious appreciation, his smile verging on flirtatiousness. Alicia was more than ready to take her mind off the flirtation still going on across the room, and her smile was warmer than was strictly necessary as she acknowledged her identity. "Yes, I am," she said simply. "Who are you?"

He laughed at her bluntness, his warm brown eyes softening with humor. "Nobody yet," he admitted ruefully. "But I hope one day to be as famous as our guest of honor." He gestured toward Ian, who stood with relaxed male grace, smiling down at another young woman who had joined the first in the circle of adoration. The young man turned back to Alicia, shaking his head. "He's really something, isn't he? He seems to have been born for this."

Alicia gave a resigned smile. "Yes, he's something," she agreed noncommittally, not spelling out exactly what she thought Ian Halsey was.

"My name is Brad Duncan," the young man finally introduced himself, holding out a well-shaped hand for Alicia to take.

Alicia did so, enjoying the fact that he held her hand longer than necessary while he shook it. "Hi," she murmured, giving Brad a small smile while she looked straight into his eyes, aware of how he would interpret that look. She was sick of being on the outside looking in, and this young man presented the perfect opportunity to take her mind off Ian's popularity with the opposite sex while she concentrated on her own.

Brad's eyes widened slightly with surprised pleasure at the reception he was getting from Alicia. He moved closer to her, wasting no time in taking advantage of her silent invitation to flirt. "Are you a writer, Brad?" Alicia asked with interest, making no effort to move away from him.

"Yes." He smiled down at her warmly, his eyes roaming the lovely planes of her face. "I've not been published yet, except in a small way, but I have hopes. My dream is to collaborate with someone like you on a best-seller like Ian Halsey's."

Alicia hid a smile, wondering if Brad was approaching her out of professional interest or male interest. Either way, he was proving to be a welcome distraction, and she didn't really care what his motivation was, since her own interest in him was only temporary.

"In case you're wondering how I got invited here, I'm Howard Talton's nephew," Brad informed her with a grin comprised of self-mockery. "Otherwise I don't think they'd have let me in the door."

Alicia laughed, liking his self-directed sense of humor and relaxing even further at learning he was related to Howard. "Oh, I'm sure they would have," she teased provocatively. "There's always a demand for handsome young men at any party."

Brad's gaze sharpened at her compliment, and his voice softened as he said, "The only thing I care about at the moment is if *you* think I'm handsome—" He hesitated, then queried, "May I call you Alicia?"

"Of course," Alicia responded with another provocative smile, feeling more reckless by the moment. "I've been calling you Brad, haven't I?"

"Yes, but that's a woman's privilege," he said, holding her gaze with his own with no attempt to hide the fact that she excited him.

"What's a woman's privilege?" Ian's lazy drawl startled Alicia as she looked up to find that he had crossed the room and approached the two of them.

Brad was equally startled at being approached by the author he admired, but when he saw the unmistakable look of male challenge in Ian's eyes, he became cautious. "Almost anything is a woman's privilege," he answered evasively, moving slightly away from Alicia.

Ian flashed Alicia a searing look that made her wince inwardly as she realized what he was thinking. "Is it?" Ian said with cool challenge, turning back to an increasingly puzzled Brad, whose look indicated that he hadn't realized he was poaching on another man's property.

Alicia bristled at that look, resenting Brad's assumption that she belonged to anyone, and resenting even more Ian's manner, which had given rise to that look.

"Brad and I were just going to get a drink and go out on the terrace for some air," she informed Ian with cold haughtiness. "Will you excuse us, please?"

Her words brought Brad's eyes to her in startled surprise, and Ian's in grim purpose. "No, I won't excuse you," he said with smooth purposefulness. "I'm ready to leave."

"Well, I'm not!" Alicia snapped back at him, having had enough of his dominance over her.

"Too bad," Ian said smoothly, taking her arm in a viselike grip. "We have something to discuss, so I'm afraid you'll just have to put off your...uh...momentary pleasures," he said with a barely polite glance at Brad. "Good night, *young* man." He dismissed Brad with an emphasis on the word *young* that Alicia realized was meant more for her ears than Brad's. Far from stinging her pride, however, it had the opposite effect. She gave Brad an apologetic, stunning smile as Ian pulled her away with him, then turned it into a glare as she was forced to follow along in Ian's wake.

"What do you think you're doing, Ian?" she hissed at him as he threw her light jacket over her shoulders and pushed her out the door of the apartment they were in. "You didn't even apologize to the hosts for leaving early!"

"Yes, I did," he answered in a voice taut with controlled anger. "I'm not quite the barbarian you think I am."

"You don't know how I think of you." She gave herself the pleasure of answering him with a double meaning. "But wouldn't you have been slightly embarrassed if I had refused to leave with you?" she continued in the heat of her own anger.

"I had no intention of giving you a choice," he answered with perfect truth, since he had, in fact, forced her exit and there had been nothing she could have done about it without creating a scene.

"What's the matter, Ian?" Alicia baited him as he thrust her into a waiting taxi in front of the apartment building. "Did you have so many offers of a home away from home tonight that you couldn't make up your mind which to accept? You don't usually leave your circle of admirers this early!"

Ian climbed in beside her and gave the driver the address of Alicia's apartment, then he leaned back against the seat and gave her the benefit of a contemptuous look. "I don't usually have to rescue unsuspecting young men from the claws of a woman who—" He broke off as he saw the color drain from Alicia's face before she turned it away from him to look out the window.

"Go on, Ian," she said in a voice muffled with strain. "A woman who . . . ?"

"Forget it, Alicia," Ian dismissed the subject wearily. "We'll talk when we get to your apartment."

She turned to look at him, her expression withdrawn and remote. "Oh, then you did have something you wanted to talk to me about?" she questioned with polite coolness. "I thought you were merely making excuses."

"No," he answered with curt dismissal, refusing to elaborate.

During the silent ride to her apartment Alicia worried over what it was Ian had to say to her. Whatever it was would be brutal, she was certain, but she would have liked to have had an inkling as to the subject matter in order to better prepare herself for the coming ordeal.

When the two of them were finally settled in her living room, Ian seemed in no hurry to broach whatever subject was on his mind, however, and Alicia grew increasingly nervous as she watched him lean his head back against the cushions of her couch, his face etched with fatigue and his body relaxing as though he might fall asleep at any moment.

In order to get her mind off the desire to touch him and soothe away the lines of fatigue on his face, Alicia broke the silence with nervous chatter. "You never told me what your mother and father thought of the book, Ian." She darted him an anxious glance, noting that he hadn't moved an inch in reaction to her question. "Was your mother unhappy at the way you wrote about her?" she persisted quietly.

A grim smile lifted Ian's mouth slightly. "My mother hasn't the faintest notion that the book *is* about her," he answered with dry cynicism. "You didn't really think she would recognize herself, did you?" He opened his eyes then and glanced over at her, his expression enigmatic. "And I don't want her to know. I didn't write the book to punish her, nor to get any long-buried neuroticism out of my system. I wrote it because I thought it would make an interesting book...that's all."

His dry assertion was all the more convincing for its lack of force, and Alicia searched his face curiously. "Does she like it?" she asked with a studious lack of emphasis.

"She loves it," Ian said with a more genuine smile. "It's on the agenda for her next literary meeting, and she's in seventh heaven at being the author's mother."

Ian sounded so unconcerned about his mother's frailties, Alicia shook her head slightly in amazement. "You don't mind?" she faltered slightly. "Or are you happy to have finally pleased her?"

Ian cocked an eyebrow at her, the strong lines of his

face creasing with amusement. "It doesn't really concern me one way or the other," he said dryly.

Alicia shook her head in impatience, not believing him. "That can't be true, Ian," she spoke quietly, careful to keep any of the sympathy she felt for him out of her voice. "Brian and Ingrid both are certain that the main reason you wrote the book was to please your mother." She glanced at his impassive expression, puzzled by his denial. "And you told me yourself she was always bothering you to write something she could be proud of."

Ian shrugged, dismissing the subject as though it held no interest for him. "Think what you like," he said in a bored tone that raised Alicia's hackles. Then he faced her, his expression taking on a firmness that made Alicia forget the subject of his book as she sensed that the time had come for Ian to discuss what he'd come here for...and perhaps to administer his final punishment.

"I believe I told you before you left California that you owed me something, Alicia," he said with a return to the cutting cruelty in his voice that he had used on her for two weeks now. "I've decided what it is I want."

Alicia withdrew into herself mentally and emotionally, searching for the courage she needed for this long-awaited interview. "I owe you nothing, Ian," she replied with stiff coolness.

His smile was unamused. "Don't you? Not even a child?"

Alicia winced at the coldness in his voice, still unable to get used to hearing it when she knew the other side of his personality...the warm tenderness that pulled at her heart. Ian had noted that wince, and his expression was coldly satisfied. Alicia retreated into remote dispas-

sion. "The child was conceived under...unusual...
circumstances, Ian. I hope you'll at least admit that."
She glanced at him for his reaction, but he seemed unmoved. "You didn't make love to me with the idea of
creating a child...." She shrugged bitterly. "As a matter of fact, you didn't even make *love* to me, you
just—" She stopped herself, unwilling to put into
words something so painful to remember.

Taking an unobtrusive breath, Alicia forced herself
to go on. "And I certainly wasn't consulted about
whether I wanted to become pregnant," she said with
dry bitterness. "I did what I had to do, Ian," she finished on a weaker note, because now she was on
grounds where her own doubts refused to furnish any
conviction for her words, then waited quietly for Ian's
reaction.

It wasn't slow in coming. "Everything you say is
true, Alicia," he responded without any softening in
his tone that she could detect. "But that doesn't change
the fact that the child was mine. If you had had the
decency to tell me about it, I would have taken it and
raised it myself, since you obviously didn't want it."

Alicia swung around to face his hard, unyielding
face, her eyes shimmering with hurt anger. "And how
was I to know that, Ian?" she asked with indignant self-
justification. "I didn't know you. And what I did know
about you, I didn't like. Just how was I to know that far
from living up to your responsibilities, you wouldn't
laugh in my face!"

"All you had to do was ask," Ian responded with soft
implacability. "But you didn't. You simply ran to a doctor and—" He broke off, the savagery that lay just
under the surface of his civilized exterior evident in his
eyes and posture. Alicia watched fearfully as he fought
it down and got himself under control

"Well, that's over and done with," he continued after a moment. "There's nothing we can do to change the past now," he said, the hard note returning to his voice. "It's the future I'm here to talk about."

Alicia closed her eyes wearily and turned away from him. "What is it you want, Ian?" she asked quietly, her tone close to despair.

"Another child." He said the words with flat conviction, as though there were no argument possible against what he meant to have.

Not comprehending what Ian really meant, Alicia responded instinctively, though the words cost her a great deal to utter. "I suggest you get married and have one then, Ian. That's the usual procedure, isn't it?"

The smile he gave her brought a chill to her spine. "That's exactly what I plan to do, Alicia. How soon can you be ready?"

Alicia blinked at him uncomprehendingly. "How soon can I—" she started, and then his meaning came clear to her in a blinding flash. "Oh, God, no, Ian, you can't be serious!" She sat frozen, willing him to tell her differently.

"I'm deadly serious, Alicia," Ian responded, holding her eyes with his own. "And the sooner the better."

"But you don't love me!" Alicia cried, jumping to her feet to put distance between them. "And I—" She started to utter the lie that she didn't love him either, but the words didn't come.

"Oh, I'm aware that marriage and children don't interest you," Ian said as he got to his feet and came to face her. "But I want my child to be legitimate. When you've given me one, you can go your own way."

"But why don't you marry someone you love, Ian?" Alicia whispered the words, not wanting to hear an answer.

"I would if there were such a person," he responded dryly. "But since there isn't, and since you owe me a child, I've decided to do it this way. If I wait much longer, I'll be too old to enjoy him—or her," he added mockingly.

"But I thought—" Alicia began, remembering Ingrid's suspicion that Ian was in love with someone.

"You thought what, Alicia?" Ian sounded impatient at her hesitation.

"Ingrid said..." Alicia hesitated, then decided to face the worst. "She thought you were in love with someone."

Something oddly disturbing flickered behind Ian's golden eyes for an instant and then it was gone, and his voice was amused and astonished when he replied, "Ingrid must have been putting you on."

Despite the relief she felt at learning that Ian wasn't in love with someone, Alicia knew that what he was proposing wouldn't work...not without love. "This is ridiculous, Ian," she protested, turning away from him to walk to a window and stare out so that he couldn't see her expression. She was afraid it would be too revealing of how tempted she was to accept such an unworkable idea simply because she loved him and wanted to take the opportunity to be near him for however short a time. "What makes you think I'd be willing to marry you, have your child, and then just walk away from it? I wouldn't even consider such an idea." The firmness in her voice was forced, though she had meant what she said.

She sensed Ian's shrug of unconcern. "That's up to you," he drawled on a dry note. "I won't deny you access to the child if that's what you want, though from your past actions, I would have thought you'd have no interest in maintaining the relationship."

Alicia swung around to face him, infuriated by his accusations. "You don't know anything about me then, Ian Halsey! I've told you before I love children. I would never abandon one of mine!"

Ian's look was coldly contemptuous. "But you did, didn't you, Alicia? Perhaps it's just that you didn't want *my* child."

Stung by the truth—at least the *partial* truth—of his accusation, Alicia raised her chin and faced him squarely. "You're right, Ian. At the time, I didn't want your child." She didn't explain that though it had been the truth at the time of the abortion, it hadn't been the primary consideration behind her decision. She honestly didn't know what she would have decided if her doctor hadn't advised her that an abortion was wise under the circumstances. But she doubted strongly if she could have found it in her to abort the child regardless of the fact that she had hated its father then. She was almost positive that after she'd had time to get used to the idea, she would have kept the child and raised it...and loved it.

Ian's face had whitened at her admission, and there was pain in his eyes, but Alicia considered his reaction to be hurt pride and she stilled her instinctive desire to comfort him. She was grateful that he didn't seem to have picked up on her prefacing her statement with the words *at the time*. They had slipped out unconsciously, and she didn't want him to know that she felt entirely differently now—that she wanted him and his child with all her heart.

"Then you won't have any problem leaving the one you're *going* to have either, since it will be mine," Ian said with harsh anger.

Alicia swayed slightly, feeling despair over what had come to pass, knowing she had to put an end to her relationship with Ian once and for all if she was ever to have any peace again. "Ian, you can't make me marry you and you can't force me to have your child," she said with weary regret. "Please...just go now. There's nothing more to be said."

Ian reached her in an instant, swinging her up into his arms and heading for the bedroom. "You're right," he grated out harshly. "I can't force you to marry me, but I sure as hell can force you to have my child!"

"Ian, no!" Alicia struggled in his arms, feeling the nightmarish sensation of history repeating itself. "Please don't do this again!" And when he ignored her, Alicia grew desperate. "What's to stop me from having another abortion, Ian?" She knew she would never do any such thing, but it was the only way she could think of to stop what was happening. "How would you be able to prevent it?"

Ian paused just outside the door to her bedroom, looking down at her with eyes that glittered dangerously bright. "I'll stop you, Alicia. You try something like that again, and I'll lock you up somewhere until the moment you have the child!"

It was crazy, but Alicia believed him. Her common sense told her that Ian couldn't possibly succeed at something like that, and her heart told her that the real Ian wouldn't even attempt it. But at that moment it was clear that Ian believed his own words, caught up as he was in some emotion she didn't understand and couldn't begin to unravel until he calmed down enough to behave rationally. Under the circumstances she did the only thing she could. "All right, Ian!" she cried out as he began to move toward the bedroom again. "I'll marry you! I'll have your child! Only please stop this. Please, Ian! Don't do this again!"

The pleading desperation in her voice got through to

him, and after a long, searching look at her face as though he were searching her soul, Ian set her on her feet, though he held her where she was. "You'd better mean what you say, Alicia," he warned her with quiet force. "If you think you're only delaying things, I promise you it won't work. One way or another, you're going to have my child."

Alicia stared up at him, fearful of the depths in him she couldn't understand, yet aching from the pain she saw in his eyes. She wanted desperately to erase that pain and even more desperately to replace it with love. In that moment, coming face to face with the depth of her own love for this man, who was such a mixture of gentleness and savagery, she made her decision, tempering it with a levelheaded respect for her own well-being.

"There have to be some rules agreed upon first, Ian. You'll get what you want, but I have to protect my own interests as well."

She almost wilted at the slashing look of contempt her words evoked in him. "Of course," he grated out harshly. "I should have foreseen that. Well, don't worry, Alicia. I'm willing to pay the price for my child. I'll make arrangements to have a generous settlement put aside for you—"

"I'm not talking about money," Alicia interrupted him with hissing fury. "I'm talking about *my* child as well as yours. Now, are you ready to listen or not?"

She faced him like a small termagant, her hands clenched, her eyes spitting fire, her posture erect and proud, and Ian's amazement at the transformation he saw in her and at her words was evident in his startled expression, but only for a moment. Then he caught himself up and his face grew emotionless. "I'm listening," he said tersely.

Alicia turned on her heels and marched back into the living room to seat herself in a chair and wait with regal poise until Ian saw fit to join her and take part in the discussion she intended to have in a civilized manner. When he was seated across from her, his eyes glinting with the merest hint of admiration, Alicia began to speak in calm, collected tones.

"First of all, there will be no attempt to start a child until at least six months after we're married." She held up a hand to stem the angry tirade she saw gathering in Ian's eyes. "During that six months," she went on with perfect calm, "we will make an effort to come to love one another, to have a real marriage." She could almost feel the jolt she had given Ian, expressed in the sudden stillness that gripped his whole body. She hurried on before he could say anything to deflect her from her purpose. "At the end of the six months, if we find we can't love one another and that there's no hope for the marriage, I will have your child, but I will retain equal custody of it." She stared at him unflinchingly. "There is absolutely no question of my abandoning the child to you totally."

Alicia could see the shock in Ian's eyes, followed by doubtful wariness. She quickly hurried on before her courage deserted her. "I want all of this in writing, especially the part about my retaining equal custody of our child. If you won't agree to it, you can take me into that bedroom and do whatever you like, but I promise you, if you do that, I'll take the baby and disappear and never acknowledge you as the father."

For long moments after she fell silent, Ian's golden eyes bored into her as though he wanted to examine her every thought, her every emotion. But when he finally spoke, in a quiet, thoughtful fashion, it was clear that it was her motivation that interested him most.

"Why are you doing this, Alicia?" he said softly, his very stillness giving the impression of his waiting for something important... something that meant a great deal to him.

But since Alicia didn't know what that something was, she considered how much of the truth she could tell him without putting herself at his complete mercy. She finally broke the silence that was growing oppressive. "I think I told you once that I believed in love and marriage and babies. That was the truth. I want a child, too," she said straightforwardly, "and since you're determined that it will be yours, I'm simply bowing to the inevitable." She turned calm, thoughtful eyes on him. "But since I'm not getting any younger either, and since I think it is in all ways preferable for a child to have both a father and a mother, I want to give this one the same chance most children have as a matter of course: the chance for a normal home with loving parents." She turned her eyes away from him then, not wanting to see his reaction to her next words. "But if, at the end of six months, you find you can't love me, I'll live up to my side of the bargain... under my terms."

Ian's response was carefully devoid of emotion. "And what if you find you can't learn to love *me,* Alicia?"

Inwardly Alicia tensed, wanting to scream at him that she already did. But, of course, she couldn't do that. If she did, her gamble would be lost before the play even began. Ian would know he could have what he wanted without making the slightest effort to live up to his side of the bargain, in which he was supposed to try to learn to love her. "Then I would expect you to let me go," she answered quietly. "That will be in the agreement as well."

She sensed that her answer disappointed him, but she attributed his reaction to her mentioning of the prenuptial agreement again. She was certain he would much prefer to do without a piece of paper that would hold him to the rules she was setting down. She reflected bitterly that she would prefer to do without it as well, but under the circumstances it would be all she had to ensure her rights to her own child!

Ian was quiet for so long, Alicia began to wonder if he was having second thoughts about his desire for a child under such onerous circumstances. She didn't know why he wanted a child so badly, but it was something she intended to discover if her gamble worked out the way she hoped it would.

At last she heard his very quiet, very final "Very well. I'll make an appointment with my attorneys tomorrow. You can come along to make sure everything you've asked for is put into the agreement." He stood up and moved toward the door, pausing with his hand on the knob. "Once it's signed, we'll be married as soon as we can get a license. You'd better turn in your notice as soon as possible, because we'll be leaving for California within the week." And without even a good night Ian opened the door and disappeared from sight, leaving Alicia limp and drained from the tension she'd been under, then trembling with reaction from the enormous step she'd just taken—a step on which the remainder of her whole life hinged. In six months she would either be happily married and pregnant... or just pregnant.

Chapter Fourteen

Alicia sat in the airplane seat next to Ian, her hands carefully folded in her lap, staring down thoughtfully at the flashing brilliance of a huge diamond nestled against the plain gold of a wedding band. The evidence of her marital state was there for anyone to see, but she didn't feel married. She felt lonely and bereft and daunted at the enormity of the task she faced.

A faint sigh escaped her as she turned to stare out the window at the white clouds and blue sky. Their natural beauty made her want to try to fight the depression that threatened to engulf her and which would be no help at all in the battle she faced. She wished Ian would at least talk to her, even if it was meaningless small talk. In that way they might find themselves beginning to communicate on a more personal level than the monosyllabic necessities they had exchanged for the past three days. And then, with a stiffening of her backbone, she decided if he wouldn't talk to her, then it was up to her to talk to him. Short of absolute rudeness, he would have to reply, wouldn't he?

"Have you made any progress on the book you were writing about the Indian couple, Ian?" she asked in a determinedly pleasant voice, ignoring the slight movement of irritation he made as he kept his eyes on the magazine he was reading.

"I'm almost finished with it," he replied in a dismissing voice that Alicia refused to let discourage her.

"Oh, good," she said with bright encouragement. "Will you tell me about it?"

"You can read it when we get to the house," Ian said in that same dismissing tone that made Alicia grit her teeth to keep from replying in kind.

"I can't wait," she replied with the barest hint of dryness in her voice. But she was determined Ian wasn't going to shut her out, and she persisted with her questioning. "Do you intend to continue writing in the same vein as you did before this last book, or will you start something else along the lines of *Portrait of a Woman*?" she asked.

Ian gave a slight sigh of impatience and set his magazine aside, turning to face Alicia with an expression of a man who was faced with entertaining a complete stranger who was an inveterate talker. Alicia faced that expression with calm fortitude, never wavering from her pose of polite interest.

"I will write what I feel like writing at any given time, Alicia," he said with obvious patience. "I enjoyed what I did before and I expect I always will. I also enjoyed writing *Portrait of a Woman,* and I expect I'll do something along those lines again. Does that answer your question?"

Alicia gave him one of her sweetest smiles, though she felt like reaching over and boxing his ears. "Yes, it does, Ian," she purred silkily. "Now would you like to discuss the weather? Because I have no intention of sitting here twiddling my thumbs while you bury yourself in that magazine again. Flying makes me nervous and talking makes me forget my nervousness. Do you think you could pretend to be a loving husband for a few moments and oblige me in this little foible?''

Seemingly against his will, a slight smile flickered behind Ian's eyes before he gravely nodded his head. "I'll do my best, Mrs. Halsey," he said with a mocking intonation that caught at Alicia's heart. Until that moment no one had addressed her by her new name, and she hated the fact that Ian had felt it necessary to do so in such a disparaging way. She refused to acknowledge her hurt in any outward manner, however, merely nodding her head with a mocking tilt that echoed Ian's mood.

For the rest of the flight Ian lived up to his word, choosing the subject of the book Alicia had inquired about earlier as a safe topic that they could discuss with mutual interest while keeping the conversation on a more or less impersonal plane. Shortly before they reached Reno Alicia decided she'd had enough of his impersonality, however, and she deliberately introduced an intimate note into the conversation.

"Do you often read the sexy parts of your books aloud to women, Ian?" she asked with mischievousness twinkling in her eyes. "The way you did to me that night in your study?"

She felt him stiffen slightly before he replied in a manner that resembled the one he'd adopted the night she'd first met him, when she'd baited him about his books in front of everyone. "Always, Alicia. I've found it a very useful tool to use in the art of seduction. Did you like it?"

His question caught her slightly off guard, but she recovered quickly, sensing something in his attitude that didn't quite ring true. In fact, she was beginning to suspect that Ingrid had been right when she'd said that most of the stories about Ian and his exploits with women were made up to sell books. While it was most likely true that he hadn't behaved like a monk, she was much more willing to accept that he hadn't been a complete libertarian either.

Now she faced the irony in his eyes with a direct look that was as provocative as she could make it. "Very much so," she murmured huskily. "And I hope you don't drop it from your routine simply because you're a married man now with no reason to practice seduction."

"What makes you think I intend to give up seduction simply because I'm married, Alicia," he drawled mockingly. "That wasn't in the agreement we signed."

His reply chilled her, chasing the soft seductiveness from her eyes and replacing it with stony shock. Alicia stared at him, realizing that he was right, and further realizing that she would not... could not... stand infidelity from Ian, regardless of the basis for their marriage, and that it was just as well that he knew it before they went any further with the dangerous game she was playing.

"It may not have been put in writing, Ian, but it's a condition nevertheless. It goes along with the part of the agreement that deals with learning to love one another. If you're ever unfaithful to me, the whole thing is off. I'll walk out, and you'll never see me again."

The quiet conviction in her voice made him frown and search her face with puzzled eyes that showed frustration as well. "You drive a hard bargain, Alicia," he finally said in a curiously flat voice. "Do I take it the same condition applies to you?"

"You have my word," Alicia said with a look that was unflinchingly honest. "I've never been promiscuous and I don't intend to start now."

Ian stared at her for a long moment, and then the captain's voice came over the loudspeaker, announcing their arrival in Reno, and in the general bustle of fastening seat belts and stowing articles away for landing, the moment was lost.

Borg met them at the airport, giving Alicia a long look that was kindly and curious and congratulatory all at the same time. Alicia was genuinely glad to see him, and in a burst of affection she gave him a hug and a kiss that brought a pleased, embarrassed smile to his craggy face.

"How are you, Borg?" she asked with a warm smile. "And how are Ingrid and Sandi?" She was even more glad now that she had written to the Johnsons after her return to New York under false pretenses to explain as well as she could why she had found it necessary to stay there instead of returning to Reno as she had said she would. Her explanation had been necessarily vague, but at least she hadn't killed all chance of reestablishing a relationship with the family.

"They're fine... I'm fine... everyone's doing well," Borg replied in his slow fashion, his kind smile enveloping her with a feeling of acceptance. "We're all happy about your marriage, of course. Ingrid swears she knew all along it would happen, and she's usually right."

Alicia gave him a startled look, remembering her conversation with Ingrid when the woman had thought Ian was in love with someone. She didn't say anything, merely reflecting that Ingrid had perhaps been right about Ian marrying, but she had certainly been wrong about his being in love.

Ian listened to the exchange with a closed expression, and now he moved them along to the luggage carousel as if he were in a hurry, though Alicia knew of no reason why he should be. They were going to spend the first night of their married life at his home, having agreed that a honeymoon at this point in their relationship would be a farce. Alicia couldn't help wishing, however, that instead of returning to Ian's home, where they would be enveloped within the loving presence of the Johnsons, they were going to some quiet hideaway where they could perhaps begin to get to know one another a little better.

There was still snow as they got up into the mountains, but it wasn't the heavy, enveloping whiteness that she had seen during her earlier visit. When at last they pulled into the driveway of Ian's home, and Alicia saw Ingrid eagerly awaiting their arrival on the front steps, she gathered her strength to make the effort to appear the happy, radiant bride the woman would no doubt expect. She was surprised when Ian placed his arm around her waist and directed a warm smile at her as Ingrid greeted the two of them.

Ingrid seemed genuinely excited and pleased about the marriage, and Alicia relaxed a little when the woman hugged her with all the affection she might have given to one of her own family, beaming and congratulating her and saying all the right things with a sincerity that warmed Alicia's heart.

"Come inside and have some coffee, you two." Ingrid at last released Alicia and, after placing a loving peck on Ian's cheek, bustled them inside the house. "There's a hot meal in the oven, Alicia, whenever the two of you are ready for it, and plenty of food for the rest of the weekend. You two won't need to leave the house for anything if you don't want to."

Alicia followed Ingrid into the living room while Ian and Borg took the luggage to the bedroom, thinking warily that if Ingrid's words meant what she thought they did, Ian wasn't going to be any too pleased at being left alone in the house with his new bride without the protective influence of the Johnsons. "Uh...you sound as though you and Borg are going somewhere, Ingrid?" she said with cautious questioning.

Ingrid looked astonished that Alicia had had to ask. "Well, of course we are," she said indignantly. "You didn't think we were going to stay here and horn in on your honeymoon, did you?" She frowned a little and added in a puzzled voice, "Such as it is. Didn't you two want to go somewhere exciting for a honeymoon?"

Alicia had to think fast. Obviously Ian hadn't bothered to come up with an explanation of his own on that score. "Well," she said slowly, "Ian is very tired from the round of publicity he's just been through. And since I went through it with him, I am, too. We've decided to wait until we are more rested to take a proper trip."

Though Ingrid still looked a little dubious at Alicia's explanation, she dropped the subject and began to explain to Alicia the preparations she'd made so that Alicia wouldn't have to cook on this first weekend in her new home. By the time she was done the men had rejoined them, and Borg was enjoining his wife to get a move on if they were going to make it to their first stop that night.

"Where are you going?" Alicia asked, suddenly nervous at being left alone with Ian and wanting to delay the Johnsons' departure if only for a few moments.

"We're going to visit Sandi at the university in Los Angeles," Ingrid supplied with beaming anticipation. "We've never been before, and I'm so looking forward to it. She sends her love and congratulations to the two of you, by the way."

"Thank her for us, will you?" Alicia smiled warmly

at the Johnsons. "But are you sure you want to leave tonight? Wouldn't it be better to start in the morning?"

Ingrid and Borg wouldn't hear of such a thing, however, both seeming a little shocked that Alicia should even suggest it. After the cheerful good-byes and the bustle of the Johnsons' departure, Alicia got control of her nervousness, and by the time the door closed behind them, she was able to face Ian with a degree of equanimity.

"Are you hungry, Ian?" she asked casually. "Ingrid left something for us in the kitchen if you are."

"Very," he answered with an enigmatic expression that brought a tingle of excitement to Alicia's spine. "But I think I'll shower first. Unless you'd like to eat now?"

"No." Alicia swallowed down a return of her nervousness. "I'd like to shower and change first, too. Shall I use my old bathroom?"

"Why?" Ian asked in a husky drawl. "There's plenty of room in my shower for two."

Alicia stared at him, wavering between uncertainty and an almost overwhelming desire to take Ian up on his invitation. She couldn't fathom the change in his attitude, but as it was the first sign he'd given in days that he felt anything more for her than complete disinterest, she was willing to forgo her doubts and use this first opportunity to get them on a more intimate basis, even if her common sense told her it sprang only from Ian's sexual nature rather than from anything more meaningful.

Her throat closed up when she tried to answer in the affirmative, however, and so she merely nodded her head and moved toward his bedroom on feet that scarcely seemed to touch the ground. Her cases were in his room, and Alicia felt a sagging relief that Ian wasn't going to put her in her old room, as she had half-feared he might do. Such an eventuality would have made her job all the more difficult, as she counted on the natural intimacy of sleeping in the same bed with him to assist the process of making their marriage into something real.

As she got out of her clothes and slipped on a soft robe, Alicia was intensely aware of Ian doing the same in the bathroom that led off of his bedroom. She didn't know whether to join him before or after he stepped into the shower, and she felt as awkward as though she were an innocent virgin rather than a woman who had been married for several years and who had already experienced Ian's brand of sexuality as well.

Ian solved the problem for her by appearing in the doorway to the bathroom, nude except for a towel around his hips. Alicia caught her breath at seeing his broad smoothly muscled shoulders, the flat plane of his stomach, and the long length of his strong legs. A patch of dark hair on his chest added to his image of male power, and Alicia felt her legs going weak with the desire to touch him with all the intimate love she was feeling for him at that moment.

"Do you like the water lukewarm or fairly hot?" he asked her casually, his eyes running over her with liquid interest.

"Hot," Alicia answered, her voice huskily suggestive, evoking a further flare of brilliance from Ian's golden eyes.

"Hot it is," he murmured, his own voice deepening with suggestiveness as he held out his hand to her. "But you'd better come and help me adjust the temperature. We may have different ideas about what constitutes...hot." The slight pause was highly suggestive, and Alicia found herself smiling at him with a lazy sensuousness that could have left no doubt in his mind about what she was feeling.

She took his hand and let him guide her into the bathroom, making no effort to move away when he slipped the robe from her shoulders and removed the towel from his hips. He bent close to her as he turned on the taps in the shower. "Is that all right?" he asked softly, holding her languorous gaze with his own as he took her hand to hold it under the water.

"Just right," Alicia whispered, letting her eyes drop to Ian's mouth with deliberate invitation. Fire sprang into his eyes at that invitation, but he didn't take her up on it. Instead he drew her into the shower and, picking up a bar of soap, he began to wash himself as Alicia stood and watched him, feeling the water on her skin with all her senses and longing to feel more.

At last she could stand it no more. "Shall I help you, Ian?" she asked softly, letting her eyes run over his body with deliberate intent.

"Do you want to?" he asked equally softly, pausing in his movements to return her inspection, his look hungrily male.

She nodded, her head feeling lazily heavy, her eyes half-closed against the water and with the sensuousness she was feeling. She held out her hand for the soap, and when Ian gave it to her, she stepped closer to begin the ritual that had little to do with cleansing him and everything to do with enjoying the feel of his skin under her hands.

She enjoyed every moment of the silent, deliberate seduction she employed as she ran her hands over him, swirling soap in intricate patterns, choosing the right moment to tease him erotically, brushing him occasionally with the tips of her breasts. She felt the tension in him increasing, watched his arousal grow into life, flicked glances up at the intent concentration in his eyes and at the taut set of his jaw.

But when she would have teased him in the most intimate way possible, he seized the soap from her hands and with a twisting smile began to do to her what she had done to him, employing her methods with every bit as much effect as she had accomplished.

At last Alicia was so weak with wanting him, she had to lean against the wall of the shower, and with a soft moan she begged for release or fulfillment. "Ian . . ." she said his name from deep in her throat. "Please . . . ?"

They had not exchanged a single kiss since entering the shower, but now Ian disposed of the soap and pinned her against the wall with both hands on either side of her, bringing his mouth close to her own. "Do you remember what I told you on that last day you were here before, Alicia?" he murmured softly, teasing her mouth with little kisses that only left her hungry for more.

Alicia shook her head weakly, wanting to capture his mouth for a real kiss, but he evaded her lips. "Remember I said I wouldn't touch you again until you admitted I meant something to you?"

Alicia came slightly awake out of her absorption with Ian's sensuality, but only slightly. Her involvement was too total for that. "You're my husband, Ian," she said softly. "Of course you mean something to me."

Ian shook his head slightly, his eyes molten, yet purposeful. "I want to know *what* I mean to you, Alicia," he said with soft insistence. "In detail."

Her frustration mounting at Ian's delay of the satisfaction she craved, Alicia had to force herself to concentrate on a reply that might satisfy him, but which wouldn't give too much away. "I want to love you,

Ian," she compromised, meaning that she wanted to love him physically, since she already loved him with her mind and her heart, but hoping he would take her words literally. "You can be kind and warm and sweet, and I'm drawn to those parts of you already," she went on under the impetus of his waiting for more. "I want you to make love to me. You know I'm drawn to you in that way, too." Still it wasn't enough for Ian apparently, and Alicia closed her eyes so he couldn't see the desperation she was feeling to have him take her without her having to bare her soul to him before it was time.

"I admire so many things about you, Ian," she said on a tight gasp as he increased the pressure she was already under by moving a hand to her breast to stroke the nipple already taut with desire. "You're intelligent," she groaned as he leaned his body against hers, letting her feel the arousal throbbing in his loins. "You're gentle," she whispered as she raised her arms to place them around his neck and pull him closer to her. "And, oh, God, Ian, I want you so!" she cried out as he placed his hands under her buttocks and lifted her into the hollow of his body, straining her to him as though he wanted to fuse her flesh with his.

"Then I guess I'll have to settle for what you feel right now," he said with harsh, masculine dominance as he brought his mouth to within a breath of hers, "and give you what you want!"

The savagery with which he took her mouth, invading it with his tongue, was exactly what Alicia needed and wanted at that moment. Ian had driven her to the point of mindless concentration on her body's needs, and she wouldn't have been satisfied with a gentler form of satiation of what she craved so intensely. There would be time for gentleness when her thirst for Ian's possession had been partially eased in this first explosive release of the desires that had been building in her over the long, long months without him.

She was scarcely conscious of his actions as he shut off the water and drew her from the shower stall to catch her up in his arms and carry her to his bed. Both were dripping water and neither cared as they landed atop the spread and Ian began to assault Alicia's senses with a rough impatience she echoed with her own caresses. Her boldness seemed to please him and excite him further, and once he lifted his head from her breast to give her a mirthless grin of satisfaction, his eyes fairly glowing with a very male light of conquering arousal.

"I've dreamed of the time when you would be like this, Alicia," he grated at her with low-toned exultancy. "I knew it was there, and I knew I could be the one to release it."

Driven by the now all-enveloping need to experience again the perfect fulfillment Ian had given her once before, Alicia acknowledged the truth of his words, her gasp a pleading ache for the mercy of his complete possession.

"You are, Ian. You have. Now, please, Ian, finish it! Take me all the way...."

She drew him, helped him, as he positioned himself above her to give her what she begged for, and her every nerve leaped with joy as she eagerly met and accepted their joining. If either noted the difference in her response from the first mating they'd shared, neither had the breath or the willingness to comment. Alicia's senses expanded, soared, and finally exploded in concert with Ian's compelling mastery of her body's rhythm and this time there was no sense of defeat that they were so perfectly matched, so exquisitely compatible, that both reached their own exclusively shared moment of ecstasy together.

Indeed, as Alicia slowly, reluctantly drifted back into the realm where she was only one again, separate and distinct from Ian, she clutched him to her body fiercely, exultant with the intimate joy she had been allowed to take and to give. Her heart expanded with hope as Ian, seemingly as reluctant as she was to let go of their intimacy, hugged her to him just as fiercely and kissed her mouth with a desperation she longed to believe sprang from his need to love as well as to want.

He said nothing, however, nor did she, each communicating whatever was in their hearts with their bodies throughout the long night that was the first of their married life and, Alicia hoped, the first of many such nights in the years to come.

Chapter Fifteen

Ian was replacing the telephone on its hook as Alicia came into his study with a tray of coffee, and his expression looked abstracted and slightly grim. "What's the matter?" Alicia asked matter-of-factly as she placed the tray on the coffee table and sat down to begin pouring out. "Bad news?"

"What?" Ian came out of his thoughts reluctantly at Alicia's question, his eyes focusing on her for the first time. "Oh, you mean the telephone call?" He came around his desk and moved to join her, seating himself beside her on the sofa and reaching a hand for his cup.

"Yes," Alicia said with a smile as she let her eyes roam over him with pleasure. "You look as though whatever was said disturbed you. Who was it?"

"Brian," Ian answered rather shortly and with none of the amused affection in his voice he usually reserved for his editor. "He wants me to come to New York to do another round of publicity for *Portrait of a Woman*. They're going to do a second printing, and he thinks it would be a good idea to remind the public about it."

Alicia responded with spontaneous pleasure. "Oh, that's wonderful, Ian!" She clapped her hands together like a child, her pride and love for her husband shining in her eyes, and then, as another thought hit her, her eyes brightened further. "I'd like to go, too. It will be nice to see all my old friends, and..."

Her voice trailed away as she saw that her proposal had provoked the closed, impatient expression on Ian's face that she hated to see, especially these days. They had been married over five months now, and on every level but one the marriage had been a resounding success. The two of them had proven to be compatible on almost every level that mattered, playing and working together with a natural smoothness and enjoyment that had increased the love Alicia felt for Ian until she honestly didn't know how she could contemplate living without him. Their relationship in bed was even more compatible, so much so, in fact, that it was becoming almost impossible for Alicia to keep from crying out her love at the moment of complete oneness and ecstasy that they never failed to reach together in their moments of intimacy.

But she was not ready to reveal her feelings to that extent and to place herself completely in Ian's power, chiefly because he had reserved a part of himself out of her keeping. He treated her with respect, easy affection, and camaraderie, but never with the depth of feeling she wanted so desperately from him. True, there were times, mostly in their bed at night, when she sensed something working on him, struggling for expression, but he always fought it down and remained in control, no matter how hard she worked to make him let go.

Now that the time was almost upon them for a decision about where the marriage was going, and whether or not the child that was a part of their bargain would grow up with two loving parents or in two separate households, Alicia was growing desperate for a resolution of their relationship. The thought of becoming pregnant with Ian's child, knowing that at the end of nine months she would be faced with another decision—the decision of whether to live with Ian, knowing he didn't love her, or whether to establish a household of her own so that their child could be shared—was preying on her mind and placing her under an increasing strain that was evidenced in the pallor of her face and the haunted look in her eyes. She was losing weight and sleep and finding it ever more difficult to maintain the pleasant, cheerful demeanor that had Ingrid and Borg loving her as a daughter and Sandi regarding her as a sister. But it was Ian's love she wanted, and it was beginning to look as though she might never accomplish that no matter how hard she tried.

Now she looked down at her coffee cup to hide the hurt she was feeling and spoke more quietly. "What's the matter, Ian? Would you prefer that I didn't come with you?" She was wondering, with a sense of despair, if Ian wanted to be apart from her so that he could be with the women who had always clustered around him.

Ian made an impatient movement, then set his cup down and got to his feet, exuding a sense of suppressed energy that was making him restless and irritable. "It doesn't matter," he said in a curt tone. "You obviously want to come, and I won't stand in your way."

Alicia looked up at him with puzzlement and hurt in her eyes, thinking his words a rather strange way to put things. "Yes, I want to come, Ian," she said with slow hesitancy, "but if you have a problem with it.. " She paused, giving him a chance to explain what the problem was.

Instead he gave an unamused laugh. "Why should I have a problem with it?" he said cynically. "It's time I got used to—" He stopped as though he'd been about to say too much, leaving Alicia wondering uneasily what he had on his mind. "I'll make the arrangements, then," he said in a distant, dismissing voice that indicated the subject was about to be closed. "We'll leave in a couple of days." He left the room then, murmuring something about speaking to Borg, and Alicia sat where she was, feeling the despair that was becoming her constant companion as the days grew shorter toward the time when she would have to face the inevitable.

Getting up from the sofa to wander aimlessly about the room, she wondered for perhaps the thousandth time if she should bring things to a head by telling Ian she loved him. But something always stopped her. She would remember the contempt he had felt for her when he'd learned about the abortion. She still didn't know why he had been so utterly condemnatory on the subject, or if it would make any difference to him if he knew the primary reason for her decision. Would he soften toward her if he knew that she blamed herself as much as he did? That she wished with all her heart now that she had waited until she was fit to make a decision of that enormity? That she woke up in the night sometimes, wondering if the child might have been healthy or at least not so severely handicapped that it couldn't have led a reasonably normal life? Or had she killed all chance for his understanding by telling him it was *his* baby she hadn't wanted?

For whatever reason, Alicia had been unable to bring herself to the point where she could be totally honest with Ian. She felt an instinctive caution about placing herself under his power even more than she already was, and an unreasoning fear that he would throw her love back in her face, or, what was worse, feel pity for her and decide to maintain the marriage for that reason instead of the only reason she could tolerate...because he loved her.

Finally she went to begin packing for the trip to New York, deciding to remain with Ian for every moment possible until the time came when she had to face up to the fact that she might never be with him again—not as his wife, at any rate, but only as the mother of his child.

Two nights later she lay exhausted in his arms in their hotel room in New York after they had made love, wondering even through her fatigue at the intensity of his lovemaking that night...the almost desperate savagery that had shaken her with its force. Ian lay quietly beside her, and she was startled when he spoke into the dark. She had thought he was asleep.

"My parents want us to stop by and visit them after we leave New York. They want to meet you."

The flat disinterest in his voice chilled her through the shock she felt at learning that she was at last going to meet Ian's parents. She didn't want to meet them. Indeed, she almost hated them, especially Ian's mother, for the hurt they had inflicted on him. "Do you want to do that?" she asked cautiously, thinking it would be unusual if he did.

He shrugged dismissingly. "We might as well. They'll kick up a fuss if we don't."

Alicia tried to see his face in the dark, but the shadows were too deep. She was wondering, as she always did, why Ian observed his duties as a son so punctiliously when he had little reason for affection toward his parents. But she was learning that he had a strong code of honor in many ways, and she supposed this was just one more case where he felt bound to observe that code. Unreasonably she wished her own parents were alive still, not only because she had loved them, but because they would have provided Ian with the same affection they gave to her, and perhaps in some small way they could have eased the damage his own parents had inflicted, though he had overcome his early up-bringing remarkably well, retaining the capacity to love that he might have been forgiven for losing under the circumstances. She sighed in the dark, wishing she knew if she were ever going to be one of the recipients of that love, or if he would one day give it to some other woman...a woman who would also be her own child's stepmother.

She was tempted to end the strain she was under by challenging Ian to discuss frankly where they were heading in their marriage. But as she heard his breathing deepen she realized he'd fallen asleep and that the chance was lost, and she didn't know whether to feel relieved or sad.

She saw very little of Ian the next day. He was sched-uled for a television interview, and she used the time to go to Talton Publications to visit with her former co-workers, except for Brian, who was with Ian at the tele-vision studio. She was sadly amused to find that most of the women were awed by her new status as Ian's wife—awed and almost universally jealous, though it was the sort of jealousy they might have felt for a movie star's wife and nothing to be concerned about. In general they didn't hold her good fortune against her, merely envying her in an abstract sort of way.

She met Howard Talton in the hallway as she was about to leave, and received an affectionate hug and a kiss in greeting, as well as a reminder not to be late for his dinner party that evening, or Samantha would have her hide. Alicia hadn't known about the dinner party, since Ian hadn't seen fit to discuss his schedule with her on the long, almost silent plane ride from Reno, but she didn't mention the fact, merely promising she would do her best to see that they got there on time.

Later, back in their hotel room, she dressed with unusual care for the evening, having stopped at a boutique to purchase a dress and bolster her spirits. She had the sense of time running out and she was unconsciously making an effort to capture Ian's interest, though she was unaware of her real purpose in adopting a new, flattering hairstyle and spending far more for her attire than she had ever thought she would.

Ian was late getting back and had to hurry to dress, but Alicia was unutterably pleased to find that her efforts had undoubtedly been successful as he gave her first a brief look, then returned his gaze to her a second time, his eyes widening with appreciation as he took in the picture she made.

She was standing before the windows in a casual pose when he entered, her heart fluttering with nervousness but her outward demeanor composed. The soft figure-hugging dress was of shell-white, and it draped over one shoulder, leaving the other bare to expose the creamy tan she had obtained in California. She had donned a gold slave bracelet on her bare right arm and that, along with dangling gold earrings, were her only accessories. Her hair was swept back from her face in a full roll at the back of her head with the glistening highlights picked out by the overhead light. She knew she looked stunningly poised and beautiful, but her confidence received an added boost when she saw the possessive sexual interest in Ian's eyes as they blazed over her.

"Is all that for me, or are you out to impress the Taltons?" he asked in a deep drawl that failed to hide the disturbance he was obviously feeling, though his words might have been calculated to hurt.

"I have no reason to impress the Taltons," Alicia answered evasively, not wanting to spell out for him that he was the only person in the world she cared about impressing.

That her answer dissatisfied him was obvious in the quick closing of his expression, but despite Alicia's instant desire to erase the effect her evasiveness had instigated, she didn't know how to make her real meaning more plain without revealing the depths of her feelings for him. "I'll try to do you justice then" was his dry comment as he left her to go and take his shower and to don the tuxedo Alicia had laid out for him.

When he reappeared, she had to catch her breath and clench her teeth over the exclamation of longing pride she felt at how handsome he looked. Instead of running to him and begging him to stay with her in the hotel room that night as she longed to do, she merely smiled brightly and nodded her head in approval. "You look wonderful, Ian," she said lightly as she put down the glass of wine she had been drinking to still her ever-present anxieties and reached for the white gossamer stole she was to wear.

Their conversation was minimal in the taxi on the way to the Taltons', and once they reached there, they became separated by the guests the Taltons had invited to meet Ian. Alicia hung on to her composure with firm discipline as the women of the party surrounded Ian, behaving as women always did in his presence. Alicia was grateful that no more than two or three of them were young and pretty enough to be considered as rivals, but it still hurt to watch as Ian charmed each and every one of them with the ease of long practice and, apparently, true inclination.

She smiled and chatted in her turn with Howard Talton and the men of the party until she looked up to see a familiar face smiling at her over the heads of the other men and looking as though he, at least, was overwhelmed by the appearance she had worked so hard to achieve that evening. Alicia smiled warmly in greeting as Brad Duncan made his way to her side and took her hand in his to kiss the back of it with continental flair.

"Where did you learn that trick?" she teased laughingly, feeling at ease with him immediately and grateful once again for the distraction he provided.

Brad wiggled his eyebrows leeringly and smiled a sly, secret smile. "Didn't I tell you the last time we met?" he said in a whisper as he looked over his shoulder in a furtive manner. "I used to be a spy over in Europe and had to seduce beautiful women right and left to get at their uttermost secrets. James Bond taught me this trick himself while I was training under him." He beamed down at her then with innocent cockiness, obviously expecting her to applaud his exploits of the past.

Alicia immediately played up to his teasing, adopting an anxious, wide-eyed look of admiration. "My," she said with breathless excitement. "I would never have suspected. You look so young." She looked around her, giving the impression of anxiety on his behalf. "But should you be telling me all this? Don't you have to maintain cover or... uh... something of that sort?"

Instantly his expression became coolly superior. "You're right," he pronounced pontifically. "I can say no more."

"Say no more," Alicia echoed solemnly before they both broke up into laughter at the parody of a scene from an old Beatles movie they had just enacted. Alicia was still laughing when she glanced up to see almost simultaneously Ian's scowling look of displeasure at her innocent teasing with Brad and the entrance of the one man who was calculated to destroy her composure utterly on this occasion. She had forgotten Dr. Hill was a friend of the Taltons, and even if she had remembered, she had no reason to expect to see him tonight. But there he was, obviously arriving late after some emergency or other, and his presence, coupled with the slashing look of disapproval Ian had just given her, combined to drain all color from Alicia's face and make her sway on her feet with a momentary bout of faintness.

"What's wrong?" Brad was asking, anxiety throbbing in his voice as he placed an arm around her waist to steady her. "Are you ill?"

Alicia closed her eyes for a moment, struggling to get control of herself and find an explanation to provide Brad that wouldn't sound too unconvincing. "I... uh...think your uncle's champagne is more potent than I'm used to," she finally managed to get out as she felt the world begin to steady around her. "If I recall, there's a terrace off Howard's library. Do you think we could go outside for a breath of air?"

She barely heard Brad murmur, "Certainly," as he turned her in the direction of Howard's library. She really wanted to be alone, but she was sensible enough to realize that Brad wouldn't leave her if he thought she needed help, and at the moment his assistance was far preferable to the alternative of asking Ian to accompany her. If she refused Brad's arm, it was entirely possible he would go to her husband to inform him of her momentary unsteadiness, and she couldn't risk that for the time being.

They were almost at the door of the library when she heard Dr. Hill's kindly voice calling her name. "Alicia! How good it is to see you again!"

She felt like running away, but after a momentary

pause of indecisiveness, she turned slowly to see the older man coming toward her, a beaming smile of greeting on his gentle face. She did her best to smile back at him, but it was a wavering effort at best, and his expression immediately changed to concern at seeing her pale, strained appearance. "My dear!" he said in a soft, kindly voice. "What's the trouble?"

Brad started to speak, no doubt in explanation, but Alicia cut him off, deciding with a burst of inspiration that she should take this opportunity to warn Dr. Hill that she didn't want any mention of their earlier dealings with one another to be made to Ian. "I—I'm not feeling very well, Dr. Hill. I wonder if I could talk to you alone for a moment?"

Brad looked startled, then concerned at her words, but he excused himself immediately after Dr. Hill's murmured "Certainly, my dear. Let's go into the library, shall we?"

The two of them entered the large booklined room as Brad disappeared, and Alicia headed straight toward the French doors leading onto a terrace, needing the air she had used as an excuse to Brad even more than she had earlier. Dr. Hill followed her out into the warm evening air and waited patiently as Alicia took in deep breaths until she began to regain her composure. Then she turned and looked at him with haunted eyes, failing to hear the soft click of the outer door into the library as it opened and closed upon a tall tuxedo-clad figure who entered the room behind Alicia and Dr. Hill and moved quietly to within hearing distance.

"Dr. Hill, there's nothing really wrong with me," she reassured him as she saw the professional look in his observant eyes. "I was simply upset at seeing you again. I hadn't expected it, you see, and it—it—"

She was having difficulty finding the words, but Dr.

Hill helped her. "Why should seeing me again upset you, Alicia?" he asked in a kindly, though chiding tone. "I thought we were friends as well as patient and doctor."

Alicia reached over to touch his arm lightly, nodding her head in acknowledgment of his words. "Yes...yes, we are. You've always been very kind to me, Dr. Hill. But I'm married now, you see, and my husband doesn't know—" She broke off again, biting her lip as she tried to get her thoughts in order.

"He doesn't know about the abortion?" Dr. Hill prompted her gently, causing Alicia to shake her head in despair.

"Oh, yes, he knows about the abortion, Doctor," she replied with a touch of bitterness in her voice. "And he—he can't stand what I did." In a lower voice, she added, "Neither can I sometimes."

Dr. Hill looked concerned and serious at this revelation. "Didn't you tell him *why* you had the abortion, Alicia? Surely he couldn't object to your decision to have it if he knew the circumstances? And there's no reason in the world for *you* to have any doubts about what you did either."

"Isn't there?" Alicia asked with a touch of the desperation she was feeling in her voice. "I had it for all the wrong reasons, Dr. Hill. Oh, it's true, I know"—she stopped him when he would have protested—"that there was a *chance* the baby would have been handicapped—not a certainty, but a *chance*. But I used that as an excuse to do what I really wanted to do...get rid of the child because...because at the time, I hated its father!" She buried her face in her hands, all of her old self-disgust welling up in her to the point where she was on the verge of breaking down.

"Alicia, listen to me," Dr. Hill said with gentleness

that was nevertheless couched in tones of firm authority. He pulled her hands from her face, then took her shoulders in his hands as Alicia looked tearfully up at him. "Regardless of your state of mind at the time—and I have no way of knowing why you felt the way you did, but knowing you, I'd say you had good reasons for your feelings—you did the right thing! I should have told you before, but I thought it would only bring you more grief. I examined the fetus, Alicia, and that child would never have been normal even if it had lived for any length of time at all." His voice was sad, but full of conviction, and Alicia held her breath, studying his face with an intent concentration that was painful to behold, willing herself to believe his words.

He nodded slowly, holding her look with steadfast honesty. "Even if you had taken the time you needed to think over your decision more thoroughly, I would have advised you even more strongly than I did to have the abortion, Alicia. If we'd waited for the tests that would have proven conclusively what I'm telling you, it might have threatened your own chances of coming through the procedure as well as you did. I should have talked to you in more detail at the time," he went on with a note of self-castigation. "I knew you seemed to be suffering from a form of shock, but I believed you had made the right decision regardless of the reasoning behind it. And I had my own reasons for failing to pay more attention at the time. My own daughter had a child that died from such birth defects shortly before you came to me as a patient. I saw how devastating carrying a baby to full term and then losing it could be. I wanted to spare you that."

Alicia sagged a little in his hands, experiencing a relief that was tainted by the sadness she felt at knowing the fetus she had carried had been damaged. Dr. Hill

held her quietly until she straightened her back and
faced him with her chin tilted up bravely. "I don't
blame you for anything, Dr. Hill," she reassured him,
noting the self-condemnation in his eyes. "You did
what you thought was right, and—and I believe you
were right now, too. I can't tell you what a burden
you've lifted from my conscience. I've felt so guilty...
so unhappy...."

Dr. Hill shook his head with impatience. "All for no
reason," he insisted. "And though it's kind of you to
absolve me from blame, I've learned enough here tonight to know that I won't make the mistake again of
withholding information like that from a patient." He
paused, studying her with the concentration of a man—
and a doctor—who wanted to do more to help. "Why
haven't you told your husband about the reason you
decided to have an abortion, Alicia?" He shook his
head when he saw that she was going to repeat her assertion that her dislike of the father was behind her
decision. "No, Alicia, don't tell me again it was because of your hatred for the father, because I don't believe that. I think you would have thought long and
hard about having that abortion if that were your only
consideration, and probably would have ended up
keeping the child. No, you had the abortion because of
the possibility of its having serious birth defects, and
you know yourself I'm right!"

Alicia pondered his statement, searching her heart
for the truth as she had so many times before. Finally
she admitted that in all probability the doctor was right.
"That may be true, Doctor. I'm almost certain it is, as a
matter of fact, though it's hard to know for sure at this
point. But I can't tell my husband...." She went back
to his original question.

"For God's sake, why not!?" Dr. Hill sounded impatiently emphatic. "Without honesty, a marriage is not good for much, Alicia. Your husband has the right to know that you're not the type of woman to be so callous, and you have the right to his unstinting regard. Why are you cutting the two of you off from honest communication this way?"

Alicia closed her eyes, wondering wearily how to explain when she wasn't all that clear about the reason herself. "For one thing"—she opened her eyes and moved away to stare out into the darkened garden—"the child was his." She paused and glanced back at Dr. Hill, seeing a light of understanding dawn in his eyes. "He hated me when he found out I'd aborted his child," she said with a break in her voice that spelled out, to Dr. Hill at least, how much that hatred hurt. "For all I know, he still does," she added more softly.

"All the more reason, then, for—" Dr. Hill started, but Alicia cut him off.

"I want him to know what sort of person I am in his heart without my having to make excuses!" Alicia cried out with more force than she'd meant to use, only then becoming aware of the real reason for her silence where Ian was concerned. Shaken by the realization, she turned back and braced herself against the bannister, leaning there with her head down and tears slipping from her eyes. "We—we have a strange marriage right now," she faltered, making an effort to control her tears, unwilling to go into detail about the nature of her and Ian's marriage. "If I go to him and tell him the truth, he'll think I'm trying to get out of a bargain we made.... At least I think he will," she added uncertainly. "And I don't want to get out of the bargain. I owe him...a child." She didn't explain that, more to the point, she didn't want to get out of the bargain because it was the only way she was likely to maintain contact with Ian...and that she wanted his child because she loved him, even if he didn't want her.

Dr. Hill sighed, shaking his head in confused sadness. "Alicia, I'm not a psychiatrist. And even if I were, you obviously aren't in a mood to confide in anyone yet about what's going on in your marriage. But I would advise you strongly to get some counseling about this matter before it's too late. Sometimes an outsider can rescue us from the disasters we all tend to get ourselves involved in from time to time. Would you consider doing that?"

Alicia surreptitiously wiped her eyes, and when she turned to face Dr. Hill, she had herself under control. She knew he was only trying to help, but she failed to see how a counselor could help her to win Ian's love. If she had that, her troubles would fade into little ones... the everyday frustrations and annoyances everyone had to put up with, but which faded into insignificance when the important things in life were obtained.

"I'll...think about it, Doctor," she promised him in order to reassure him that his efforts to help hadn't gone unheeded. "And—and thank you for what you've told me. It helped enormously. I'm grateful to have run into you here tonight."

"If I had told you this before, I could have saved you months of agonizing worry." He still seemed unwilling to let himself go blameless. "But we can't change that now," he went on, accepting the fact with the sound common sense he exuded. "I'm only happy to have eased your mind on one point at least, even if—" He hesitated and let whatever he'd been about to say go, though Alicia knew what it had been. "Now, if you feel up to it, I think we'd better rejoin our hosts and the other guests. They must be wondering what has happened to us."

Alicia felt a start of alarm as she realized she had forgotten all about everyone else during her conversation with Dr. Hill. Ian must be wondering where she was...if he wasn't too caught up with the adulation of the female guests to even notice she hadn't been around for a while. Outside the library she left Dr. Hill to rejoin the others, while she made her way to a bathroom to repair the damages her tears might have caused. When she rejoined the party a few minutes later, it was to see that Ian was still surrounded by a bevy of female admirers, though he seemed to have lost some of his enjoyment in their attentions. He sent her a searching glance as she entered the room that was curiously subdued and withdrawn, though unhostile, and Alicia felt both gratified that he apparently had noticed her absence and relieved that he didn't seem angry about it.

The rest of the evening passed in a normal manner, though Brad, upon noticing Alicia's change of mood, was less pronounced in his attentions to her, as if he understood that she was not feeling very lighthearted, and Ian was uncharacteristically quiet and withdrawn for the remainder of the night, his mood continuing even after they had left the party and returned to their hotel. Alicia was unable to fathom the reason for his mood and unwilling to ask about it, as her own emotions had undergone about as much strain as they could take for one night. But she longed for the comfort of his arms and came close to tears again when he turned on his side away from her after the lights were out, not even giving her the unsubstantial comfort of his passion, which she would willingly have accepted as a substitute for his love on this night when she was so confused...so unhappy...so fearful of what was to come.

Chapter Sixteen

Alicia was desperate by the time they flew to Boston to see Ian's parents, wishing for some miracle that would open Ian's eyes to the wealth of love she felt for him and to the kind of marriage they could have if only he could bring himself to love her, too.

When she caught her first glimpse of the tall, stately, handsome woman who was Ian's mother, and the equally tall, but less awesome figure of his father, Alicia felt a surge of bitterness toward the couple, wondering if they were the key to Ian's inability to respond to the love she was offering him. She had thought Ian had overcome his early upbringing, but perhaps these people had scarred him irreparably and left him with a cold void in his heart...a void she so desperately wanted to fill with love.

Her bitterness waned, however, to be replaced by puzzled confusion when Mrs. Halsey stepped forward to embrace her son with hearty warmth.

"Ian, darling!" the woman exclaimed with pleasure. "How good it is to see you!" She held him off for a moment while he smiled down at her with an enigmatic expression that could have been fond amusement, indifference, or any number of emotions. Alicia couldn't decide, and before she could wonder about it too long it was her turn to be enveloped in the woman's embrace. Mrs. Halsey's hug was nothing like the warm affection Ingrid could impart, but it was nevertheless genuine, and Alicia stepped back from it feeling more confused than ever. It was clear that Ian's mother was not the cold harridan she had envisioned, though she had a stately reserve that was perhaps not as motherly as a young boy might wish for.

Alicia replied to Mrs. Halsey's eager queries about their trip and Ian's publicity venture in New York while, out of the corner of her eye, she watched Ian shaking hands with his father, the older man smiling vaguely, yet with a light of affection in his brown eyes that was restrained but genuine.

The Halseys hustled them into a hired limousine, explaining that they didn't like to drive in Boston's traffic, and then they were on their way to the Halsey residence, with Ian's mother dominating the conversation. Fortunately she addressed her rapid questions to Ian in the main, so that Alicia was able to sit back quietly and observe mother and son with wonderment. Ian was unfailingly polite to his mother, treating her with fond respect, though without the relaxed, uninhibited warmth he gave to Ingrid, Borg, and Sandi. Mr. Halsey came out of his thoughts occasionally to address his son as well, but he seemed content to let his wife manage the conversation for the most part. When he did say something, however, it was evident that he was a highly intelligent and sensitive man who didn't fit the image of selfish preoccupation Alicia had imbued him with, any more than his wife fit her image. He was preoccupied, yes... but Alicia somehow couldn't picture him as selfish, though she imagined he was often simply unaware of what was going on around him.

By the end of the first day in the Halseys' company

Alicia was filled with frustrated curiosity about what the real relationship of the family entailed and was longing to talk to Ian about it, but as he seemed even more withdrawn into his brooding thoughts than usual, she couldn't find the courage to bring up the subject. She lay for long hours staring up at the dark ceiling beside Ian, trying to sort things out and reaching no clear conclusions. From time to time she turned her eyes toward his dark shape, worrying about what was going on inside him, and feeling frustrated because he seemed to have lost all physical interest in her since that first night they had spent in New York. She wanted to offer him the comfort of her body if she could give him nothing else, but his behavior was such that she felt unaccountably shy about being the aggressor. Besides, there were only a few short days left before their six-month agreement was up, and she was beginning to feel coldly anxious that Ian might have changed his mind about wanting anything from her... even a child.

By the middle of the next afternoon, after Ian and his father had gone off to visit the university, Alicia felt her frustration growing by leaps and bounds as she sat on the screened-in porch at the back of the Halsey home, going over old family albums and listening to Ian's mother extol her son's virtues with restrained, but enthusiastic, pride. "Look at this one, Alicia," Mrs. Halsey was saying with fond amusement. "Ian was five here and mad as hell at me because I canceled his birthday party after he misbehaved. See that ferocious scowl?" She laughed fondly as she leaned toward Alicia and pointed out the picture of Ian in her hand.

Alicia stared at her, then at the picture, her heart contracting at the pain she fancied she could see in Ian's young face. Without volition she found the words forming that she had longed to ask ever since she had met Mrs. Halsey. "Did you love your son, Mrs. Halsey?" she inquired with a hint of the puzzled, painful frustration she was feeling coming through in her voice.

Iona Halsey looked up with surprised affront in her cool blue eyes. "Why, whatever do you mean by that, Alicia?" she asked, her tone assuming the daunting formality that was entirely in keeping with her statuesque dignity. "Of course I loved Ian." She sat back then, her face composed into coldness for a moment before her expression changed slowly to inquiring shrewdness. "I love him now, Alicia. What makes you ask such a question?"

Alicia had watched the woman closely during the exchange, and though the woman was intimidating, she was obviously sincere. Alicia stood her ground, determined to get at the truth. "Ian doesn't think you did... or that you do," she said with quiet firmness. "I'd like to know why."

She felt guilty as she saw the pained dignity in the older woman's eyes, and then uneasily sympathetic when she saw the expression change to puzzled hurt. "Are you sure, Alicia?" Iona asked faintly, her daunting exterior softening for the first time since Alicia had met her. At Alicia's nod she seemed to sag a little, her dignity still evident but less stiff and off-putting. She shook her head slightly, her eyes abstracted and regretful. "I don't know why he should feel that way," she said almost to herself. "I may not have been a stereotyped example of a warm mother, with cookies in the kitchen and a tendency to kiss hurts away, but I always thought he knew I loved him... in my own way."

She then turned her now cloudy blue eyes on Alicia and spoke hesitantly. "I never wanted a child, Alicia. That much is true at least. Ian's father was enough to

look after. I love him. I always have. And he is so..."
She waved her hand vaguely, then found the words.
"He's so lost in his own little world much of the time,
it is left to me to do all the things I can to ensure he has
the recognition he deserves and to take care of him in
the way he needs to be taken care of." She looked at
Alicia for understanding, and Alicia gave it, having the
disorienting feeling of hearing the Halsey marriage described as so much like her own to Ben, that it was
uncanny. Except for the fact that Alicia *had* wanted
children, Mrs. Halsey might almost have been describing word for word what Alicia had felt for Ben.

"Ian was an accident," Mrs. Halsey went on, her expression indicative of remembrance. "And I panicked
when I realized I was pregnant. Forrest—Ian's father—
was at a critical point in his career and needed all the
help I could give him, and I thought I couldn't manage
both his needs and a child's at that point." She turned
her head away, almost as though she were ashamed, as
she continued her story and her voice was soft with
regretful humility. "I did a very foolish thing then. I
tried to have an abortion." After a moment of silence
between them that Alicia made no attempt to break,
Mrs. Halsey continued, her voice strengthening, her
posture firming. "Fortunately in those days it wasn't
easy to find someone willing to break the law in that way,
and I ended up going to a midwife who was less than...
effective." She smiled wryly without humor. "When I
stepped into that room and saw the primitive, unsanitary
conditions..." She shrugged. "Well, I turned right
around and walked out again. And I've never regretted
doing so."

She turned her gaze on Alicia then, leaning back in
her chair and looking introspective. "I tried to be a
good mother to Ian and I did love him, but he was

always such an exuberant, affectionate boy, while I've never been one to let my feelings show. Perhaps he did interpret my reserve as an indication that I didn't love him. But it wasn't—and isn't—true. The trouble is, I don't know how to go about letting him know that, since I find it as difficult now to show my feelings as I ever have. It's only with his father that I can..." She let her voice trailj off, a wry smile coming and gdng briefly before she seemed to gather herself together and put an end to the unaccustomed emotionalism she had been displaying. She started to get to her feet, but Alicia stopped her, wanting to finish what had been started before the moment was lost.

"Why did you think it was so important for Ian to write the kind of book *Portrait of a Woman* is, Mrs. Halsey? Weren't you proud of him before?" She spoke with gentle understanding, taking the hand of the older woman in her own, but her gaze was firm as she looked into the blue eyes, which now showed surprise.

"Of course I was proud of him!" Iona said somewhat indignantly. "But—" She shook her head with impatience. "The thing is, Alicia, *Ian* would never have been satisfied until he proved he could write something like that. I know him, you see. He has such high expectations of himself, but there's also a sort of fear that he won't be able to live up to those expectations." She looked momentarily uncomfortable as she added, "Perhaps because his father and I always pushed him to do better, knowing he *could*!" And then she gathered her rather awesome dignity about herself once more and her face grew sterner. "I pushed Ian to do what I knew would ultimately make him happy. And now that he's done it, I don't care if he never does it again. He's shown himself he could, and that's all I was trying to accomplish!"

She got to her feet then, and Alicia sensed that the

time for confidences was over. "I'm going out into the
garden to do some weeding before dinner, Alicia. I
hope you'll excuse me, but I feel the need to be alone
for a while."

Alicia murmured, "Of course," feeling sorry for the
woman whose personality made it so difficult for her to
express the feelings that lay within her heart in abun-
dance. She got to her own feet, meaning to go out the
front way to take a short walk and do some thinking of
her own, but Mrs. Halsey stopped after pushing the
screen door open and looked back at her with a smile
and a look of wry understanding shimmering in her
clear blue eyes.

"I think you'll be good for Ian, Alicia," she said quietly. "It's clear you love him." She hesitated, then
added, "In fact, you remind me of myself at your age.
You have high standards. But I think you have a more
open nature than I can ever hope to have, and I think
Ian needs that. He won't ever have to wonder whether
you love him or not."

She walked away then, leaving Alicia pondering her
words thoughtfully as she realized for the first time that
Ian didn't know any such thing. She hadn't had the
courage to tell him. Her pride had been on the line and
she had counted that pride more important than anything else. Had she been wrong? she wondered with a
sad sense of frustration. Should she tell Ian how she
felt about him?

A slight sound behind her interrupted her thoughts,
making her swing around to face the open doorway behind her. She gasped as she saw Ian standing there, his
hands in his pockets and a withdrawn, brooding look on
his handsome face. "Ian!" Alicia faltered, wondering
how much he'd heard, and how badly his mother's
revelations had affected him if he had heard them.

"How—how long have you been there?" she asked with uneasy discomfort.

"Long enough," he answered, his eyes wearily cynical. "I seem to be making a habit of eavesdropping lately." His enigmatic comment meant nothing to Alicia except as it applied to the present circumstances, and she took a step toward him, wanting to wipe out any hurt he had felt at what his mother had said.

"Then you know that your mother does love you?" she said gently, letting the hand she had raised toward him fall when he made no move to accept the comfort she offered.

Ian raised a hand to rub the back of his neck, a weary gesture that went with the tired look in his eyes and the vulnerable twist to his lips. "Yes, I know," he answered coolly, his eyes flicking to where his mother was now bending over a rosebush in the backyard. "I suppose I always did know it in a way, though it was hard to accept after I learned about the abortion." His smile was crooked as he turned his gaze back to Alicia. "Or rather the attempted abortion."

Alicia frowned in puzzlement, struggling to sort out the implication in his statement. "You—you knew about your mother's attempt before now... before today?" she asked cautiously.

"Oh, yes, I knew," he said with a hard inflection that seared Alicia's heart.

"Oh, Ian..." she murmured softly. "I'm so sorry. How did you find out?"

He shrugged, a curiously boyish movement that caught at her heart. "I had a habit of eavesdropping when I was twelve years old, too. I came home unexpectedly one day when my mother was talking to her pastor. I suppose she wanted to know if she was forgiven for the attempt, though I didn't stick around to hear the whole conversation once I got the gist of what she was talking about.''

Close to tears, Alicia stared at him, aching for the boy he had been and for the man he was now. "Have you forgiven her, Ian?" she asked softly, knowing that it was important that he did so for his own sake.

Ian looked down at her, a whole series of emotions flashing through his eyes in succession...anger, doubt, and then the maturity of reflection. "Yes," he said finally, his voice quietly convincing. "I thought I had long ago, but it seems I was wrong until today. But it's over now. I can look at her as a person instead of just as my mother, and care for her as she is, not as I used to wish her to be."

Alicia stood quietly, believing him and grateful beyond words that she had been at least a part of bringing him the new peace she saw in his eyes. Then he brought his attention to her, and instantly she felt uneasy again as she saw the grim determination in his face. "Come on, Alicia. Let's go for a drive. We have something to talk about."

He turned on his heels, leaving Alicia to follow him, and she did so after a moment's hesitation, her legs feeling wooden as she forced them to move and carry her to what she was afraid would be the end of her marriage.

Ian took his father's car, an old sturdy model no longer being made, and headed toward the open countryside, Alicia sitting silently beside him, afraid to speak the fears that were filling her with dread. After a while Ian took a turning that led to an open meadow surrounded by trees and stopped the car by the side of the road. Alicia climbed out to follow him to the edge of the meadow, watching him as he stood with his hands on his hips, surveying the area with reminiscent eyes. "I used to come here when I was a boy," he said abstractedly. "My father would bring me out sometimes on a Saturday and sit reading while I explored and pretended I was a frontiersman being stalked by Indians."

He turned to her, looking down with a rueful, ironic expression that spelled out the fact that he was a man now...very much a man in Alicia's eyes. Then his expression sobered and he turned his face away again. "I'm canceling our bargain, Alicia," he said with a hard note of strain in his voice.

Alicia's breath left her all of a sudden and she swayed where she was until, spying a fallen log nearby, she moved on wavering legs to seat herself before she fell. "What—what exactly do you mean, Ian?" she asked with a lack of expression that belied the riot of feeling going on inside her.

He moved closer, though he still wouldn't look into her eyes. "I mean you're free to go," he answered grimly. "You don't have to have my child...and you don't have to stay married to me."

Alicia closed her eyes for a second, clenching her hands and willing herself to maintain control. "I see," she said in a dull, lifeless voice. "Then—you've decided—" She faltered, opening her eyes to gaze with a tortured look at Ian's profile. "You've decided you can't love me, then?" she asked faintly, drawing in her breath on a painful sob that she just barely saved from being audible.

Ian swung around to look at her, frowning ferociously, a stormy look in his eyes that made her draw back slightly. "What the hell are you talking about?" he gritted out harshly. "I've loved you since the first night I met you!"

Alicia froze, blinking up at him in astonishment,

afraid to believe her own ears, afraid to give way to the instant surge of joy his words invoked for fear she might be wrong. "Then, why—" She stopped, licking her lips, which had suddenly gone dry. "Why do you want a divorce then, Ian?" she asked, her voice cracking on his name.

Ian swung around to pace a few steps, then turned and came back to where she sat to stare broodingly down at her before he seated himself on the log next to her. He bent forward, his hands hanging loosely between his knees. "I overheard you and Dr.—Hill, was it?" he asked, not really caring about an answer. "At the Taltons' the other night. I know now why you had the abortion."

Alicia tensed, then made herself relax, sensing that her whole life hung on this first real communication she and Ian had shared in so long, she had given up hoping for it. "I . . . see," she said slowly, giving herself time so that she wouldn't make a mistake. "And . . . and how do you feel about what you overheard?" she asked hesitantly.

"Like a goddamn bastard!" Ian bit out with suppressed violence. He turned toward her then, reaching out to grip the hand on her knee with bruising force. "If only you'd told me, Alicia!" And then he let go of her to face forward again, his profile looking as though it were carved in stone. "But I can understand why you didn't after all I'd put you through. I can see why you hate me," he said with hard self-contempt.

Alicia licked her lips again and placed a hand on Ian's forearm, gently, afraid as yet that he might toss it off. "I don't hate you, Ian," she said quietly. "I—"

But before she could take the momentous step of telling him she loved him, he interrupted her, shaking his head with impatience. "No, I suppose you don't.

But you don't love me either, and I can't force you to live with me any longer. You're free to go anytime you like, Alicia.''

Alicia closed her mouth on the words she wanted to say, electing instead to clear the air between them once and for all. "You...you said you loved me the first time you met me, Ian. Will you...tell me...why you behaved as you did?" She hastened on as she saw the tortured pain in Ian's eyes indicating that he thought she wanted her pound of flesh. "I'm just trying to understand, Ian. I'm...confused."

He gave a little movement of self-disgust, then raked a hand through his auburn hair with impatience. "I suppose you are," he said with weary cynicism. "And I suppose I owe you an explanation. You can't be blamed if you think I didn't act as though I loved you." He settled down then to a certain degree, explaining in a tight voice that hurt Alicia to hear.

"I was attracted to you from the first moment I saw you, but you looked so cool and untouchable, I decided I wouldn't get anywhere if I came on strong to you. Then you started baiting me, and I realized you thought I wasn't good enough for you." Alicia made a slight movement of protest, but Ian didn't see it and went on talking. "That made me angry," he said with a flat note of understatement in his voice. "I realize now that I reacted to you with some of the anger I'd always felt for my mother. She always gave me the impression I wasn't good enough for her either."

Alicia did protest then, her tone aching with hurt for him. "Oh, Ian, that isn't true. You know that now, don't you?"

He shrugged, a grim smile twisting his mouth as he glanced down at Alicia with a hard expression. "Yes, I do now, but that wasn't the case when I met you. I really only intended to scare the hell out of you, not to—'' He hesitated, then made himself continue. ''Not to hurt you,'' he added more quietly. ''But you were so damn beautiful that I couldn't stop, especially when I sensed that you were responding to me physically, despite all your verbal protests.''

Alicia dropped her gaze, remembering that long-ago humiliation but not with any of the hatred she had felt in the past. ''You were right,'' she said with quiet acceptance. ''I couldn't help myself, though I didn't want to—to feel that way about you. I had a lot to learn about myself in those days.''

Ian chose to take her words in a negative way. ''Yes, well, I helped your education along considerably, didn't I?'' he said with dry self-disgust. He didn't see Alicia's frustrated shake of her head. ''Anyway,'' he went on doggedly, ''despite how it started out, it was the most moving, beautiful experience I'd ever had with a woman, and by the time it was over I was in love with you.'' His voice had dropped to a husky whisper, tinged with regret, and Alicia's eyes softened joyfully at his admission. ''But by then it was too late,'' Ian went on quietly. ''When I looked into your eyes afterward, I knew I'd ruined the chance for anything between us, and my pride took over. I wanted to make you not feel so badly about yourself, but you were in no mood to listen to me, and I thought the best thing I could do was to get out of your life....'' His voice changed to wry hardness. ''Only I found out I couldn't get you out of my mind.''

He turned his eyes to her then, looking at her with a ragged, possessive love that turned her bones to water. ''There's one point I want to clear up, Alicia. You said once—you asked, rather—who I'd taken to bed that night. I'll repeat what I answered then. It wasn't my

mother. I may have reacted to you with some of the
anger she inspired in me, but what I felt that night once
I had my hands on you was nothing remotely con-
nected with her. There was nothing Freudian about it
then...nor has there ever been.''

Alicia gave him the answer she saw him asking for.
''I believe you, Ian,'' she said quietly. ''I was hitting
out at you any way I could that night, because you—
you were showing me a part of myself I didn't want to
look at...not then.''

Ian nodded, smiling wryly but with gratitude that she
understood that part of him...and herself. He leaned
back to get more comfortable then and went on with
his explanation. ''I knew when I saw you in Brian's office that day that I couldn't leave things as they were.
I'd been thinking about you for months, wanting you,
hating myself for what I'd done to you and for what I'd
spoiled. I'd already decided to do *Portrait of a Woman,*
and when you walked in, I knew I had the perfect opportunity for a second chance. It was your kind of book.
It might win your respect, and while you were working
on it I thought I could win you over.''

Alicia's lips tightened at his reference to winning her
respect, but Ian didn't give her a chance to comment.
''Only I kept making the same mistakes over again with
you,'' he admitted ruefully. ''I couldn't keep my hands
off you, and I couldn't keep from trying to break
through that shell of yours and get at the woman I
sensed was there. As a result I ended up making you
respond to me physically, while I drove you further
away from me emotionally.''

''That's not true, Ian...'' Alicia started to say, but
Ian wasn't listening. He was at the part of his most
painful reminiscences by then, and he wanted to get it
over with.

"When I found out about the abortion," he went on with grim quietness, "all I could think of was that you were more like my mother than I'd thought. I told myself I hated you, and when you ran away, I began to lay plans to get revenge. A child seemed the perfect way, since I was certain you didn't really want one, and learning that I'd lost one made me realize how much I wanted to be a father. I thought I could accomplish both goals at once—getting even with you and starting a family at the same time. I didn't think I'd ever find another woman I could love, but at least I could have a child." He sighed wearily and looked at her with haunted eyes. "It was about the most stupid piece of reasoning I've ever come up with, and I realize now that I can't go through with it. It wouldn't be fair to the child, and it wouldn't be fair to you."

He fell silent then while Alicia thought over how to proceed. "How have you felt all this time we've been married, Ian?" she asked hesitantly. "You've said you loved me...then you hated me...and now I don't know how you feel. I need to know, Ian."

Ian glanced over at her, his eyes expressing his thoughts before he spoke. "You'll never know how hard it's been not to tell you I loved you these past months, Alicia," he said with quiet torment. "The hate I felt didn't last past the first day. But I couldn't make myself say the words, even though you were unfailingly sweet and pleasant and trying so hard to make a go of things. I thought you were just trying to make the best of a bad situation because that's your nature. I still do."

It was time at last, Alicia thought, a slow smile beginning as her joy flooded her being and was reflected in her clear blue eyes. "Then you were wrong, Ian," she said softly, all her love for him coming through in her voice. "It's been as hard for me to stop myself from saying I love you as it has been for you. I never would have married you if I hadn't loved you."

Ian's eyes widened, then narrowed as he raked her face, his doubt that happiness was within his grasp as strong as Alicia's had been earlier. Alicia nodded to reassure him, then laughed as she saw the light of comprehension dawning in his eyes and loosening the tautness with which he'd been holding his body.

"You mean we've wasted the past six months, each thinking the other wasn't in love?" he asked with incredulous frustration.

Alicia leaned forward to wrap her arms around his neck and bring her face close to his. "Oh, I wouldn't say it was wasted," she teased archly, her eyes glowing with love for him. "I've learned your favorite foods, you've taught me how to keep up with you on skis—and in bed...." she added softly, her look an open invitation for him to teach her more.

Ian moved then, pulling her up against him with such force that they both toppled over the back of the log and ended up sprawled on the grass behind it, laughing and holding one another with all the fierce possessiveness of two people incredibly in love and never wanting to let each other go.

Then Ian was above her, looking down into her eyes with a fierce blaze of sensuality that Alicia felt clear down to her toes. "I think it's about time we made *love* for the first time, don't you?" he growled on a ragged note of arousal.

Alicia smiled up at him with lazy sensuousness. "I don't know what you mean," she said from deep within her throat. "I've been making *love* for the past six months."

"So have I," Ian acknowledged, echoing her lazy

smile. "But this is the first time we'll do it knowing how we both feel...and being able to say it. I'm looking forward to that," he said in a husky whisper as he brought his mouth down to hers.

Alicia was sinking down into the depths of her own sexual arousal before a thought brought her groping to reality again. She moved her head away from Ian's marauding lips, gasping out her thought. "Ian, what about a baby? We can have one the right way now."

Ian shook his head, his smile slumberously sexual, his hands already unbuttoning the blouse Alicia wore. "Not yet," he growled on a husky note. "Now that I know you love me, I want your uninterrupted attention for a while before I share you, even with my own son or daughter." He bent his head to nuzzle her breast, causing Alicia almost to lose the train of thought that struggled for her attention.

"How long, Ian?" she murmured on a moan of desire.

"Mmmm? How long what?" he asked abstractedly, preoccupied as he was with other, more interesting matters.

"How long do you want to wait before I get pregnant?" she gasped out as his teeth gently closed on the nipple he had captured.

"At least another six months," Ian muttered impatiently, raising his head to capture her mouth and close it against her distracting questions.

When he at last freed her lips, his look turned to puzzled frustration as he saw that she was wide-eyed and much too alert to be ready for what he intended.

"What's the matter, Alicia?" he asked with growing anxiety, which prompted Alicia to capture his face in her hands and kiss his cheeks before she answered.

"Oh, nothing serious, Ian," she assured him with

suspicious solemnity. "I just want to make certain you don't plan to take me to court for breaking our agreement. I've experienced your talent for revenge before, remember, and you're too good at it for me to take chances."

Ian's look was a mixture of chagrined amusement at her bringing up his past regretful behavior and frustration at her timing in doing so. But then his mouth turned up in a sly smile as his eyes began to glint with the same mischievous laughter that danced in Alicia's. A second later he had her pinned helplessly beneath him while he scowled threateningly down at her.

"You're right, woman," he growled menacingly as she struggled laughingly beneath him. "Taking you to court might be a little drastic, but I *am* entitled to some revenge for the torture you've put me through these past months, and I think I know just how to go about it." He held her wrists while he raised himself slightly to rake a leering, appraising glance over her body. "Am I correct in assuming you're not indifferent to me physically?" he inquired in the tones of a prosecuting attorney who had sensuous appetites.

"You are correct, Mr. Halsey," Alicia replied on a gurgle of laughter, then rounded her eyes in mock fear as Ian's expression turned to exaggerated malevolence.

"And am I correct in my assumption that you're not a stranger to sexual frustration just because you're a member of the . . . uh . . . *weaker* sex?" he asked sternly as he moved his hand to her inner thigh.

'Oh, you are *soooo* correct, Mr. Halsey," Alicia gasped out in a weak whisper as she closed her eyes against the stab of arousal he had invoked.

"Then my duty is clear," Ian growled on a deep note of satisfaction as he dipped his head to tease the nipple he had uncovered earlier.

"What—exactly *is* your duty?" Alicia murmured brokenly, feeling her entire body fill up with the heat of response to Ian's provoking mouth and hands.

"I'm going to make you pay," Ian said on a low growl as he began to undo the buttons of her skirt. "I'm going to have my revenge for your wasting six months of my valuable time with mere sex when I could have had all of you anytime I wanted it." Impatient with the complicated fastenings of her skirt, Ian finally abandoned his attempts and resorted to the simple expediency of pushing the material up over her thighs, revealing the objective he sought to his entire satisfaction. And as he began a tantalizing, beautifully timed exploration of what he found there, he murmured with bland provocativeness against the trembling sweetness of Alicia's mouth, "It's my duty to the male sex to teach my wife her place."

Alicia allowed him to bring her to within a breath of the peak of ecstasy, knowing all along that he planned to leave her hanging there after he'd derived the dual satisfaction his nuzzling, probing, nipping, tantalizing, mouth and hands were evoking in both of them. Then, just before she sensed he was about to administer his final revenge, she thrust upward with both hands against his chest, toppling him off of her and following up her surprise attack by landing on top of him with a force that had him laughingly gasping for breath.

"All right, Mr. Halsey," she said with threatening menace that was somewhat spoiled by the ragged arousal in her voice. "I'm entitled to revenge, too!" She began to unfasten the buttons of his shirt, her gaze firmly holding his as she fired questions at him. "Did you or did you not plan the seduction of this poor, defenseless female lying atop you now fighting for her rights?"

Ian shook his head at first, his chest still heaving with his laughter, but at Alicia's fierce scowl he adopted an expression of meek shame. "Yes, I did, madam," he admitted manfully, through his laughter.

"And did you or did you not plan to keep her barefoot and pregnant against her express wishes to the contrary," Alicia demanded as she began working on his belt.

Ian tried weakly to fight her off, but his efforts were remarkably futile in the face of Alicia's determination. "I did not," Ian responded in highly offended tones. "I remember distinctly buying her not only an ungodly number of shoes, but even a specially ordered pair of ski boots!" His mouth took on a sly twist as he added, "And besides, I don't remember that she expressed any wishes to the contrary. In fact, if I recall, she drew up a contract *ordering* me to learn to love her and to give her a baby within six—"

Alicia clapped her hand over his mouth, crying out, "Oh, you cad!" before she removed her hand and seized his mouth with her own, giving him a kiss that would have rocked him on his toes had he been standing up. By the time she raised her head to gaze with shining, liquid love down into his eyes, neither of them were inclined to continue their argument about which of them was entitled to wreak revenge upon the other.

"I love you, Ian," Alicia murmured, her heart in her eyes and voice.

"I love you too, Alicia," Ian responded, his expression at once serious and possessively loving. "I want you now... I want you with love.... I always will." He was bringing her head down to his slowly as he spoke, his eyes caressingly warm and seductive. "Now suppose we work out a solution to this common desire for revenge together for a change. This moment is too precious to waste working at cross purposes."

Alicia gave him a slow, sweet smile of understanding before his mouth covered hers and she lost herself in the promise of his kiss. She felt his strong hands on her ribs as he lifted her off of him and placed her gently onto the soft green grass that was to be their first real marriage bed. And this time she didn't have to censor or stifle the emotional love and the need to express it verbally as she had in the past, and neither did Ian. Their muted, hauntingly expressive whispers enhanced and made whole their physical communication as they came together for the first time with their mutual love acknowledged to God and nature and one another.

"Ah, my darling—my precious Alicia," Ian faltered humbly as they lay together afterward, letting the breeze in the meadow cool the heat their passion had instigated. "How sweet...how very sweet is the taste of love's revenge," he misquoted, his voice breaking with emotion as he spoke.

"Yes, dearest Ian," Alicia responded through tears of happiness. "Love is the sweetest revenge of all."

HARLEQUIN
PREMIERE AUTHOR EDITIONS

6 top Harlequin authors—6 of their best books

1. **JANET DAILEY** Giant of Mesabi
2. **CHARLOTTE LAMB** Dark Master
3. **ROBERTA LEIGH** Heart of the Lion
4. **ANNE MATHER** Legacy of the Past
5. **ANNE WEALE** Stowaway
6. **VIOLET WINSPEAR** The Burning Sands

Harlequin is proud to offer these 6 exciting romance novels by 6 of our most popular authors. In brand-new beautifully designed covers, each Harlequin Premiere Author Edition is a bestselling love story—a contemporary, compelling and passionate read to remember!

Available in September wherever paperback books are sold, or through Harlequin Reader Service. Simply complete and mail the coupon below.

A Harlequin
ROBERTA LEIGH
Collector's Edition

A specially designed collection of six exciting love stories by one of the world's favorite romance writers—Roberta Leigh, author of more than 60 bestselling novels!

1 **Love in Store**
2 **Night of Love**
3 **Flower of the Desert**

4 **The Savage Aristocrat**
5 **The Facts of Love**
6 **Too Young to Love**

Available in August wherever paperback books are sold, or available through Harlequin Reader Service. Simply complete and mail the coupon below.

Harlequin Reader Service

In the U.S.
P.O. Box 52040
Phoenix, AZ 85072-9988

In Canada
649 Ontario Street
Stratford, Ontario N5A 6W2

Please send me the following editions of the Harlequin Roberta Leigh Collector's Editions. I am enclosing my check or money order for $1.95 for each copy ordered, plus 75¢ to cover postage and handling.

☐ 1   ☐ 2   ☐ 3   ☐ 4   ☐ 5   ☐ 6

Number of books checked_____ @ $1.95 each = $_____

N.Y. state and Ariz. residents add appropriate sales tax $_____

Postage and handling $___.75___

                       TOTAL $_____

I enclose_____

(Please send check or money order. We cannot be responsible for cash sent through the mail.) Price subject to change without notice.

NAME_____
                   (Please Print)
ADDRESS_____ APT. NO. _____

CITY_____

STATE/PROV. _____ ZIP/POSTAL CODE_____

Offer expires 29 February 1984.   30856000000